The World's Best Tennis Vacations

The
World's Best
Tennis Vacations

ROGER COX

The Stephen Greene Press
PELHAM BOOKS

THE STEPHEN GREENE PRESS/PELHAM BOOKS

Published by the Penguin Group
Viking Penguin, a division of Penguin Books USA Inc., 40 West 23rd
    Street, New York, New York 10010, U.S.A.
Penguin Books Ltd, 27 Wrights Lane, London W8 5TZ, England
Penguin Books Australia Ltd, Ringwood, Victoria, Australia
Penguin Books Canada Ltd, 2801 John Street, Markham, Ontario,
    Canada L3R 1B4
Penguin Books (N.Z.) Ltd, 182-190 Wairau Road, Auckland 10,
    New Zealand

Penguin Books Ltd, Registered Offices: Harmondsworth,
    Middlesex, England

First published in 1990 by The Stephen Greene Press/Pelham Books

Distributed by Viking Penguin, a division of Penguin Books USA Inc.

10 9 8 7 6 5 4 3 2 1

Library of Congress Cataloging-in-Publication Data
Cox, Roger.
    The world's best tennis vacations
    / by Roger Cox.
        p.   cm.
    ISBN 0-8289-0705-6 : $12.95
        1. Tennis resorts.   2. Tennis resorts—Evaluation.   3. Tennis
    resorts—Directories.   I. Title.
    GV998.C69   1990
    796.342′025—dc20   89-29807
                                                                  CIP

Printed in the United States of America
Designed by Cope Cumpston
Set in Galliard by Compset, Inc.
Produced by Unicorn Production Services, Inc.

To my family and the Kezers,
who always believed that I would write a book

Contents

Acknowledgments

I could never have written this book if it had not been for the editors at *Tennis* magazine, specifically Alex McNab, Donna Doherty, and, though he has since retired, Shep Campbell. Most of what I know about tennis resorts I owe to their willingness to ship me off on travel assignments for the magazine, an odyssey that has taken me throughout North America and the Caribbean and as far away as Wimbledon and Australia. They have given me an opportunity to pursue my passions for tennis and travel and call it work.

Another valuable contribution was made by the scores of people who took the time to talk to me about their experiences with particular camps. There is no way to name every one of them without sounding like someone who's just won an Academy Award, but they'll know who they are and I want them to know I appreciate their help.

Finally, there is Tom Begner. A strong tennis player himself and a veteran of several tennis camps, Tom was looking for a writer to do a book about tennis programs at the same time I was looking for a publisher. Sheer luck and Jim Loehr brought us together. Tom contributed his intelligence to the overall shape of the book, and a combination of patience and prodding as I worked to get it written. I'm grateful that he did.

The
World's Best
Tennis Vacations

Introduction

· ·

A friend of mine looked at me in disbelief recently when I said I needed a vacation and wouldn't mind going to tennis camp. Writing about tennis camps and resorts is what I do for a living, and in a typical year I travel to scores of them in the course of researching travel assignments. The notion that I would turn around and do for fun what I do as a profession struck her as bizarre bordering on the obsessive. She thought of camp as a kind of repair shop for tennis strokes, a place to take one's game for a tune-up or overhaul. Thus, it seemed to her that, as often as I attended, whatever the tennis-camp pros could do for my game must already have been done. What was the point, she asked, in my going again?

In one sense it is true that I get far less out of a standard camp now than when I started attending a decade ago. Then every one of my strokes needed major work, and virtually everything the pros told me was new information. Today, while my strokes are far from perfect, their flaws are fewer, and only rarely does a pro tell me something I haven't heard many times before. Yet if anything I am even more enthusiastic about tennis camps now than I was ten years ago. Why?

The major reason is that I have never attended a tennis camp without meeting players I liked. Like all specialized vacations, it brings together a mixture of people who share a very particular interest, in this case a passion for tennis. More often than not these players come to camp because they think running and sweating and doing drills is fun. They look forward to the challenge of trying to get better, and they like feeling tired at the end of the day, knowing it's because they worked hard. The fact that everyone is there to try to improve his or her game contributes to the unusually high degree of compatibility.

That camaraderie is the most often overlooked aspect of a tennis-camp vacation. That's what keeps me going back. Strictly speaking, I've reached a level of play where, unless I attend one of the camps for advanced or tournament players (see "The Best and the Worst"), it might make more sense for me to spend that money on private lessons, but it wouldn't be nearly as much fun.

1

Besides there are advantages to a camp's group drills. Personally I tend to work harder, especially if someone else in the group seems to be making faster progress. While the pro feeds balls to one or two campers, the others in the group can be picking them up, so there is relatively less down time than in a private lesson. A group of four also makes it possible to work on doubles. And most important of all, once the day's drills are over I don't have to look far to find players at my level when I feel the urge to play. For someone like me who loves tennis, a camp makes an ideal vacation.

The question is where to go. Because I cover travel and resorts for *Tennis* magazine, people often ask me for suggestions, knowing that I've been through most of the best-known programs. They assume that I'll tick off the names of my three favorites, and that will be it. Instead I barrage them with questions. Do you have a particular part of the country—or the world—in mind? How much money are you prepared to spend? What time of year is your vacation? How many hours a day do you want to devote to instruction and drills? Do you have a preference for clay or hard courts? Are you going alone or with a spouse or friends? Are you taking your kids? What do you require besides tennis in the way of other recreation? In particular, do you need a beach or golf course? Is a lively social atmosphere and/or nightlife important? Would you consider staying in a dorm room and eating cafeteria food or do you insist on posh digs and elegant cuisine or a condominium with its own kitchen? Once they answer all those questions, I can usually suggest a few camps with appropriate programs and amenities. All I ask in return is that, wherever they ultimately go, they report back and let me know how they liked it.

Since 1981, when I joined *Tennis* magazine as a contributing editor, I have been to more than 200 tennis resorts and schools on five continents. Not all of them offered the kinds of full-scale tennis programs that are the subject of this book; but when they did I was there, if not on court as a participant then alongside it as an observer. As a result, much of what I know about tennis programs comes from first-hand experience.

At the same time, in traveling to resorts I constantly come in contact with vacationing tennis players. Whenever that happens I steer the conversation toward a discussion of tennis programs in an effort to find out which they liked best—or least—and why. So ultimately my sense of which programs deserve to be called the world's best derives not only from my own experience but from that of hundreds of other tennis players as well.

Anyone who scans the table of contents will notice that many well-known and highly regarded tennis resorts do not appear. The reason is that my subject is not tennis *resorts* but tennis *programs*. A resort may have acres of courts, a stellar pro, a calendar full of tennis events, and drop-dead amenities and still not be included in this book if it lacks a well-thought-out, multi-day curriculum of group instruction for *adults*.

Something happens when players come together to work on their games, and this book is about the places where that magic is most likely to break out. Thus, a great resort with mediocre programs has no hope of being included here; a great program that put campers up in tents and fed them pemmican and hardtack would be.

Because of the critical nature of this guide, however, I'm not going to steer you toward any program without pointing out its assets and drawbacks, whether they are tent accommodations and cafeteria food or a grueling regimen of drop-dead drills. At the same time this is not a *Consumer Reports* guide to every existing tennis camp. Only the best places appear here. So, when I launch into them for shortcomings, my negative criticism needs to be kept in context. They wouldn't be in the book at all if they weren't outstanding.

Much of that criticism is aimed at sorting them out, one from another. After all, the best place for someone looking to get ready for a tournament is not likely to also be the best place for a family of low intermediates more interested in having fun, nor is an intimate tennis resort with a clientele of older couples any place for thirtysomething singles. In each of the reviews, I try to make clear what makes a particular resort or school one of the best and, at the same time, what kind of players are most likely to find it alluring. In essence, I've tried to provide the kinds of information needed to answer the questions I ask when people want to know where they should go to tennis camp.

Although I sought advice from as many people as possible, the final selection of the world's best is mine alone. All of them are places I can comfortably recommend to friends, even those who are not shy about letting me know when they think I'm wrong. I'd appreciate hearing about your experiences, whether you agree or disagree with my recommendations and especially if you attend a program that is not included here but you believe deserves to be. If we don't get a chance to meet at tennis camp somewhere, drop me a line care of the publisher.

A Guide
to the Guidebook
· ·

Tennis players headed on vacation fall into two broad categories: those who want to play and perhaps take a few private lessons, and those who crave an actual tennis program, consisting at the very least of several hours a day of group instruction. Finding a resort with courts and a pro is relatively easy, but sorting out the differences among scores of tennis programs is not. If the goal of the programs is always the same—to help campers improve their strokes and broaden their understanding of the game—the methods and amenities differ widely.

This book developed from my sense that tennis players needed help making that decision. Some I talked to had had the bad experience of showing up for the group instruction expecting to find fifteen people, only to discover that just three had enrolled. Others turned up in a t-shirt and running shorts to confront a sea of designer tennis outfits. Still others imagined they were in for three days of fun and games when in fact they'd signed on for tennis's version of a boot camp. All of these problems resulted essentially from a lack of reliable information, not only about the instructional programs themselves but about the cuisine, lodging, and overall tennis atmosphere as well. I set out to write a book that would make sorting out those differences easier.

▶ *The Method*

There are an estimated 150 full-scale adult tennis camps and clinics in North America, the Caribbean, and Europe offering instruction in English. The U.S. Tennis Association publishes a partial directory, as do *Tennis* and *World Tennis* magazines in their January issues. All three list the names, addresses, and phone numbers of the various clinics, along with the dates, number of daily hours devoted to instruction, and the maximum number of participants. What those lists lack is any kind of qualitative evaluation of the camps' and clinics' assets and drawbacks.

What I've sought to do in this book is to flesh out those skeletal listings, but only for the best of the programs. After nearly a decade of covering travel and resorts on assignments for *Tennis* and other national magazines, I have a first- or second-hand knowledge of a substantial number of the camps in those directories, because I have been through their program, talked to people who had, or interviewed the directors who ran them. When I set out to write this book, I drafted a tentative list of some 60 camps and clinics that my research and experience and the recommendations of other tennis and travel journalists and tennis players suggested belonged among the world's best tennis programs.

At that point, I began to delve more deeply into their virtues and drawbacks. When I had not personally been through a program, I either made a point of attending or sought out people who had. I also talked to the directors of tennis or heads of camps about their philosophies of teaching and credentials. I checked into the kinds of players most likely to benefit from the individual programs. I also sought out specific information about how many campers attend—not the theoretical maximum a camp can accept, but the actual number likely to be there during any given week.

Eventually, I established a few objective criteria to reduce the field of candidates. All of them are programs for adults, although a few conduct concurrent sessions for juniors. The program itself has to last at least two days and offer a minimum of three hours of group instruction daily; in those few cases where I've included one whose basic session is only two hours long, it is only because campers have the option of more. I have left out a few well-known programs—like Terry Addison's Australian Tennis Institute in Florida—because they rarely get more than a few campers at a time, too few, in my opinion, to generate a lively tennis atmosphere. And finally, the resort or school needed a proven track record of luring passionate players. Several that opened recently—or are about to open—obviously haven't had an opportunity to do that. Rather than seem to have omitted them unfairly, I've listed them in the section "Too New to Rate."

Slightly more than half of the original 60 made the final cut. Any listing of this sort ultimately comes down to a subjective judgment, and I take full responsibility for the final selection. It reflects my prejudice for larger camps with comprehensive programs. At the same time, it is a deliberately eclectic mix that runs the gamut from low-key family affairs to tennis boot camps and from the spartan to the luxurious.

5

▶ *The Reviews*

To make it easier to compare one program with another, I've adopted a standard format for each of the reviews. An overview of the basic information contained within each section of the profile follows.

SEASON: This section notes the dates the program is in operation and, where appropriate, the periods when attendance in the clinics is most likely to be at its highest.

RATES: Although resort packages differ widely in what they include, I've estimated how much it will actually cost per person per day for lodging (double occupancy), breakfast and dinner, and at least three hours of daily group instruction. The categories are:

> *Very Inexpensive,* less than $80 per person per day
> *Inexpensive,* less than $110 per person per day
> *Moderate,* $110–$160 per person per day
> *Expensive,* $160–$210 per person per day
> *Very Expensive,* over $210 per person per day

When resort packages themselves do not include meals, I've added $35 to $45 a day to cover breakfast and dinner (or whatever the resort's MAP rate is), depending on my best guess of what it will actually cost if you eat in the resort's middle-range restaurants. You may be able to get by on much less. I've also summarized what's included in the basic clinic package.

COURTS: For the most part this is a straightforward account of how many courts there are, the kind of surface they have, and how many are indoors or have lights. If there's a stadium, I've made note of it, as I have of any distinctive features of the layout and of any courtside amenities, like swimming pools, restaurants, lounges, or fitness centers.

COURT FEES: Many resorts have a detestable policy of charging fees for court use. I've used the following categories to indicate how much:

> *Inexpensive,* up to $7 per court-hour
> *Moderate,* $7–$14 per court-hour
> *Expensive,* over $14 per court-hour

However, those fees are often avoidable on packages. If so, I've made note.

PRO STAFF: Tennis programs live and die by the quality of their teaching staffs. For each school or resort, I've outlined the teaching and playing backgrounds of the director of tennis and, in some cases, of the head pro as well. I've also generalized about the credentials of the assisting staff.

A few of these resorts have contracted with a big-name player to be their touring or resident pro. If so, I've assessed how much time he or she actually spends on site conducting clinics, giving exhibitions, or playing with guests. Wherever possible, I've noted the specific times when such personal appearances are most likely to occur.

INSTRUCTIONAL PROGRAMS: Each section on instructional programs provides answers to some or all of the following questions. How many hours a day do the sessions last? Is it all group instruction or are there private lessons as well? Are there special provisions for beginners or advanced players? What is the ratio of students to pros (the industry standard is 4:1)? Do you stay with the same pro all week or rotate through several members of the staff? Are there special weeks or packages for singles, advanced players, or people over 40? Do they simultaneously run camps for juniors and, if so, for what ages?

SPECIAL FEATURES: This category inventories the equipment available, like videotaping, ball machines, hitting lanes, and match-charting devices. This is where I describe the game-matching services, especially if they're outstanding.

SEASONAL TENNIS EVENTS: Depending on your point of view, special tennis events can be a reason either to visit or to avoid the resort while they're in progress. In this section I've included names and approximate dates of pro tournaments, pro-ams, open amateur tournaments, and any other tennis events that recur perennially on the resort's calendar.

PRO SHOP: Since every resort ought to have a pro shop, I haven't bothered to include a description unless it is unusual or inadequate.

LODGING AND FOOD: This section is both a survey and qualitative review of the options for accommodations and food within the resort.

OTHER RECREATIONAL AMENITIES: For those who do not live by tennis alone, I've provided a catalog of everything else there is to do at the resort.

GESTALT: This is a subjective review of the resort, based on all the information I've been able to compile. To the extent that it was possible, I've tried to give a sense of overall tennis atmosphere.

TRAVEL INSTRUCTIONS: On the assumption that most people will arrive by plane, I've included the location of the nearest airport and information and advice about getting from there to the site of the clinic.

Too New to Rate

As I was completing the research for this book, I came across more than half a dozen promising camps that had either opened too recently to be accurately evaluated or not yet opened at all. It's too soon for me to rank any of them with the world's best, but each has many of the qualities I look for in a top contender. They're listed below by region with a summary of their assets.

▶ Northeast

NEW HAMPSHIRE

▷ *New England Tennis Holidays,* New England Inn, P.O. Box 1648, North Conway, NH 03860. Phone: (603) 356-9696 or (800) 869-0949. Former British junior champion and international circuit player Clare Grabher and her husband Kurt run two-day and five-day camps on the four courts at a century-old 40-room inn in New Hampshire's White Mountain National Forest.

▶ Mid-Atlantic and Southeast

FLORIDA

▷ *Gerulaitis Tennis Resort,* 1601 Congress Ave., Boynton Beach, FL 33436. Phone: (407) 732-0044. Vitas Gerulaitis, who ranked as high as Number 4 in the world, plans to run adult and junior clinics at this new 16-court facility on Florida's east coast.

▷ *Naples Bath & Tennis Club,* Bill Beverly's Tennis Academy, 4995 Airport Rd. North, Naples, FL 33942. Phone: (813) 261-5777 or (800) 225-9692. Although Bill Beverly is a fixture at Naples Bath & Tennis, his academy is new. He has hired a director and pros (Beverly himself does not teach the academy programs) to run the five-hour-a-day sessions. The curriculum varies according to the needs of each particular group of campers. With 37 courts, Naples Bath is known for attracting a tennis-hungry crowd, but campers may find that they have to stay somewhere else because there's a chronic shortage of guest accommodations at the resort.

NORTH CAROLINA

▷ *Pinehurst Tennis Advantage School,* Pinehurst Hotel & Country Club, P.O. Box 4000, Pinehurst, NC 29374. Phone: (919) 295-6811, (800) 334-9560, or in N.C. (800) 672-4644. Though best known as a golf resort, Pinehurst has introduced adult tennis clinics during the spring and fall. Sessions run five or more hours a day; so far turnout has been small, but early reviews are very enthusiastic. During the summer the school conducts junior clinics.

▶ *Midwest, West, and Southwest*

CALIFORNIA

▷ *John Gardiner's Rancho Valencia Resort,* P.O. Box 9126, Rancho Santa Fe, CA 92007. Phone: (619) 756-1123 or (800) 548-3664. The director of tennis for this newest John Gardiner venture (see "The Designer Labels") is Ken Rosewall, who in his long career won all the major Grand Slam events. Plans call for him to be at this posh new tennis resort ten to twelve times a year.

TEXAS

▷ *T Bar M Tennis Ranch,* P.O. Box 310714, New Braunfels, TX 78131-0714. (512) 625-7825 or in TX (800) 292-5469. Former international touring pros John Benson and Mark Turpin run six-hour-a-day clinics consisting of instruction in the morning and supervised matchplay in the afternoon. You have a choice of staying in an inn or condominium on all-inclusive packages that even provide complimentary beer, wine, and soda. Clinics take place on the ranch's 14 hard courts; however, Turpin has a grass court in his front yard and makes it available to campers curious to try out the game's original surface.

UTAH

▷ *The Vic Braden Tennis College at Green Valley,* 1515 W. Canyon View Dr., St. George, UT 84770. Phone: (801) 628-8060 or (800) 237-1068. Set in the scenic desert canyonlands of southwestern Utah, the resort has a growing reputation both for its tennis programs and its spa. Although Vic Braden himself (see "The Designer Labels") is not personally involved, the staff has been trained in his methods. The college has 19 hard courts, 4 of them indoors, and 13 of Braden's hitting lanes. It is definitely worth looking into.

WYOMING

▷ *John Gardiner's Tennis Center at Teton Pines,* Star Rte. Box 362A, Jackson, WY 83001. Phone: (307) 733-9248 or (800) 238-2223. Set 6,000 feet above sea level on a posh real-estate development backdropped by the Teton mountains, Gardiner's Teton Pines operation has magnificent scenery, an Arnold Palmer–designed golf course, and a fly-fishing school to recommend it. Only recently, however, with the completion of sixteen luxury suites, has this ten-court tennis center been able to offer all-inclusive packages.

MEXICO

▷ *Club Med–Ixtapa,* Zihuatanejo, Gro. 40880. (212) 750-1687 or (800) CLUB-MED. The newest Club Med to offer their version of an "intensive" tennis clinic is in Ixtapa on Mexico's Pacific Coast (see "The Designer Labels" for an overview of the basic Club Med tennis formula). The club has 12 hard courts, four with lights.

The Designer Labels

Hard-core tennis vacationers instantly recognize All American Sports, Braden, Bollettieri, Gardiner, Hopman, and Van der Meer as some of the designer labels of the tennis-camp industry. Each of those brand names evokes not only a particular style of camp but a distinctive teaching methodology as well. Knowing that can ease the task of choosing a tennis camp.

▶ *All American Sports*

All American Sports was founded in 1968 by Nick Bollettieri and a group of investors. As the name suggests, the original intention was to operate a variety of summer sports camps for juniors. The first to open was the Nick Bollettieri Tennis Camp at Wayland Academy in Beaver Dam, Wisconsin. Shortly thereafter the organization brought in U.S. Davis Cup captain Donald Dell; team members Stan Smith, Arthur Ashe, Dennis Ralston, and Marty Riessen; the Australian Davis Cup coach Harry Hopman; and touring pros Bob Lutz and Charlie Pasarell. Together they designed a tennis program geared to the needs and athletic abilities of amateurs, and launched it in 1969 as the Hopman-Bollettieri tennis camp, choosing as a site the green, rolling campus of Amherst College in Massachusetts.

Unlike the original Bollettieri camp, Amherst ran clinics for both juniors and adults. The program devised by that stellar crew combined two diametrically opposed philosophies of teaching: Bollettieri favored having students stand in one place and practice good-looking strokes; Hopman believed in making them run, with form taking a backseat to hitting out. The hangers-on added encouragement—*"Come on, come on, come on. You can get it. Go, go!"*—as a way of making drills more fun, and the classic All American Sports drills were born.

All American soon dropped its multi-sports orientation to specialize in tennis. Although most of the original staff has gone on to pursue other tennis interests, All American continues to operate the original Amherst summer camp and now runs a half-dozen others besides, in sites from Vermont to Florida and from the Caribbean to Europe.

All American can accommodate almost every type of tennis enthusiast, from families interested in a fun tennis vacation to hard-core players. The format of its adult program varies slightly according to the environment in which it is offered: at Amherst, the clinics run more than five hours a day; at resorts, guests have the option of a three-hour morning clinic, a two-hour session of supervised match play, or both.

Full-scale junior programs take place during the summer at Amherst; Swarthmore College in Pennsylvania; and Hurstpierpont School in Brighton, England. They combine five hours a day of tennis instruction with a wealth of other supervised activities. Although these camps may lure a few very strong junior players and expose everyone to tournament play, All American does not structure its camps around hardcore competition. This is a summer camp in the classic sense of a place to get away and have fun. It just happens that the main activity is tennis.

The junior programs also serve All American as training ground for its pros. It is there that they learn All American's teaching methods and drills and hone their skills as instructors. Only the best of them have any hope of being hired for one of the resort positions. Those who remain with the organization full-time must now be certified as competent to teach by either the U.S. Professional Tennis Association or the U.S. Professional Tennis Registry.

Beyond that, there are certain characteristics common to all All American programs. The student-pro ratio never exceeds 4:1, and it's often less for beginners. None of its pros will try to impose major changes in strokes unless the camper requests it or the errant stroke risks causing injury. The most basic three-day program begins by teaching and videotaping the major strokes, moves on to specialty shots (overheads, return of serve, lobs, and approach shots), and ends with an introduction to strategy and tactics. Every group of four works on the same thing at the same time but at a pace and difficulty geared to their playing level. As the week progresses, so do the drills, becoming more demanding as students master techniques. Every program includes one or more half-hour private lessons. From time to time at various of its sites All American stages special weeks for singles, advanced players, or those over 40, supplementing the usual clinic program with special events and activities.

Nick Bollettieri runs hard-core programs for juniors and soft-core programs for adults at his academy in Bradenton, Florida.

▶ *Nick Bollettieri*

No junior tennis academy in the U.S. has a higher profile than Nick Bollettieri's, especially now that Andre Agassi has cracked the world's top ten. Yet the man himself remains a controversial figure. His supporters point not only to Agassi but to his other successful protégés, among them Brian Gottfried, Paul Annacone, Jimmy Arias, Carling Bassett-Seguso, and more recently Monica Seles and Jim Courier. His detractors insist that he is little more than a vigorous self-promoter, far better at associating himself with up-and-coming talent than he is at nurturing greatness.

A former Marine paratrooper, Nick Bollettieri turned to teaching tennis in the late 1950s after dropping out of Miami Law School. In subsequent years, he served as a personal pro to the Rockefellers and helped found both the famed Port Washington (N.Y.) Tennis Academy and the All American Sports camp operation. His rise to international prominence as a maker of tennis stars dates from the mid-1970s when he established a school for aspiring juniors, first at the Colony Beach and Tennis Club on Longboat Key in Florida and subsequently at his Nick Bollettieri Tennis Academy in Bradenton, Florida.

Bollettieri has a reputation as a tough taskmaster and his academy is often described as a tennis boot camp. In spite, or perhaps because of that, as many as 200 juniors from all over the world come to him, opting to live there in condominium-style dormitories just for the privilege of enduring a daily regimen of drills, exercises, and supervised matches. Laggard behavior is not tolerated, and those who let up during the daily workouts risk having Bollettieri bark orders at them, even if he's several courts away. Bollettieri himself describes it as "a total program of competitive play," comprising instruction, drills, and weekend tournaments. In practice the kids eat, drink, talk, and sleep tennis, and dream of greatness—or of the day their parents let them leave.

Many adults come to Bollettieri's expecting to endure a similar regimen, only to find that his adult programs are cut from much softer cloth. Bollettieri himself has little or nothing to do with the adults on or off the courts. The five-hour-a-day format looks intensive, but more than an hour of that is spent in the classroom. So instead of a grown-ups' version of the juniors' industrial-strength workouts, this turns out to be a resort program in tennis academy clothing.

▶ *Vic Braden*

No tennis teacher is better known than Vic Braden. His beaver grin and comic patter made his syndicated television series *Vic Braden's Tennis for the Future* a favorite of millions when it appeared on PBS in the early 1980s. Not only did he add a dimension of fun to the sport, but his jokes also helped to deflate the little fears and anxieties that made learning a complex game even harder. He became a master of the tennis one-liner and the patron saint of the weekend hacker.

What underlies the methodology at the Vic Braden Tennis College and its satellites is Braden's extensive research into "the physical properties of tennis, the laws." At his college in Coto de Caza, California, he has a research center crammed with computers and technological equipment for measuring athletes in action. Rather than speculate about how Roscoe Tanner hits his serve at 140 m.p.h., for example, or whether a looping backswing on groundstrokes is better than a straight one, Braden and Dr. Gideon Ariel, the sports scientist who heads his research center, amassed reams of biomechanical data in search of the perfect tennis strokes. Having found them, Braden teaches only what science tells him is absolutely *the* most efficient way to hit a tennis ball. "To make a ball do a certain thing," Braden insists, "you have to hit it in a precise manner, no ifs, ands, or buts about it. . . . You can't strike the ball in two ways and produce the same desired result."

The distinguishing characteristic of any Braden clinic is that uncompromising approach to what is taught. With that comes a heavy emphasis on strokes and very little on strategy and tactics. His clinics typically have a 6:1 student-pro ratio and make extensive use of hitting lanes and videotape. Those at Coto de Caza run roughly 6 hours a day, but the sessions are often extended for anyone who wants more help. However, even at Coto de Caza—where Braden lives—he rarely shows up in person, except once or perhaps twice a week to give introductory lectures into his theories and research. At other resorts with Braden clinics, he is always present on videotape but only rarely shows up in person.

▶ *Peter Burwash International*

When Peter Burwash talks about hitting a tennis ball, he steadfastly avoids cliches like "get your racquet back" and "watch the ball." Instead he talks about things like "contact zone," "balance," and "control." His basic premise is that players cease to improve because they lack a common-sense understanding of the game. "Tennis is a game of emergencies," says Burwash. It isn't perfect form that determines who wins a tennis match but knowing how to respond when an opponent has you in trouble. And for that you need to understand the theory behind sound strokes.

Burwash lays out his theories and the "simplicity checkpoints" for each of the various strokes in *Tennis For Life,* the book he wrote with John Tullius. Along the way he debunks a few myths—like *never bend your wrist*—and, almost as an afterthought, launches into the virtues of a vegetarian diet.

Tennis For Life is the Bible of the teaching pros of Peter Burwash International. Burwash founded the organization in 1975 to supply clubs and resorts with pros who had been trained not only to teach but also to manage every aspect of a tennis operation, from running tournaments to merchandising the shop. The training is so thorough— it runs for 35 days, some of which run to fourteen hours—that it ensures graduates can type and take photos.

Today there are more than 86 pros in 23 countries worldwide, not just in U.S. tennis resorts like the Royal Lahaina in Hawaii, but also in exotic locations like the Jakarta Hilton in Indonesia and the Oman

Sheraton in the Sultanate of Oman. From time to time Burwash personally conducts a "Tennis For Life" clinic at a PBI resort, but most of the time he travels the world introducing the joy of tennis in the most improbable places: Third World countries, prisons, and mental hospitals. Few PBI sites, however, run the kinds of ongoing programs available from All American Sports or Dennis Van der Meer. That's odd to me, because one that does, Hotel Stanglwirt, near Kitzbühl in Austria, is enormously successful. And many of Burwash's theories and methods—though not his pros—contribute to the solid program at the Inn and Tennis Club at Manitou in Canada.

▶ *Club Med*

Club Med offers tennis clinics everywhere it has courts. These typically last an hour, with separate sessions for beginners, intermediates, and advanced players. Class sizes can reach 20 or more. Rather than serious instruction, the clinics' real function is to introduce tennis players to one another.

At a few sites, however, Club Med runs what it calls an intensive tennis program. "Intensive tennis" *chez* Club Med does not mean concentrated and rigorous, as it does in programs at resorts or on college campuses; what it really means is longer—that is, two-and-a-half-hour—clinics supplemented by almost daily tournaments and special tennis events. Club Med itself subscribes to no particular teaching philosophy, nor does it dictate a set program. The decision about how to structure the clinic rests instead with the head of the program—or *chef de tennis*—who, like the entire teaching staff, changes clubs every six months. Reviewing a Club Med tennis program is like reviewing a restaurant when you know the chef will leave before the review appears.

Still, it is possible to make a few generalizations. The two Club Meds with well-established intensive programs—Paradise Island in the Bahamas and Sonora Bay in Mexico—strive to have one teaching pro for every ten people in the clinic. Because the staff is much larger than that at an ordinary Club Med, the odds are greater that there will be several strong teaching pros on hand. It is, therefore, not unusual to find a few on staff who played in college or on the satellite tour, others who have advanced degrees in exercise physiology or other sports-related fields, and still others who have U.S. or foreign certifications.

The Club Med format has you stay with one pro throughout the week. For the most part, each pro decides what to teach and how, based on the needs of his or her particular batch of players. Styles and approaches differ widely from pro to pro. The best are students of the game with their own clearly defined philosophy of how to teach the

16

kinds of players they routinely encounter at Club Meds. The worst, unfortunately, can be embarrassingly mediocre. You take potluck.

In my experience, the stronger pros tend to be given charge of the better intermediate and advanced players. That's good news for everyone but beginners, and it's one reason I don't recommend any Club Med to a beginner who's serious about taking up the game. The classes at the lowest level are too big, the quality of the technical instruction too hit-and-miss. But, having said that, I should point out that a Club Med intensive program also affords beginners something they'll have trouble finding anyplace else: as many as 20 people struggling along with them to pick up the game and tournament sections open only to novices. Whatever reservations I personally have about the instruction don't alter the fact that the beginners I talked to were having a lot of fun.

Ultimately, the lure of a Club Med program derives from more than the on-court instruction. Its pros are more than usually willing to hit with the campers outside of the clinics. There are daily tournaments and contests, which may include pro-am Calcuttas (you bid for the right to play with your favorite pro in a doubles tournament) and challenge-the-pro events. The courts have lights so you can literally play all night if you want to. But, most of all, the two Club Meds I've reviewed—Paradise Island in the Bahamas and Sonora Bay in Mexico—stand out for their ability to lure large numbers of tennis players.

▶ *John Gardiner*

In the mid-1950s, John Gardiner was a teaching pro in Monterey and frustrated. Parents sent their kids to him for an hour a week, viewing tennis, like horseback riding, as one of the social graces. A dilettante's superficial skill was essential; mastery unnecessary. But Gardiner wanted a means to do more, so in 1957 he purchased a 25-acre apricot ranch in California's Carmel Valley and opened the nation's first camp to specialize exclusively in tennis. Though he originally catered to juniors, he soon had to add clinics for adults, when parents, inspired by their children's progress, began asking for a similar kind of instruction. Thus the tennis camp was born.

Although Gardiner himself no longer teaches, his clinics continue to reflect his pragmatic approach to instruction. Much of the emphasis falls on doubles since that's what his generally older clientele tends to play. What people really want out of tennis camp, Gardiner believes, is to improve enough to be able to "beat the guy in their club or their neighbor." They aren't looking to undertake a major overhaul of their strokes. They want to be sufficiently tired at the end of the day to feel like they got their money's worth. So, according to Gardiner, the three

17

Since 1957, when he started his Carmel Valley Tennis Ranch, John Gardiner has been the first name in luxury tennis camps.

most important attributes of a clinic are "to get some exercise, have fun, and learn something about tennis," in that order.

Gardiner's pros all go through a nine-week training program and apprenticeship to learn both his methods and his catch phrases, so that they not only teach alike but use exactly the same vocabulary. They become masters of positive reinforcement. Every one is unfailingly polite. One thing they do not do, however, is socialize with the guests outside the context of the clinic itself. At lunch and once the day's workouts are over, the entire teaching staff disappears, with the occasional exception of the director of tennis and head pro.

In the demeanor he demands of his pros it is easy to see Gardiner's nostalgia for the era when tennis was played by refined ladies and gentlemen in tennis whites. To this day he dresses his teaching staff in impeccable tennis whites, and even goes so far as to request it of clients. Under "Apparel" in his brochures it reads: "Thank you for wearing the traditional tennis attire of predominant whites while on the courts," a request that goes largely unheeded. But Gardiner's impulse to create a particular atmosphere, even mystique, suffuses his ranches in Carmel Valley and Scottsdale, Arizona, and perhaps will at the new Rancho Valencia in California.

▶ *Harry Hopman*

Harry Hopman was the architect of the Australian tennis dynasty that ruled Davis Cup play during the 1950s and 1960s. During his 19 years as coach the Aussie squads won the cup 15 times. His methods had less to do with the technical fundamentals of stroking than with training, motivation, and discipline, and for that he's been called "the greatest coach ever."

Hopman died in 1985, but not before helping to launch the careers of John McEnroe, Vitas Gerulaitis, Peter McNamara, Paul McNamee, Andres Gomez, and Ramesh Krishnan, to name only a few. The tennis school he started after coming to the United States continues. Located at Saddlebrook, a golf and tennis resort north of Tampa, Florida, Harry Hopman International Tennis has, like Nick Bollettieri's Tennis Academy, a reputation for being a tennis boot camp. You wouldn't know it from looking at the posh condominiums where the kids live, or at the swimming pools and Jacuzzis. But the brochures do warn that "Beginners, intermediates, and tournament players are put through the rigorous paces that champions demand." Hopman's beloved running drills and his minimalist's approach to technical instruction remain hallmarks of the program.

That's as true for adults as it is for juniors. There is no more physically demanding adult tennis clinic than the five-hour-a-day sessions at Hopman's. There are never more than four students for each pro; often there are fewer, which makes the workouts even more grueling.

As long as the ball goes in, the pros don't bother with much technical instruction. "Just hit out" is the most frequently heard phrase in a Hopman clinic—that and "Just five more balls. Hit five more and you're done."

▶ *John Newcombe*

John Newcombe's stellar career as a player, signature mustache, Australian drawl, and television commentary for CBS make him a household word—at least in houses with tennis players. He was the

19

Number 1 player in the world for four years in the late 1960s and early 1970s. In the course of his career he won the Wimbledon singles championship three times, the Australian four, and the U.S. once as well as the doubles championships in all three of those events and the French.

Newcombe's name and trademark mustache appear prominently at John Newcombe's Tennis Ranch in New Braunfels, Texas. He is a part owner; however, except for conducting a very rare clinic, he has no personal involvement with the actual programs. That does not diminish their quality—see my review of the Texas ranch—but it is a clue to the slippery nature of Newcombe as a brand name. It may mean nothing more than that Newcombe is an investor or licenser, as is the case with the John Newcombe Tennis Clubs in Puerto Vallarta, Mexico, and in Fiji. It does not guarantee that the facility will subscribe to a particular Newcombe-inspired teaching methodology or will offer a program unique to Newcombe properties.

▶ *Dennis Van der Meer*

In more than three decades of teaching and coaching, Dennis Van der Meer has established himself as one of the foremost tennis teachers in the world. A former top player in his native South Africa, he went on to coach Margaret Court and Billie Jean King and then established his own teaching center on Hilton Head Island. In 1988, the President's Council on Physical Fitness and Sports established a "National Master in Tennis" award and designated Van der Meer as one of the very first recipients.

But Van der Meer's distinction in the world of big-name pros is his willingness to spend vast amounts of time teaching club players. He personally conducts roughly half of the major clinics offered at his tennis centers, and the schedules make explicitly clear which are his and which are led by senior staff. He doesn't just show up, make a brief personal appearance, and disappear. When Van der Meer runs a clinic he is there for the duration, on the court, actively teaching from the first minute to the last.

Whether it's Van der Meer or his senior staff running the clinic, the teaching methodology is the same. Van der Meer has developed a highly programmed, step-by-step teaching method he calls the Official Standard Method of Instruction. It breaks each of the basic strokes down into a series of specific steps. Students start by mastering simple skills (like bouncing a ball off the ground with their racquet), which can then be combined to produce whole strokes. The idea is to create confidence by building on successes and thus minimize the frustration of learning a difficult sport. Van der Meer believes that his methods

20

Dennis Van der Meer, who coached Margaret Court and Billie Jean King, spends more hours teaching club players than any other big-name pro.

"can teach a beginner the basics of the game faster and more efficiently than any other method."

Moreover, he insists that it has other advantages. For one thing, he maintains that his method is "teacher-proof"; that is, simple enough to be demonstrated and taught even by a novice instructor. What he'd really like to see, however, is his method become the standard used throughout the U.S.—and, for that matter, the world. That would eliminate, he insists, the frustration of taking lessons from two different pros and having each of them recommend something different.

To that end, he has established a program called TennisUniversity I to teach pros his methods, and an organization called the United States Professional Tennis Registry (USPTR) to certify their competence. What Van der Meer has not managed to do is get the tennis-teaching establishment—namely, the United States Professional Tennis Association (USPTA), itself a major certifying body—to adopt his methods as the U.S. standard. The USPTA's position is that Van der Meer's method of instruction is one among several with merit, no one of which is perfect. Recently, the USPTR moved its headquarters from the Van der Meer Tennis Center to another location on Hilton Head Island, hoping to find more widespread acceptance by distancing itself from Van der Meer.

Stymied there, Van der Meer has lately begun to expand his influence by contracting to manage resort tennis complexes. His organization supplies USPTR-certified pros and gains additional venues for its clinics. Van der Meer himself typically shows up to conduct one or more clinics a year at each of those subsidiary sites.

The Best and the Worst

In this subjective world, one player's great tennis resort can just as easily be another's tennis hell. It depends on which criteria are used to make the judgment. Advanced players require far more demanding and sophisticated clinics than beginners. Vacationers traveling alone have nightmares about being the only single person at a resort of romantic couples. Tennis players who favor running shorts and t-shirts will never find happiness among those who regard designer clothing as a major weapon in their psychological arsenal. The drill-til-you-drop crowd measures a resort by the number of hours devoted to tennis clinics and the ready availability of free courts and perhaps hitting lanes, while less fanatic tennis vacationers may also crave amenities like a beach or golf course. Perspective is everything.

▶ Best Programs for Beginners

Boca Raton Resort & Club, Florida
Vic Braden Tennis College, California
Inn & Tennis Club at Manitou, Canada
Killington School for Tennis, Vermont
Sugarbush Tennis Club, Vermont
Total Tennis, Massachusetts
Van der Meer Tennis Center, South Carolina

▶ Best Programs for Advanced Players

Advanced Weeks at Amherst College/All American Sports Clinics, Massachusetts
Harry Hopman/Saddlebrook International Tennis, Florida
"Championship" program at John Newcombe's Tennis Ranch, Texas
Match-play drill clinics and mental toughness clinics (Tennis-University II) at Van der Meer Tennis Center, South Carolina

▶ *Best Value for Dollar*

Amherst College/All American Sports Clinics, Massachusetts
Gray Rocks Inn, Canada
Total Tennis, Vermont
Van der Meer Summer Camps, Virginia
Van der Meer Tennis Center, South Carolina

▶ *Friendliest Camps*

Amherst College/All American Sports Clinics, Massachusetts
Inn & Tennis Club at Manitou, Canada
John Newcombe's Tennis Ranch, Texas
Reed Anderson Tennis School, Nevada

▶ *Best for Those Vacationing Alone*

Amherst College/All American Sports Clinics, Massachusetts
Nick Bollettieri Tennis Academy, Florida
Club Med–Paradise Island, Bahamas
Club Med–Sonora Bay, Mexico
Killington School for Tennis, Vermont
John Newcombe's Tennis Ranch, Texas
Total Tennis, Vermont
Van der Meer Summer Camps, Virginia

▶ *Most Romantic*

Inn & Tennis Club at Manitou, Canada
John Gardiner's Tennis Ranch, California
The Palace Hotel, Switzerland
Topnotch at Stowe Resort & Spa, Vermont

▶ *Finest Cuisine*

Colony Beach & Tennis Resort, Florida
John Gardiner's Tennis Ranch, California
Inn & Tennis Club at Manitou, Canada
Rancho Bernardo Inn, California
Topnotch at Stowe Resort & Spa, Vermont

▶ *Best Accommodations*

Beach Club at Boca Raton Resort & Club, Florida
Junior suites at Inn & Tennis Club at Manitou, Canada
Houses with their own courts and the *casitas* at John Gardiner's
  Tennis Ranch on Camelback, Arizona
Casitas at Wickenburg Inn Tennis & Guest Ranch, Arizona

▶ *Best All-round Resorts*

Amelia Island Plantation/All American Sports Clinics, Florida
Boca Raton Resort & Club, Florida
Gray Rocks Inn, Canada
Lodge of Four Seasons, Missouri
Palmas del Mar, Puerto Rico
Sea Pines Plantation, South Carolina
Stratton Tennis School, Vermont
Wild Dunes, South Carolina

▶ *Best Beaches*

Amelia Island Plantation/All American Sports Clinics, Florida
Club Med–Paradise Island, Bahamas
Colony Beach & Tennis Resort, Florida
Sea Pines Plantation, South Carolina
Wild Dunes, South Carolina

▶ *Best Golf Courses*

Harry Hopman/Saddlebrook International Tennis, Florida
Sea Pines Plantation, South Carolina
Wild Dunes, South Carolina

▶ *Best Daycare or Activities for Kids*

Amelia Island Plantation/All American Sports Clinics, Florida
Ian Fletcher Tennis School, Vermont
Sea Pines Plantation, South Carolina
Sugarbush Tennis Club, Vermont
Wickenburg Inn Tennis & Guest Ranch, Arizona

▶ *Worst Places to Take a Non-tennis-playing Companion*

Amherst College/All American Sports Clinics, Massachusetts
John Newcombe's Tennis Ranch, Texas
Total Tennis, Vermont
Van der Meer Summer Camps, Virginia

The Fine Art
of Choosing a
Tennis Resort

. . . .

Choosing a resort for a tennis vacation seems to demand all the fore-thought of picking out a can of balls. Any resort with a respectable number of courts seemingly ought to do. Golfers may travel halfway around the world to challenge a particular course, but tennis players' battles are not with the peculiarities of the courts, which adhere to absolute standards, but with the skills of an opponent. And for that, any court will do.

At the same time, no ardent tennis player is about to book a resort that has only one court. Courts are generally interpreted as a metaphor for the resort's commitment to tennis players. Any respectably large complex—say, ten or more courts—seems destined also to have essential services like lessons, clinics, game-matching, and on-court social events; thus, as the number of courts increases, so does a resort's tennis mystique. And therein lies the Great Tennis Resort Fallacy: acres of courts, by themselves, do absolutely nothing to distinguish great resorts from those that are merely large.

Subconsciously, tennis players know that. Ask those just back from a tennis vacation what they liked about the resort and not one will so much as mention the number of courts. Instead, they'll rave about how many hours they played, the people they met, the quality of the instruction, the friendliness of the staff—in short, all those aspects that made their stays memorable. The soul of a resort lies not in its courts but in that most intangible of assets: tennis atmosphere. But without actually visiting the resort, how do you go about assessing something as nebulous as "tennis atmosphere"?

The obvious solution of asking friends and acquaintances for recommendations works only to the degree that they have personal experience with the resorts you're considering. If they are avid, well-traveled tennis players, their advice can be invaluable. As backup, however, you must know how to evaluate a resort's tennis assets when no one you know has been there.

Over the years I've worked out a method for getting a sense of a resort before I ever go. Gathering brochures helps, but too often they fail to include much of the information I regard as critical. So what I do is telephone the pro shop (which you can sometimes reach on the resort's toll-free number) pretending to be a run-of-the-mill vacationer in the throes of planning his holiday. After letting them know which particular week I'm planning to visit, I ask questions about what to expect in the way of game-matching services, social-tennis events, and instruction. As important to me as the specific answers is the attitude of the person in the shop. If he or she is friendly, helpful, and seemingly eager to have me visit, that tells me much of what I need to know about the resort's enthusiasm to lure tennis players.

The tennis atmosphere that distinguishes a great resort from a merely good one cannot exist unless nurtured by a superb staff, but its source lies elsewhere. In nearly a decade of reviewing tennis resorts, I've come to recognize five other criteria as the building blocks of a great resort.

▶ *Availability of Courts*

The law of supply and demand applies to tennis courts just as it does to economics. Thus, the issue is not how many courts a resort has, but whether enough exist to meet the needs of the people wanting to use them. A clue to the adequacy of the supply lies in the ratio of courts to rooms.

In the best of all possible worlds, resorts would build one court for every room, thus ensuring every tennis-playing guest what amounted to a private court. In this world it has happened only once: John Gardiner's Tennis Ranch in Carmel Valley, California, has fourteen courts and fourteen rooms. But not even the most fanatical of tennis players spends every daylight hour on court, so there is no reason to hold a typical resort to anything like that theoretical ideal. A realistic target is one court for every ten or twelve rooms. That is more than adequate even at a tennis resort destination having few other recreational amenities.

Even that standard becomes too rigid, however, at resorts with much more to offer than tennis. If there is also a beach, golf, watersports, sightseeing, and shopping, then a smaller percentage of the guests will be tennis players and fewer of those will be fanatics. A resort with a beach and one or more golf courses can safely get by with one court for every twenty-five rooms and still satisfy its tennis-playing guests.

Several other factors influence court availability. The demand for courts burgeons during holiday periods and high season. Hot climates may make playing at midday unthinkable, forcing guests to vie for the same morning and evening court times. Lighted courts, on the other hand, extend playing hours and thus help spread out the demand. All these factors go into determining whether the court-to-room ratio is adequate to the circumstances.

▶ Court Fees

Court fees are the bane of every ardent tennis lover's vacation. Nothing is worse than to step onto the court feeling as though the meter is running, clicking off $10 or $15 or even as much as $20 for every hour spent on court. This benighted policy emerges when management insists that the tennis courts be a "profit center." It's much easier to show how many dollars come in as court fees than it is to demonstrate that players who spend more time at the courts also end up spending more money in the pro shop, restaurant, and bar. The policy is aggravated by the Rich Guests Syndrome; namely, the assumption that anyone who can afford to spend $250 a night for a room at the resort can certainly afford to shell out an additional $100 or $200 or $300 a week in court fees and probably should be made to.

Unless a resort's brochure touts a policy of not charging for court time, assume you will have to pay. Also assume that the more expensive the room, the higher the court fees. If you only intend to play an hour a day, it may not matter. But if you plan to play more than that, or are taking your family of four, then you need to do one of two things. Either request a higher limit on your credit cards or look for a resort that offers unlimited free court time, if not as a general policy, then to guests on its tennis packages.

▶ Game-Matching Services

There are two major categories of tennis resort: the higher order, which does everything it can to make sure guests who need opponents find them; and the lower order, which does not. The distinguishing feature is a conscientious game-matching service. It is not unlike a dating service, except the goal in this case is to get two or four roughly equal players together on court.

All systems are essentially alike: the pro shop staff takes down your name, date of arrival and departure, ability level, the time of day you want to play, and your preference for singles, doubles, or mixed doubles. What happens next is an excellent barometer of the resort's overall dedication to the tennis player. The worst of them hand you their list and suggest you phone anyone who looks promising. Many people have an aversion to telephoning strangers, but there is an even deeper flaw in that system: it can be extremely difficult to catch guests in their room. Leaving a message is fruitless since they'll have equal difficulty getting back to you. Instead of playing tennis you may end up playing telephone tag, and who wants that kind of aggravation on vacation?

Resorts that understand the logistical problem take charge of making the calls themselves, and very often have someone on staff whose sole duty it to set up matches. All you have to do is decide when you want to play; the staff makes the calls in search of an appropriate opponent. The best of them go so far as to guarantee to find someone for you to play, and back up that guarantee by promising to supply a hitting pro, free of charge, if they fail.

▶ Social Tennis Events

Many resorts supplement their game-matching services by scheduling social tennis events to bring players together. Having met, the players can work out their own arrangements for later matches. More than that, however, events like round-robins, singles and doubles tournaments, exhibitions, tennis-wear fashion shows, cocktail parties, and the like, add to the social fabric of a resort, sometimes to the point of making it feel like a club. A resort with a strong game-matching service can do without such events but will never have the same impalpable tennis mystique as one that thrives on bringing tennis players together on and off the courts. When you phone to inquire about game-matching services, ask the pro shop staff what's on the schedule during the week of your vacation.

▶ Instruction

A good argument can be made for including instruction in vacation plans because there's so much time to practice. How much instruction and what kind can dictate the resort you choose. Some, like those reviewed in this book, run full-fledged camps, which have anywhere from two to six hours of daily instruction and drills. But all will have one or more pros available for private lessons and probably clinics. If you're traveling with children, you may want to check on the availability of junior camps or tiny-tot lessons. Your choice of resorts may in part be dictated by your instructional needs. If you're contemplating private lessons, you may first want to look into their cost. At some luxury resorts, rates can run more than $50 an hour.

A few resorts advertise a well-known pro as their resident professional, touring professional, or director of tennis. None of those titles guarantees he or she will even be on the property, much less giving lessons. If you've chosen a particular resort convinced that its big-name pro can cure your errant volleys, then make sure he or she will be there and available to teach.

What to Pack

. . . .

The cardinal rule of packing light—leave out anything you only *think* you'll wear—does not apply to tennis clothing. It is virtually impossible to pack too many changes of tennis wear. Nothing is easier than to go through two complete outfits a day: one during the clinic in the morning and another playing matches or social tennis in the afternoon. If the resort has a reliable overnight laundry service, you may be able to get them cleaned in time for the next morning's clinic. You will also have to take out a second mortgage to pay the cleaning bill and wonder whether anyone notices that you're wearing the same two outfits every day.

What's worse, if their overnight service turns out not to be reliable, you won't have any clothes to wear at all, which means you'll have to buy them in the pro shop, where prices are double what they are anywhere else. If the resort has guest laundry facilities, you can avoid going into debt, but still have to contend with your vanity. One ruse is to pack outfits that are exactly alike. That way no one can ever be certain whether you're wearing the same outfit over and over or simply have an obsessive preference for one particular style. Or you can do what I do, which is pack every article of tennis clothing I own.

The ease and expense of getting clothing laundered and your own vanity ultimately conspire to determine how minimally you're willing to pack. What specifically goes into your luggage can depend on the resort you've chosen. Many of the better ones require "Proper Tennis Attire," which essentially means tennis rather than jogging shoes and collared shirts with sleeves (sleeveless blouses, on the other hand, are perfectly acceptable), although there is definitely a trend toward accepting t-shirts as proper attire. While a few old-line private tennis clubs still require tennis whites, no resort does.

When it comes to shoes, most experts suggest that you take two pairs. By wearing them on alternate days, you let one pair dry out thoroughly. Not only are they more comfortable that way, but they also last longer. Taking a backup tennis racquet also makes sense in case you pop a string or the handle gets wet from perspiration.

So, with all of that in mind, here is a checklist of crucial items to get you through a three- or four-day clinic with little or no need to do laundry. If you find that laundry can be done often and easily, then you can obviously cut back. Use the following as a guide, adding or subtracting as you see fit.

2 tennis racquets
3–4 shorts or skirts
6–8 shirts or blouses
8–10 pairs of socks
tennis shoes, 2 pairs if you have them
wristbands, especially in hot, humid climates
griptape
warmups (optional)
waterproof sunscreen (at least No. 15)
hat or visor
a swimsuit
insect repellent (where necessary)

NORTHEAST

Massachusetts

▶ Amherst College/All American Sports Clinics, Amherst

▶ Total Tennis, Easthampton

Vermont

▶ Ian Fletcher Tennis School, Bolton Valley

▶ Killington School for Tennis, Killington

▶ Stratton Tennis School, Stratton

▶ Sugarbush Tennis School, Warren

▶ Topnotch at Stowe Resort & Spa/All American Sports Clinics, Stowe

Amherst College/All American Sports Clinics

Amherst, MA
Information: All American Sports
116 Radio Circle Drive
Mt. Kisco, NY 10549

(914) 666-0096 or outside NY (800) 223-2442

SEASON: Early June to late August.

RATES: *Moderate.* On-campus rates include accommodations, full board, all tennis instruction, and free court time; off-campus rates include lunch daily, all tennis instruction, and free court time. Full-week packages run Sunday to Saturday; mini-sessions are available from Sunday to Wednesday or Thursday to Sunday.

▶ *Profile*

COURTS: Amherst College has 45 courts in all. The lower complex, where the adult clinics take place, consists of 6 HarTru and 14 all-weather courts partly bordered by forests of hardwoods and evergreens. Another 16—half of them hard, all-weather courts badly in need of resurfacing, half a mixture of red clay and dirt—occupy a terraced hillside between the college's newer buildings and its sports fields; this complex is used for the junior clinics. The recreation center houses the remaining 9 courts, all of them indoors and available in case of rain.

COURT FEES: None.

PRO STAFF: Director of tennis Reiny Maier has been part of the AAS summer clinic program at Amherst since 1970. He played Number 1 for a Wisconsin college and was one of the pros at Nick Bollettieri's (see "The Designer Labels") original camp in Beaver Dam, Wisconsin. Later he worked for Harry Hopman, when the legendary Australian Davis Cup coach was running the program at Amherst. Now, as direc-

35

All American Sports' first and most successful adult camp still runs every summer on the wooded campus of Amherst College in Massachusetts.

tor himself, he heads a staff of roughly 25 teaching pros from all over the world. Most are or have been college players; a few may have done stints on the satellite circuits. Although Amherst serves as a kind of

36

farm system for pros within the All American system, none of those teaching adults are novices, and some have impressive teaching credentials and ten or more years of experience. All have been through a training program to learn All American's drills and teaching techniques.

INSTRUCTIONAL PROGRAMS: All American Sports runs an intensive program at Amherst. At least five hours a day are spent on court, doing instruction and drills, and that does not count the three half-hour private lessons included in a full-week package, or the additional three hours per day left open for free play or ball-machine drills.

The standard intensive clinics take place throughout the summer. You can opt for an abbreviated session (which runs either Sunday to Wednesday or Thursday to Sunday) or a full seven-day session (which runs Sunday to Saturday). In addition, during certain weeks All American offers specialized programs. In the past these have included sessions for beginners, for advanced players, and for players who want to concentrate on doubles (whether men's or women's).

All American also runs junior clinics at Amherst for kids aged 8 to 17. This is not a hard-core junior academy like Hopman's or Bollettieri's but a summer camp where tennis is the major focus, though not to the exclusion of other organized sports, like softball, volleyball, and soccer. It's very social, with dances and movies every week and supervised lounges in the dorms where kids can watch TV. It attracts an international clientele. Adults and juniors eat in the same restaurants, but the two camps are otherwise completely separate.

SPECIAL FEATURES: Videotaping is an integral part of every week's program. Ball machines are available for anyone who for some unfathomable reason hasn't had enough drilling by the end of the day.

SPECIAL TENNIS EVENTS: While no major events or tournaments take place, the teaching pros occasionally put on exhibitions and the weekly calendar typically has some kind of social round-robin.

PRO SHOP: Set up in what looks like it may be an office during the regular school year, Amherst's pro shop is very small. It carries a limited supply of t-shirts, shoes, AAS logo clothing, sweatbands, griptape, and a few racquets, including demos. Twenty-four-hour restringing is available. The shop is open only during non-clinic hours.

LODGING AND FOOD: All American packages this clinic with or without on-campus accommodations and food. Opting to stay on-campus means bedding down in an un air-conditioned but private dorm room, one of a suite of four that shares a bathroom (with shower but no tub) and a very spartanly furnished living room. The dorm room itself measures ten feet by eleven. Each has a single bed, large closet, built-in drawers and, of course, a desk. It's up to you to bring your favorite posters to liven it up. You should also bring insect repellent since there are no screens on the windows. Couples who want to stay together can have both beds in one room, using the other as a dressing room. Most of the dormitory buildings have coin-operated washers and dryers.

Meals are served in the cafeteria. Though not in danger of winning culinary awards, the food is better and more varied than you might expect. Dinner entrees range among meat, chicken, and fish, almost always supplemented by pastas or other foods high in carbohydrates. There is a salad bar at both lunch and dinner and a general abundance of fresh fruits and liquids, including lemonade, orange juice, various sodas, and a dispenser of Poland Spring water. Eating well is easy. So is socializing. Since all the tables are for six or eight, you get plenty of opportunity off court to meet other campers. No one who comes alone needs to fear eating alone.

Alternatively, you can book your own accommodations off campus (AAS provides a list—the Lord Jeffrey Inn is the best among them). Lunch is included in the clinic package but not breakfast and dinner (though they're available at a very reasonable surcharge), which means missing out on the major occasions for off-court socializing. In practice, only about 10 percent of the campers opt to stay off campus.

OTHER RECREATIONAL AMENITIES: Amherst has a gym which contains a swimming pool and Nautilus equipment. Arrangements can be made for massages.

▶ *Gestalt*

Amherst College is a 150-year-old, ivy-covered institution set amid the green rolling farmland and wooded hills of central Massachusetts. The town's main street borders the north end of campus, and its shops, restaurants, and pubs are thus within walking distance of the dorms.

The All American Sports camp at Amherst is in its own way as venerable as the college. Now entering its third decade, it is the oldest and best known of the campus programs. Many of its drills date to the early years when Harry Hopman was director, but its emphasis has changed. "This is not a run-and-hit camp; it's a teaching camp," says current director Reiny Maier. By that he means that the primary goal is less to get you fit than to give you a solid grounding in all the essential strokes. At the same time, All American recognizes that there's only so much that can be done in a week, so the pros focus on making the strokes you already have more efficient. Unless what you currently do may cause injury or unless you express a desire to make a major change, they'll work to refine what you have rather than alter it entirely.

The week's progression reflects that philosophy. You start out by hitting balls while standing still. Only later, as the stroke becomes grooved, do you have to start moving to get in position. Then as you become more proficient, the drills become longer and more demanding. Finally toward the end of the week, the emphasis shifts again toward match-play situations, singles and doubles strategy, and some actual matches. (See "The Designer Labels" for a more detailed discussion of All American's philosophy and approach.)

As tennis programs go, this one ranks among the more rigorous but stops well short of being a boot camp. The pros look across the net and see not recruits but vacationers, so it's imperative that they make the drills fun as well as productive. Even people who don't ordinarily play often get through the week without missing a session.

The smoothly honed instruction is only part of what makes Amherst appealing, however. There is something very relaxing about being on a college campus—especially when it's for courses that don't involve any homework. The uniform of the day—and often evening—is far more likely to be t-shirts and running shorts than Fila or Ellesse outfits. Everyone has the same schedule of meals and clinics, and those constant encounters help to foster an easy familiarity. If Amherst campers as a group seem to have more than usual in common, it's probably because they not only share an enthusiasm for tennis but have also opted for a relatively demanding, five-hour-a-day program and against luxury appointments.

The social aspects draw sustenance from the relatively large turnouts. Even a slow week is likely to have at least 40 adults in the camp, and a busy week may have twice that many. The campers typically range in age from the mid-twenties to the fifties and sixties. Singles outnumber couples, and, except during the special weeks for advanced players, women usually outnumber men.

TRAVEL INSTRUCTIONS: The nearest airport is Bradley International in Hartford, Connecticut, about 50 miles to the south. All American will arrange transportation from there to Amherst; the cost is roughly $20 each way.

Late news: Amherst College rather than All American Sports now runs Amherst's summer camp program. They will follow exactly the AAS format and employ many of the former AAS staffers, including director Reiny Maier. For information contact the college at (413) 542-8100 or (800) 256-NETT.

Total Tennis

· ·

Williston-Northampton School
Easthampton, MA
c/o Box 1106, Wall Street Station
New York, NY 10268-1106

(718) 636-6141 or outside NY (800) 221-6496

SEASON: Mid-June to Labor Day.

RATES: *Inexpensive.* The package includes dorm accommodations, all meals, tennis instruction, one or two private lessons, unlimited court time, and free transportation from the bus station in Holyoke. Tennis-only packages (which include lunch) are also offered.

▶ *Profile*

COURTS: There are 15 courts in two locations. Directly behind the dorms is a line of 4 red clay and 5 hard courts; a few minutes' walk away there are another 6 red clay courts near a lake. None have lights. If it rains, Total Tennis has access to two clubs with indoor courts in nearby Springfield.

COURT FEES: None.

PRO STAFF: Ed Fondiller founded Total Tennis in 1978 after several summers of teaching and directing other summer tennis camps. He now oversees a staff of 23 teaching pros, a few of whom have taught for Total Tennis more than a decade. Chief among them is John Kahane, the assistant director, who has a Ph.D. in psychology and coaches the Williston girls' tennis team. Many of the remaining staff have four to five years experience with the operation.

INSTRUCTIONAL PROGRAMS: Total Tennis runs three-, four-, six-, and seven-night programs, all of which include six hours a day of instruction and drills. No pro ever has more than four students (the optimal maximum) and stays with his or her charges throughout the week.

40

Total Tennis is distinguished by its red-clay courts, economical prices, and high percentage of returning campers.

SPECIAL FEATURES: Videotaping is done once each session and ball machines are available for use on the hard courts after class.

PRO SHOP: There is a tiny room that sells t-shirts, gloves, hats, wristbands, and other accessories. It has demo racquets for rent but none to sell (though if you find one you like, the staff will arrange to get you one). Restringing can be arranged; however, if you need something like shoes or other clothing, you'll have to buy that in town.

LODGING AND FOOD: Total Tennis uses the dormitories of the Williston-Northampton School. The rooms are unusual in having air conditioning and maid service but typical in their small size. Most have two single beds (expect to share a room unless you pay a single supplement), two student desks, and two closets. A few have one double

41

bed instead. The bathrooms are down the hall. Campers universally complain about the insufficient number of showers (on average one for every eight people), which creates a bottleneck as everyone needs to clean up about the same time. Each dorm has a lounge with a television and a heavily utilized washer and dryer.

The brochures for Total Tennis describe the food as "delectable" when in fact it is pretty much the pedestrian fare you'd expect in a dorm. There is a minimal salad bar at both lunch and dinner (iceberg lettuce, tomatoes, mushrooms, pickled beets, jello with fruit, pasta salad, and cottage cheese). The dinner entree may be prime rib, steak, or turkey, with fish always available as an alternative (though several campers I talked to had never heard about the optional fish). Given prior notice, the kitchen will prepare special vegetarian or diabetic meals. You can bring your own beer and wine into the dining room. On Sundays there's a barbecue on the lawn. What you won't find on campus is an after-hours soda or snack machine; nor is there a refrigerator in your room to keep things cold. You may want to bring a small cooler.

OTHER RECREATIONAL AMENITIES: The school has a swimming pool, squash courts, basketball and volleyball courts, and a running track. You wouldn't want to set foot in the lake on campus, but there are lakes to swim in within two or three miles. There's also a lounge with a fireplace and a ping-pong table.

▶ Gestalt

Total Tennis is one of the most popular summer programs in New England. More than half of its clientele are repeats, and throughout much of the summer it runs close to its maximum capacity of 60 people.

Part of the allure is the setting on 150 acres of lawns, trees, and rolling hills near the Berkshire Hills of western Massachusetts. Part is the low-key, unpretentious, very social atmosphere. And part is the extraordinarily economical price.

What you will not find at Total Tennis is a sharply defined teaching methodology. There are some broad guidelines. "Our basic philosophy is to keep the ball in play," says Fondiller. "Our theory is most people at this level lose tennis matches, so we stress consistency." What his pros do not do is make major changes in strokes.

Since the pro works with the same group of people throughout the week, it is the individual pro who establishes a curriculum based on the needs of each particular group and the pro's own preferences. Kahane, the assistant director, circulates from court to court to help

"Most people at this level lose matches," says Total Tennis director Ed Fondiller. "So we stress consistency."

out. He also occasionally introduces mental toughness techniques like visualization or relaxation exercises. Mainly, though, this is a nuts-and-bolts camp whose emphasis is on strokes. In addition, among the large staff are two or three instructors who love teaching beginners, so Fondiller encourages novices to come.

The inherent danger in any program that saddles you with one pro throughout the camp is that you may end up with someone whose teaching style doesn't suit you. If that happens, speak up and insist on being moved, even if it's to a weaker group.

You'll be videotaped at least once during the week. Unfortunately, you're likely to have to wait until much later that day or even until early the next before seeing the footage and having it analyzed. By then it loses much of its impact and some of its value as a teaching tool.

That is a minor criticism of an otherwise solid program. The six-hour-a-day format packs a lot of instruction and drills into even a long-weekend session. Courts are available afterwards for those who want to play. There is a round-robin mixer a couple of afternoons a week. And occasionally the pros play among themselves, providing a kind of impromptu exhibition.

After dinner roughly every other night, there is some kind of social gathering planned, like a cocktail party or tennis movie, but people are mainly left to their own devices. Some form carpools and head off dancing or pub crawling, others take advantage of nearby summer stock or the Tanglewood summer music festival (about an hour's drive away), still others seem lost. Easthampton and its ice cream parlor are within walking distance, but Northampton, which is livelier and has a movie theater, is four miles away—a problem for those without cars.

The crowd here is evenly divided between men and women, singles and couples. They range in age from the late twenties to the mid-fifties, with the largest contingent somewhere in their thirties. Like most New England camps, Total Tennis draws heavily from the New York-Boston corridor.

Though far from luxurious, Total Tennis is one of the best tennis-for-dollar values around.

TRAVEL INSTRUCTIONS: Easthampton, Massachusetts, is roughly 150 miles north of New York City and 100 miles west of Boston. The nearest airport is Bradley International near Hartford, Connecticut, 40 miles to the south. Bus service is available from there to Holyoke, Massachusetts, where someone will pick you up if you let them know you're coming.

Ian Fletcher Tennis School

Bolton Valley Resort
Box RS
Bolton, VT 05477
(802) 434-2131 or (800) 451-3220

SEASON: Mid-June to the weekend after Labor Day.

RATES: *Inexpensive* until roughly July 4, then approaching *Moderate* through the remainder of the season. The rates include accommodations in the Bolton Valley Lodge, country breakfast and dinner nightly at a choice of restaurants, two hours of daily instruction, and one hour of additional court time.

▶ *Profile*

COURTS: Bolton Valley has 10 hard courts, all surfaced with Decoturf II, the same rubberized paint used at the U.S. Open. Of those, 8 are outdoors on a terraced hillside backdropped by forested mountains. The remaining 2 are indoors in the Sports Center.

COURT FEES: *Inexpensive.*

PRO STAFF: A native of Australia, Ian Fletcher played on the pro tour from 1968 to 1976, reaching the fourth round of both Wimbledon and the French Open. He later trained the New Zealand, Japanese, and Israeli Davis Cup teams and coached Johan Kriek. He personally conducts every clinic. His associate is Brooke Becker, a superb tennis teacher who played for Skidmore College and held a Top-ten ranking in Quebec.

INSTRUCTIONAL PROGRAMS: Change is endemic to Fletcher's program, but as currently conceived it consists of a two-hour morning session focusing on the basic strokes and an optional two-hour afternoon session, which could be videotape analysis of your strokes, lectures and drills on singles and doubles strategy, or work on return of serve. Each day's work is independent of what has gone before, which

Former international touring pro Ian Fletcher personally conducts a low-key, family-oriented tennis camp at Vermont's Bolton Valley.

means that you can arrive on any day of the week and stay as long as you want (packages require a two-night minimum booking). The newest addition is a concurrent junior program for kids who are there with their parents. It consists of a one-hour daily session for those aged 5 to 11, two hours for those 12 and over.

SPECIAL FEATURES: Videotaping is done at least once during each clinic. Ball machines are available free of charge to anyone on a tennis package.

PRO SHOP: None. A shack at the courts handles court reservations and ball-machine rental but doesn't sell anything, not even tennis balls. A shop called Pleasures in the lodge complex has rental racquets and a very limited selection of accessories. Rather than regular tennis clothes, however, it carries only t-shirts, sweatshirts, running shorts, and the like. Rental racquets are available but on-site restringing is not.

LODGING AND FOOD: Though you have the option of upgrading to a condominium at extra cost, the basic tennis package includes accommodations in the relatively new wing of the Bolton Valley Lodge, just uphill from the courts. Bright and spiffy, the rooms are furnished in Conran-ish style with oak, butcher's block, overstuffed chairs, and quilts. All have televisions, full-length balconies, and mountain views. There is no air conditioning, but nights are almost always cool enough for that not to matter. One-to-three-bedroom condominiums are available as an alternative to the Lodge. There is evidently a third option, though it is not mentioned in Fletcher's brochures. Some of the campers stay at the Black Bear, a 24-room inn decorated with handmade quilts and antiques, and rave about the personal service and home-cooked fare. It is located a short distance down the access road (phone: 802-434-2126).

Two restaurants in the resort village remain open during the summer: Lindsay's, a small, casually elegant *boîte* open only for dinner, whose eclectic menu ranges from seafood pasta to steak au poivre; and Fireside, an informal cafe open for breakfast, lunch, and dinner. The food in both is generally very good. In addition, a barbecue lunch and salads are served outside around the pool at the Sports Center. The bar at the Fireside is a sometimes lively gathering place at night.

OTHER RECREATIONAL AMENITIES: Bolton Valley Resort is a tiny outpost in a 6,000-acre mountain wilderness laced with hiking and jogging trails. The resort village has a Nature Center staffed by professionals from the University of Vermont School of Natural Resources. Throughout the summer they schedule a variety of activities, including guided nature walks, wildflower tours, and historic trips up Bolton Mountain. The resort itself has a Sports Center that consists of indoor and outdoor swimming pools, exercise room, saunas, a whirlpool, and a bar and restaurant. Conscious of its family clientele, it runs an excellent all-day children's camp for kids aged three months to 12 years. Golfers can arrange to play on two nearby courses.

▶ *Gestalt*

The Bolton Valley Resort nestles in a landscape of mountains, forest, and sky roughly 23 miles from Burlington and a little more than half

47

that distance from Ben & Jerry's Ice Cream Factory in Waterbury. Of the many places to play tennis in Vermont, this is one of the loveliest and most serene. The tiny resort village consists of a U-shaped lodge, a few shops and restaurants, a tiny market, and several clusters of condominiums. Immediately behind the village rise what in another season are the ski slopes but in summer wear a mantle of grass flecked with wildflowers.

Except for a two-year hiatus, Ian Fletcher has run his summer school on these courts since the early 1980s. Behind his approach to teaching is a system he calls Economy of Motion. All you have to do is look at the former touring pro's compact strokes to see where it comes from. "It's sort of based on the way I used to play on the circuit," says Fletcher. "I had very economical strokes. I believe in simplicity, basically: the fewer number of movements the better."

Fletcher speaks volumes with his classical strokes. However, when it comes to explaining actual mechanics he sometimes also seems to believe in Economy of Words. It is at those moments that Brooke Becker, who shares teaching responsibilities with him, takes over. An actress and model when she's not teaching tennis, she summons up a theatricality and expressiveness that perfectly complement Fletcher's laid-back reticence. They work well as a team. Fletcher introduces and demonstrates the strokes and then relies on Becker to elaborate. And it's really her animation that infuses the clinics with vitality.

Fletcher's system goes back to the basics. His goal with campers, he says, is to "make their shots a little bit better by making sure their contact is good, their footwork is good, and make sure their balance is good." He is not out to make drastic changes in players' games.

The two-hour daily sessions are not at all demanding. Those who want more—and about one-third do—can sign up for the intensive program, which adds a two-hour afternoon session. Either way, what is missing from these clinics is a sense of progression, of one day's work leading logically to the next. That is deliberate on Fletcher's part. He set out to design a program in which each day stood alone so that guests could come and go at their own convenience. "We're pretty flexible," says Fletcher, "because the morning sessions are all pretty similar."

The clinics have been getting ten to fourteen participants, about two-thirds of them couples, most in their twenties, thirties, and forties. No one needs a state-of-the-art racquet or the latest in tennis fashions to fit in. Rarely do the clinics attract anyone stronger than intermediate, partly because of the family-oriented nature of the resort and partly because Fletcher sees them as his target audience. "We cater the program mostly to the intermediate," says Fletcher. "They tend to get on a plateau and it's very tough to get off, so they try to do too many fancy things." He also tries to lure them with two or three social round-robin tournaments each week, which are run with an idea that competition is fun.

Fletcher is hoping the numbers will go higher as people realize that he's back at Bolton Valley (for two summers in the mid-1980s he did not run his school). As it is, however, he hasn't been sticking to the 4:1 student-pro ratio his brochure advertises. Some clinics have been running 6:1 or 7:1. He justifies that by saying that campers are better off having him and Becker teach than they would be if he brought in another pro less familiar with his methods. That may be so, but it doesn't change the fact that his brochure's misleading. It's a tiny and unnecessary blight on an otherwise solid program.

TRAVEL INSTRUCTIONS: The nearest airport is in Burlington, about a 20-minute drive from Bolton Valley. Transportation can be arranged through the resort. If you rent a condominium, buy your groceries (especially fresh fruits and vegetables) at the last major town before you hit Route 2. The tiny market at the resort is fine for snacks and beverages but won't do to stock a larder.

The Killington School for Tennis

Killington, VT 05751

(802) 422-3101 or (800) 343-0762

SEASON: Late May to mid-September, with slightly higher rates in effect during July and August for the five-day programs.

RATES: *Moderate.* The basic package includes lodging, all meals, tennis school, gratuities, and sometimes chairlift rides to the top of Killington Mountain, but not taxes on rooms or meals.

▶ *Profile*

COURTS: The school has 8 courts in all—half of them clay, the other half hard. Five have lights. In the midst of this cluster are two covered sheds, each containing four hitting lanes with ball machines. There is talk of adding additional courts, some of which will be indoors. As of now, when it rains everyone heads for a small indoor complex in Rutland, about sixteen miles away.

COURT FEES: None.

PRO STAFF: Barry Stout, the director of tennis, has worked at the school since 1978. Head pro Marc White played for Towson State University in Baltimore before coming to Killington in 1983. The other 18 pros are mainly school teachers and ski instructors. "On the whole I don't hire college players," says Stout.

INSTRUCTIONAL PROGRAMS: Killington's program, which runs five hours a day, comprises three elements: classroom instruction, hitting lanes, and on-court drills. Student-to-pro ratios never exceed 4:1. You stay with the same pro throughout the week.

SPECIAL FEATURES: Few tennis schools do as fine a job of videotape analysis as Killington. The secret is that not only does it have a video specialist (who has worked with people like Dennis Van der Meer and former touring pros Gene and Sandy Mayer) to set up the system and train the camera people, but it also shows the videos at courtside immediately after they're shot. Often the camerawork is done clandestinely. The result is that what you see on tape is more likely to be typical of your strokes, unaltered either by video tension or on-camera histrionics.

Another popular feature is the hitting lanes, which remain open all night for anyone who wants additional work outside of class.

LODGING AND FOOD: The Killington package includes a room at The Villager, which is just steps from the courts. These are not much different from standard motel rooms, functional rather than luxurious, with two twin beds (or a twin and a double) and a television. It's a place to sleep. There are coin-operated washers and dryers in the Villager complex.

Meals are served in Pogonips, a restaurant about a five-minute walk from the rooms. Breakfast and lunch are buffets and, like dinner, have an abundance of carbohydrates, fresh fruits and vegetables, cereals, and whole-grain breads as well as traditional fare. The dinner menu is the same every night except for the two or three daily specials. You get a choice of soup or appetizer (like smoked trout or black and white pasta in two sauces), salad (mixed greens, hearts of palm, tomatoes with pesto), and an entree, which might be grilled tuna, steak, seafood marinara, or stuffed breast of chicken. Wine by the glass and beer are available. Overall the food is better than at the tennis academies on college campuses and reasonably healthy, but it still falls short of the fare at most resorts. On the five-day program, one night each week is an outdoor barbecue.

OTHER RECREATIONAL AMENITIES: Killington has an 18-hole golf course, a small health club, and a seven-acre pond stocked with trout, but the most inviting facilities from the point of view of the tennis-school students are the small swimming pool and outdoor heated whirlpool that are part of the Villager complex.

▶ Gestalt

The backdrop for the courts at the Killington School for Tennis is Vermont's Green Mountains. This is a quintessential New England landscape, the rounded hills forested with hardwoods and conifers and accented by outcrops of granite. The heat and humidity of the lowland summer rarely reach this altitude, which makes Killington an ideal place to swing a racquet at the 1,400 tennis balls the school estimates each student hits daily during the course of its five-hour-a-day clinics.

The curriculum at the Killington School for Tennis consists of videotaped lectures, hitting lanes, and on-court drills.

Any notion that the Killington School is a clone of other intensive tennis camps is dispelled the first morning of classes. Killington doesn't start by teaching forehands and backhands but the volley, arguing that it is an easier stroke to learn because it has fewer moving parts. More than that, however, the volley is the cornerstone of Killington's Accelerated Teaching Method, because it provides a simple and graphic means of introducing ball control. And ball control—the ability to control the direction, pace, and spin on a ball—is fundamental to Killington's teaching philosophy.

Those philosophical underpinnings aside, the very format of a Killington clinic is unusual. A typical session begins in the classroom, where you watch an overly long videotaped lecture about how to hit a particular stroke. From there you move to the hitting lanes, where you practice the stroke without having to worry about distractions like the net, the baseline, or an opponent. Only then do you graduate to the court for drills.

During those on-court segments, the pros frequently use a ball machine to do the feeding so that they are free to work directly with the students. Videotaping is done during almost every one of these sessions, sometimes overtly, sometimes clandestinely, and the tapes are shown and analyzed at courtside immediately after they're shot. Then, with the images still fresh in your mind—both of what you're doing right and what still needs work—you go back to the court to continue the drills. I know of no program that uses videotape as well.

Because all of this movement is so well orchestrated, Killington can actually take twice as many students as a normal eight-court facility and still keep student-to-pro ratios at the optimal 4:1. The classroom sessions provide a natural break and a chance to rest and have some fresh fruit or juice (there's water available near all of the courts), while the hitting lanes give you a chance to hit huge numbers of balls without having to move far to get into position. The result is that this program turns out to be far less grueling than its five-hour-a-day format suggests. In fact, despite the long hours, this is not nearly as demanding or as aerobic a program as, say, the All American Sports clinics at Amherst. Depending on your needs, that is either an advantage or a drawback.

"The way the program is designed," says Barry Stout, the director of tennis, "it really is a beginning tennis program, because the methodology is geared to beginners." What Killington is finding, however, is that tennis players as a whole have grown much stronger since the program was developed. "Intermediates feel that they're only going to get better by being on the court hitting tennis balls," Stout admits, "but our system doesn't allow them enough court time."

As a result the Killington program is in transition. In an effort to attract more strong players, there is talk of altering the sessions to better cater to the needs of Killington graduates and others who need advanced instruction. Among the options under consideration is adding more courts in order to reduce the time spent on the hitting lanes and in the classroom. But, as this book goes to press, the exact nature of those new programs has not been finalized.

Far more troubling to me than the format is the quality of some of the instruction I experienced on my last visit. The best of the pros are superb and have extensive teaching experience and sometimes even coaching credentials. But I ran into a few whose flimsy technical knowledge and lack of commitment and interpersonal skills made me wonder how they ever got hired. Given that Killington's format calls for you to remain with the same pro throughout the week, this is the last place you want to be stuck with a poor one. If you don't like yours, insist on being moved to another group.

The relatively large number of students—they average 60 weekends, 50 during the week—means a good distribution of players at all levels. Women generally outnumber men, Stout told me, and there's always a mixture of couples and singles. "On weekends we seem to get the yuppie crowd from Boston and New York City," said Stout. Most range in age from thirtysomething to fiftysomething.

The atmosphere is thoroughly relaxed. No one dresses for dinner or for the summer-stock theater productions at the Killington Playhouse (tickets are included in the five-day packages). After the clinics, there may be a social round-robin or an exhibition. Though most people are tired, a few players inevitably want competition when the day's drilling is over. Most are content to head for the swimming pool and Cabana Bar, which overlooks the courts. The bar is also an easy place to hook up with people for dinner (that's important if you've come alone, because tables in the restaurant are for however many there are in your party). Nights tend to be pretty quiet except when a group decides to drive down the access road to one of the bars with music.

At the end of either session, you get a personal critique and a booklet summarizing the Accelerated Teaching Method.

TRAVEL INSTRUCTIONS: Killington is in central Vermont, at the junction of U.S. 4 and Vermont 100 in Sherburne, about 16 miles east of Rutland. The nearest major airport is in Burlington, about 60 miles north; however, limited commercial service is also available into Rutland.

54

Stratton Tennis School

Stratton Mountain Resort
Stratton Mountain, VT 05155
(802) 297-2200 or (800) 843-6867

SEASON: Memorial Day to early September, but busiest during July and August.

RATES: *Expensive.* The basic package includes accommodations at the Stratton Mountain Inn, lunch, three hours of daily clinics midweek, five hours of daily clinics weekends, unlimited additional court time, and admission to the Sports Center. It is also possible to book the school separately, without accommodations, leaving open the option of staying in one of Stratton's other inns or numerous condominiums.

▶ *Profile*

COURTS: The resort, with 23 tennis courts altogether, is the largest complex in New England. All but 4 are at the Stratton Sports Center, which has 7 hard courts, surfaced with Decoturf II, the same coating used at the U.S. Open; 8 clay courts outdoors (none with lights); and another 4 hard courts indoors. In addition, there are 2 hard and 2 red clay courts behind the Stratton Mountain Inn.

COURT FEES: *Expensive,* but complimentary on packages.

PRO STAFF: The director of the program is Kelly Gunterman, a former college and satellite circuit player who turned to giving lessons when, as he puts it, "I found out I was either going to be real skinny or do something else." In more than a decade of teaching he has worked for Peter Burwash International in Hawaii, Nick Bollettieri in Florida, and at several of the John Newcombe camps, including the one that used to take place at Stratton. He heads a staff of five pros, a couple of them older and very experienced teachers who have been coming back from year to year. One or more of the others is likely to be a college player.

55

INSTRUCTIONAL PROGRAMS: There are two formats: a five-day midweek and a more intensive three-day weekend. The midweek program runs three hours each morning, leaving afternoons free for sightseeing or social tennis (those who want more on-court work can opt for additional clinics or private lessons in the afternoon, though there is a surcharge for this extra instruction). The weekend program, by contrast, is more demanding, with three hours of instruction and drills scheduled before lunch and another two hours after. In both cases, the student-pro ratio never exceeds the optimal 4:1.

SPECIAL FEATURES: Videotaping is part of both clinic formats, and ball machines are available for rent. The Sports Center staff can also set up competitive tennis matches by drawing on its stable of local members.

PRO SHOP: In the Sports Center is a complete pro shop, which carries not only tennis clothing, shoes, accessories, and equipment (on-site restringing is available) but also running gear, racquetball paraphernalia, and sunglasses.

LODGING AND FOOD: The tennis school package includes accommodations at the Stratton Mountain Inn, which is about a five-minute walk from the tennis courts at the Sports Center where the clinics take place. To call this 125-room hotel an "inn" is misleading, if, like me, you think of an inn as a place personally run by its owner. But the rooms are spacious and pleasant, if untroubled by anything that could be called character. All have a few deluxe toiletries and televisions with pay video channels. The best are on the back, with narrow balconies overlooking the swimming pool and the forest beyond. The inn has its own whirlpools and saunas; the Sage Hill Restaurant, which serves breakfast, lunch, and dinner; and a nightclub/bar, which sometimes has live entertainment.

Besides the Sage Hill, there are another half-dozen restaurants at Stratton. The best of them is the Birkenhaus, whose changing menu has dishes like Wiener schnitzel, grilled herbed Cornish hen, *tournedos poivrade,* and scallop quenelles in orange-saffron buerre blanc. For something livelier, try Mulligan's in Stratton Village. It has seafood and Mexican and Italian dishes at reasonable prices. It's also a disco on weekends. Beyond Stratton, but within easy driving distance, are three or four country inns.

OTHER RECREATIONAL AMENITIES: Stratton is a major-league summer sporting destination. It has 27 holes of golf and a golf school, stables and a horseback riding school, a lake and a sailboarding school, and freshwater fishing. Its Sports Center has a 75-foot indoor swimming pool, a whirlpool, three racquetball courts, a tanning salon, and a fitness center with Nautilus equipment, exercycles, and rowing machines. Finally, Stratton runs summer day camps for kids aged 3 to 12, so parents can pursue their own interests knowing that their children are being entertained and supervised.

▶ *Gestalt*

Once known mainly for its skiing, Stratton has emerged in recent years as a four-season destination with multiple dimensions. Nothing in New England can match the depth and diversity of its summer sports facilities. One reason for choosing this tennis school over others in Vermont is that there is so much else to do in Stratton's resort playground besides knocking yellow spheres back and forth across a net.

Each day's session of the Stratton Tennis School begins indoors at the Sports Center with a chalk-talk about some aspect of singles and doubles strategy. From there, you move out to the hard courts for warmup exercises and an introduction to that session's curriculum by director of tennis Kelly Gunterman. The school starts out by working on the volley, moves on in subsequent sessions to groundstrokes, and finishes with serves and return of serve. The progression is the same whether you're on a five-day midweek or two-day weekend program.

Once all the strokes have been covered, Gunterman shifts to what he calls "Special Help" sessions as a way of tailoring the program to the specific needs of the students. It works this way: one court is designated for forehands, another for backhands, a third for volleys, a fourth for serves and returns. Each has a pro. You simply head for whichever court offers the kind of instruction you feel you need most. You may stay for the whole session or move on to something else: it's entirely up to you.

Students are videotaped at least once during each clinic. The analysis, which takes place outdoors on a covered porch of the Sports Center, is excellent. The pros make good use of slow-motion and freeze-frame to pinpoint what is both right and wrong. Now all they need to do is shorten the time between the shooting of the videotape and its analysis.

The actual on-court instruction is at its best very good. Gunterman and his two senior staff (who come back year after year) have solid credentials and engaging courtside manners. They avoid dogmatism. "We don't have a set style that we think is right," says Gunterman, so the changes they introduce stay within the context of the strokes you already have.

But perhaps because some of his pros are themselves very experienced, Gunterman has never formulated a distinctive methodology.

Thus as your group moves from pro to pro, you may find one telling you one thing, another another. He defends that approach, saying, "Yes, you are going to hear some different things. If one pro says one thing on your forehand, it may not click. If another says another thing, it may." At the same time, he recognizes the drawbacks of his laissez-faire approach, adding, "but I am looking for more consistency." It wouldn't hurt either if he taught his younger pros not only the drills but also the teaching methods he favors. Gunterman has yet to put his personal stamp on the Stratton Tennis School.

Thus the program and Gunterman's philosophy of what the school ought to be are still evolving. Although the school has existed for years, Gunterman's tenure dates from 1988, when he was called in to take over its operation on very short notice. His priority during that first year was just to get it going.

One thing that is clear, however, is his attitude about what a camp should be. "People are here on vacation, so they not only want to learn to play tennis but they want to have fun while they're doing it," he says. "So we try to keep it fun and still have people hit a lot of balls."

The school takes a maximum of sixteen people midweek and twenty on the weekends, though don't expect a full camp except during July and August. Couples make up the largest segment of the group. Most come from the Boston-to-New York City corridor and are intermediates in their thirties, forties, and fifties. Gunterman does not exactly discourage beginners from enrolling in the school, but he believes that it is a difficult place for them to begin acquiring racquet skills. Instead he recommends private lessons and the personal attention that goes with them.

Apart from a cocktail party and, on the five-day program only, a graduation banquet, there is no organized social activity, so how much you see of campers after class depends on you. If you want more tennis after the clinics and can't find other campers to hit, the staff at the Sports Center has a lengthy list of local members eager for matches. Logging a full day on the court should not be a problem.

TRAVEL INSTRUCTIONS: The nearest major airport is in Albany, N.Y., 81 miles away; the regional airport in Rutland, 52 miles distant, is closer.

LATE NEWS: Stratton has tentatively—but not absolutely—decided to eliminate its tennis school. Unfortunately, the final decision will not be made until after this book goes to press, so check with the resort for the latest word about just what types of programs they will be running.

Sugarbush Tennis School

· ·

Warren, VT 05674-9993

(802) 583-3333 or (800) 53-SUGAR

SEASON: July to August, although there are plans to offer winter tennis/ski packages as well.

RATES: *Moderate.* The two-day weekend and five-day midweek packages include accommodations in a one-bedroom condominium, all meals, tennis instruction, unlimited court time, admission to the sports club, and a fitness evaluation. Those on the five-day package also get a private lesson and a massage.

▶ *Profile*

COURTS: The tennis school operates out of the Sugarbush Sports Center, a spiffy tennis and fitness club that has 13 courts, 3 of them indoors. Except when it rains, the teaching is done outdoors on 6 hard courts terraced into the hillside just above the sports center. The remaining 4 courts, all clay, are across the road in a creek-laced forest of hardwoods and evergreens.

COURT FEES: *Moderate,* but complimentary on packages.

PRO STAFF: The school's director is Christophe Delavaut, a former college player who went on to work for All American Sports, among other things running their summer camp at Topnotch at Stowe. He heads a staff of seven pros, several of whom play for his alma mater Franklin Pierce College in New Hampshire. "The pro has to have a great personality and good strokes and be able to pick out the basics," insists Delavaut, but beyond that they are put through a preseason training program to ensure that everyone follows the same teaching methods. Delavaut himself is certified by the U.S. Professional Tennis Registry.

INSTRUCTIONAL PROGRAMS: The instruction sessions run roughly five hours a day, equally divided morning and afternoon. The sessions begin in a classroom with either a videotape of Delavaut introducing and demonstrating the day's strokes or a chalk-talk about strategy and tactics. From there it's out to the courts for drills and videotape analysis. The student-pro ratio never exceeds 4:1. Those on the five-day program also get a half-hour private lesson and a massage as part of their package. In addition, several evenings each week there is a lecture on such subjects as mental toughness, equipment, and strategy and tactics.

Although the Sugarbush Tennis School is essentially an adult program, the staff also runs a separate, ongoing tennis camp for children aged 4 to 16. That program mainly gets local kids, or the children of people with summer homes, but welcomes the children of guests as well. Contact the school for more details about how it works and what to expect.

SPECIAL FEATURES: No tennis camp can match the Sugarbush Tennis School for the sheer variety of special features that are a regular part of every one of its sessions. They take videotape analysis one step further by providing you with a tape of your video sessions to take home. On that tape, the pro dubs his critiques over your shots, using freeze-frame and slow motion whenever appropriate. Also included are examples of Delavaut hitting the ball in the proper way. Beyond that, the school has six computerized ball machines, which are used to feed balls during the clinics. They are also used in a series of aerobic drills designed both to mimic tactical situations and raise your heart rate to target levels. There is a fast-serve contest using a speedgun to measure velocity. They sometimes use a system called TNT® to chart strokes and thus show statistically where your strengths and weaknesses lie. They provide a basic cardio-fitness evaluation by measuring percentage of body fat, blood pressure, resting heart rate, flexibility, and the number of situps and pushups you can do in one minute. They even send you home knowing your NTRP level.

SEASONAL TENNIS EVENTS: The Celebrity Classic, a tennis and golf event to raise money for Vermont's Special Olympics, takes place in late August, drawing stars from television, movies, and sports.

PRO SHOP: The sports center has a limited selection of tennis racquets, shoes, and accessories for sale but no shop to sell them from. Instead, what merchandise they have—much of it swimsuits and aerobics gear—is on display behind windows in the sports center and sold over the counter as you enter. On-site restringing is available, but plan to drive to Waitsfield, which is 5 miles away, if you need to do any significant shopping.

LODGING AND FOOD: The school usually puts up campers in either the Glades or Paradise condominiums, which are among the nicest on the mountain and within walking distance of the Sugarbush Sports Center. These are one-bedroom/one-bath, or two-bedroom/two-bath, units with contemporary furnishings *à la* Conran's. The bedrooms tend to be on the small side, but the living space is comfortable, with a fireplace, cable television, a small dining room, a fully equipped kitchen, and an outside deck. Individual condos do not have laundry facilities, but each complex does, along with a common lounge and a game room.

About the only kitchen appliances you're likely to need are the refrigerator (for cold drinks) and coffee maker, since all three meals are included in the school's package. Breakfast is served every morning at the Sugarbush Inn, a few miles down the hill. Lunch is poolside, just steps from the courts. Every night except one (when there's a barbecue around the pool), the group meets Delavaut or another member of the staff for dinner at a different local restaurant, among them the Phoenix (which has fabulous desserts) and Sam Rupert's, which are generally regarded as the best in the village. The catch is that you need to decide what you want for dinner in the morning when the clinics start. Typically you have a choice of three entrees—often meat, fish, and poultry—which are served with soup or salad and dessert.

OTHER RECREATIONAL AMENITIES: Besides tennis courts, the Sugarbush Sports Center has a heated outdoor swimming pool with two whirlpools (one for adults only) and a pool bar and snack bar. Inside is another swimming pool and whirlpool, two squash and two racquetball courts, locker rooms, saunas, massage rooms, and a fitness center with Nautilus and Universal equipment, freeweights, computerized exercycles (with heart-rate sensors), treadmills, rowing machines, Nordic track machines, aerobics, and stretch-and-tone classes.

Not at the club but available to the public is an 18-hole Robert Trent Jones golf course. Families can also enroll children ages 1 to 10 in the Valley Day Camp, which entertains (rather than merely babysits) them from 8 A.M. to 4 P.M.

▶ *Gestalt*

The name Sugarbush Tennis School is much too pedestrian for one of the most imaginative and diverse tennis programs in the country. The two teaching pros who founded it—Christophe Delavaut and Joe Santisi—should have called it something else. They should have invited Tom Wolfe up for a clinic in exchange for an evocative name, like the Sugarbush New Wave, Holistic Tennis Center.

Delavaut and Santisi are much too mainstream to ever go for a name like that. Yet they have designed their school to be more than merely a place to take group lessons. They are interested not only in everything else that can affect performance—like physical conditioning and mental toughness—but also in making the time on and off the court enjoyable. And they have shown a remarkable willingness to experiment with old and new technologies as a way of making the clinics more efficient and simply more fun.

Both have impeccable credentials. As noted earlier, Delavaut came out of the All American Sports organization. Santisi was head pro at the Killington School for Tennis. In establishing their own school, they naturally began by fusing the best elements of the two operations they knew intimately. Knowing they had a solid base, they then began looking for ways to create an original program.

It is not so much one single aspect that sets the Sugarbush Tennis School apart as it is the cumulative effect of many sometimes subtle features. The day begins with a ten-minute videotape of Delavaut introducing and demonstrating the stroke you're about to work on. As at the Killington School for Tennis, the instruction focuses first on the volley, which has fewer working parts, before moving on to the rest of the strokes, including specialty shots like lobs and overheads, and finally to strategy and tactics.

The on-court work consists of two two-hour sessions, one in the morning, one in the afternoon. You stay with the same pro throughout each two-hour period but change pros from session to session. Every court has a ball machine, which the pro often uses to do the feeding so that he can come around on your side of the net to teach. Instruction, drills, and superb use of videotape typically take up the first 90 minutes of each session, and are followed by half an hour of playing situations, often with the pro as one of the competitors. The routine varies, however, during the very last session of both the two-day and five-day programs, when each court becomes a "station" devoted to a particular stroke, forehands on one, volleys on another, specialty shots on a third, and so on. You can head to whichever court is working on the shot you want more help with.

However well thought-out, that basic format contains nothing original. What makes the Sugarbush school impressive is that it does not stop there. From time to time, the staff breaks up the normal routine by throwing in a session of aerobic drills (using the ball machine) or a fast-serve contest. They are experimenting with other ways to use the speedgun, like helping better players develop more pace as they rally. Visualization (a mental-toughness technique) is introduced as a means of placing the serve. Off the court there is an optional fitness test, lectures on mental toughness by a sports psychologist, and seminars on equipment and strategy and tactics. The school is even experimenting with computer-enhanced learning using tennis video games.

With so much going on, Sugarbush may sound like a school for the tennis-obsessed but it isn't at all. Most of the people who attend are intermediates, and when beginners turn up they're given lots of special attention until they are ready to join a lower intermediate group. The object in the clinics is not only to learn something but also to have fun.

Delavaut personally participates in all the clinics, sometimes teaching one of the groups, sometimes roving from court to court to help out. (Santisi directs the sports center and does not participate in the actual teaching.) His approach is flexible, leading him to modify routinely the program to fit the needs of a particular group of campers. He clearly loves teaching and cares deeply about seeing campers make progress.

The crowd at the Sugarbush Tennis School comes mainly from the northeast, especially the Boston-to-New York City corridor. Most are couples; however, because of the dine-around program no one who comes alone has to worry about having dinner alone (on the other hand, anyone who comes alone should be aware that Sugarbush has no nightlife at all in summer). Attendance has been averaging twelve to sixteen people, though as it gets better known, it seems inevitable that those numbers will go higher (24 is the maximum they can take). It is too exciting a program not to attract more attention.

TRAVEL INSTRUCTIONS: The nearest airport is Burlington, approximately 45 miles away; limited commercial service is also available into Rutland, 50 miles away.

Topnotch at Stowe Resort & Spa/All American Sports Clinics

Mountain Rd.
P.O. Box 1260
Stowe, VT 05672
(802) 253-8585, (800) 451-8686,
or in Canada (800) 228-8686

or

Information: All American Sports
116 Radio Circle Drive
Mt. Kisco, NY 10549
(914) 666-0096 or outside NY (800) 223-2442

SEASON: Year-round (indoor in winter), but busiest from July through Labor Day.

RATES: *Very Expensive* in season (late June to mid-October), *Expensive* the rest of the year. The basic package includes accommodations, full breakfast, three hours of daily clinics, unlimited additional court time, and a gift pack of sportswear.

▶ *Profile*

COURTS: Topnotch has 12 hard courts in two locations. The main complex of 7 courts is directly adjacent to the hotel and its European spa. The remaining 5—one of which is a 4,640-seat stadium, the other 4 indoors—are across the road next to the equestrian center. Only the indoor courts have lights.

COURT FEES: *Moderate,* but complimentary on AAS packages.

PRO STAFF: The director of tennis is Lorie Zacharias-Verdi, who played Number 1 for the University of Arkansas before joining All

American in 1981. She heads a staff of six or more pros, some of whom are or have been college players. Regardless of their playing backgrounds, however, all have had previous All American experience and training at Amherst or one of the other resort sites.

INSTRUCTIONAL PROGRAMS: All American Sports has three-, four-, five-, and seven-night packages that combine accommodations with tennis instruction. There are basically two types of program: a three-hour "Top Seed," which consists of group clinics and drills, plus one or more private lessons; and a two-hour "Match Point" clinic, during which the pro functions as a coach, providing tips about strategy and shot selection while you're actually playing matches. You can sign up for one or the other or both. In no case does the student-to-pro ratio exceed 4:1.

AAS does not run a junior program at Topnotch, but they do run two in the town of Stowe. So, although the regular clinics at the hotel are for adults only (that is, 18 and over), it is possible to arrange for your children to be fed into one of the local programs (or for a special family clinic, in which all of you are together on one court at Topnotch itself).

SPECIAL FEATURES: Like other All American resort sites, Topnotch has a tennis concierge, whose duty it is to make sure all of your tennis needs are met, from clinics and private instruction to competitive matches. In addition, Topnotch has ball machines for rent and does videotaping as a regular part of the clinic program.

Topnotch is occasionally the site, often in June, of Singles Weeks and 40s Plus Weeks, during which they offer a 10 percent discount on the usual single-supplement rate. Those weeks typically get a larger-than-usual turnout, many, though by no means all, of them singles. AAS beefs up the program with additional social activities and large, well-attended round-robins. The 40s Weeks, despite the name, are open to adults of any age. They are distinguished by a greater willingness for good players to play with the weaker ones, as though the very name repels people with ego problems.

LODGING AND FOOD: The rooms at Topnotch are almost everything you could want in an elegant inn: uncommonly spacious, each slightly different, with some antique furnishings, original artwork, fresh flowers, a small library of books, Crabtree & Evelyn soaps and shampoos, a makeup mirror, and a blow-dryer, plus air conditioning (something few Vermont inns have), remote-control color television, and direct-dial phones. Those who need something even more spacious can opt for one of the fifteen kitchen-equipped townhouses.

65

Topnotch has three restaurants: the Dining Room, Le Bistro, and a spa dining room called Evergreens.

The menu in the Dining Room changes daily but may feature such appetizers as glazed seafood crepes or *shiitake* mushrooms with roasted garlic; soups like strawberry champagne and tortellini; salads of mixed local greens with sage bleu and cottage cheese with fruit; and entrees of half rack of Vermont lamb, broiled New York sirloin with herb butter, breast of chicken with saffron sauce, and steamed or broiled salmon with lobster sauce. The waiter can give suggestions about which of these dishes the kitchen can prepare in keeping with the American Heart Association's guidelines for low cholesterol, low fat, and low sodium. Jackets are preferred for men in the dining room at night but not required.

The informal Le Bistro serves lighter fare, including a few items with a heart symbol to indicate their AHA approval. And Evergreens has yet another dimension in healthy, low-calorie cuisine.

Finally, coffee is available in the lobby from 6:30 to 7:30 A.M. and again from 10 A.M. to noon, and there is afternoon tea between 4 and 6 P.M.

OTHER RECREATIONAL AMENITIES: Apart from the courts, Topnotch has an outdoor swimming pool, an equestrian center (offering trail rides, lessons, and a training ring for experienced riders). Its newest amenity is a 23,000-square-foot European spa, which opened in the fall of 1989. There is talk of integrating aspects of the All American program with the spa regimen. If that interests you, check with the inn for the latest information.

▶ Gestalt

Though a little too large to pass for a country inn, and in many ways too elegant, Topnotch still manages to exude an almost homey character. The lobby looks more like a giant living room, with a scattering of leather sofas and chairs, a few miscellaneous antiques, vases of fresh flowers, and a giant moosehead hung on a wall next to the floor-to-ceiling windows looking out on the garden. What appears to be missing is any place to check in, until you realize that that's taken care of at a tiny counter in an alcove library.

Just out back is a small swimming pool surrounded by beds of flowers and anchored by a white-lattice Gazebo Bar. A few of the courts and the bluff-top pro shop are visible through the trees. The wooded deck surrounding it on three sides provides a good vantage point for the action on Court 1, which now stands between the pro shop and the spa.

Some tennis resorts just feel right from the moment you arrive, and Topnotch is one of them. The pro shop almost looks festive, as sunlight streams through the windows to fall between neat shelves of merchandise. Mainly, however, it's the friendly welcome and the staff's quickness to ask what they can do for you.

The tennis clinics at Topnotch are rock-solid (see "The Designer Labels" for details of the All American Sports formula). They include an interesting variation on the standard videotape session: once the pros have the entire class on video, they pull students off the court one by one, turning stroke analysis from a public into a private affair.

Topnotch clinics get a respectable turnout. Between Memorial Day and Labor Day attendance typically ranges from sixteen to 24 campers. The well-dressed crowd is a mix of couples and singles, mainly from the Northeast and ranging in age from the mid-thirties on up. During special promotions, like Singles and Over 40s weeks, the attendance may go even higher and when it does so do the number of *après*-clinic social activities.

The intimate nature of Topnotch makes bumping into the other campers outside the clinics inevitable, if not around the swimming pool, then in the lobby or restaurant. Evenings at Topnotch, however, tend to be very quiet. The Buttertub Bar and Lounge just off the lobby occasionally has live entertainment, though if it's nightlife you want you're better off heading into Stowe, which is five miles away.

Stowe also has scores of restaurants, shops, and art and antique galleries. A bike-and-recreation trail runs from near Topnotch to the white-steepled church in the center of town. Stowe's June-to-August calendar includes summer-stock theater, an antique and classic car rally, a dog show, the Highland Games, and, over the Fourth of July, the "world's shortest marathon." And the fall foliage can be spectacular, so spectacular that very few people enroll in the clinics.

All American Sports actually runs its Topnotch programs year-round, shifting to the four indoor courts after the weather turns cold and inclement. But as a tennis destination it is truly in its glory in summer, especially July and August. During those two months, no American tennis camp east of the Mississippi can match its combination of sterling instruction and creature comforts.

TRAVEL INSTRUCTIONS: The nearest airport is in Burlington, 35 miles away. Sullivan Transportation (802-253-9440) provides transfers.

MID-ATLANTIC AND SOUTHEAST

. . . .

Florida

▶ Amelia Island Plantation/All American Sports Clinics, Amelia Island

▶ Boca Raton Resort and Club, Boca Raton

▶ Nick Bollettieri Tennis Academy, Bradenton

▶ Colony Beach & Tennis Club, Longboat Key

▶ Harry Hopman/Saddlebrook International Tennis, Wesley Chapel

South Carolina

▶ Sea Pines Plantation, Hilton Head Island

▶ Van der Meer Tennis Center, Hilton Head Island

▶ Wild Dunes Beach & Racquet Club, Isle of Palms (Charleston)

Virginia

▶ Van der Meer Summer Camps, Sweet Briar College, Lynchburg

Amelia Island Plantation/ All American Sports Clinics

Highway A1A S.
Amelia Island, FL 32034

(904) 261-6161, (800) 874-6878
or in Florida (800) 342-6841

or

All American Sports
116 Radio Circle Drive
Mt. Kisco, NY 10549

(914) 666-0096 or outside NY (800) 223-2442

SEASON: Year-round, although busiest from mid-March into June.

RATES: *Expensive.* The basic package includes room or villa accommodations, three hours of daily tennis clinics, one or more private lessons, free court time, and a gift pack of sportswear.

▶ *Profile*

COURTS: The Plantation has 25 tennis courts, 3 of them lighted, in two locations. The main complex, known as Racquet Park, consists of 19 clay courts, one of which is surrounded by a permanent stadium, and 2 hard courts. These fan out from a clubhouse containing a fitness center, an indoor swimming pool, two racquetball courts, the tennis pro shop, a conference center, and the Verandah restaurant and bar. The remaining 4 courts—surfaced with an artificial grass called OmniTurf—are two miles away near the Dunes Villas.

COURT FEES: *Expensive,* but avoidable on resort and AAS packages.

PRO STAFF: Kathy Rinaldi is the resort's touring pro. She made headlines in 1983 by turning pro at the age of 14 and has since ranked as

71

high as the women's Top 10. She now lives at Amelia Island when not on the pro tour, making two or three official appearances yearly to help conduct clinics or give exhibitions. The timing of those visits is unpredictable, but they are most likely to occur during the Bausch & Lomb Championships in April and over Fourth of July weekend.

The day-to-day operation of the tennis facility falls to John Morris, a USPTA-certified pro who played for Boston College and then began teaching full-time for All American when he graduated in 1975. From September through May, however, the All American Sports Clinics camps are run by Maureen Rankine, a Jamaican-born USPTA-certified pro and former college player.

INSTRUCTIONAL PROGRAMS: All American Sports has three-, four-, five-, and seven-night packages that combine accommodations with tennis instruction. There are basically two types of program: a three-hour "Top Seed," which consists of group clinics and drills and video-taped analysis of your strokes, plus one or more private lessons; and a two-hour "Match Point" clinic, during which the pro functions as a coach, providing tips about strategy and shot selection while you're actually playing matches. You can choose to do one or the other or both. In all cases the student-pro ratio never exceeds the optimal 4:1.

SPECIAL FEATURES: The Plantation's staff includes a tennis concierge, whose job it is to see to all your tennis needs, from working out an individualized instruction program to meeting other players or arranging use of the ball machine. When it comes to game-matching, the concierge at Amelia has an easier job than at many other resorts. Even during weeks when the number of campers is small, the staff can always draw on a stable of local players to provide appropriate competition, whether for singles, doubles, or mixed doubles. In addition, there are social events such as a weekly mixed doubles round-robin and occasional exhibitions.

SEASONAL TENNIS EVENTS: The most prestigious tournament at Amelia is the Bausch & Lomb Championships, a Kraft General Foods clay-court event that consistently attracts several of the top-ranked women in the world. It usually takes place in mid-April.

LODGING AND FOOD: The AAS package offers a choice of rooms or villas adjacent to the Racquet Park. By "room" they mean one of the Courtside Villa's bedrooms, which has a separate entrance and can be locked off from the living room and kitchen you'll also get if you opt for villa accommodations. Those who prefer oceanside, oceanfront, or pool villas can upgrade at additional cost. Each of the villas has its own washer and dryer.

There are five restaurants on the plantation, but not one of them serves inspired cuisine (and all automatically add a 17 percent mandatory service charge to their bills). Plan on stocking your condo with whatever you'll need for breakfast and lunch (there is a market at the plantation). For dinner, the best bet on the property is the seafood at the Verandah restaurant adjacent to the courts. A better option still, provided you have your own transportation, is to head for the tastier and less pricey restaurants in Fernandina Beach, Ft. George, or Mayport. Ask the pros for suggestions.

OTHER RECREATIONAL FACILITIES: Amelia epitomizes a resort playground. Chief among its assets is a four-mile-long Atlantic-washed beach backed by great mounds of sand dunes. Pete Dye and Tom Fazio contributed 27 challenging holes of golf, framed by lakes and live-oak forests. Adjacent to the tennis courts is the spiffy Health and Fitness Center with an indoor lap pool, racquetball courts, an aerobics room, Kaiser exercise equipment, saunas, steambaths, and whirlpools. There is another large outdoor pool at the Beach Club, and many smaller pools at the various villa complexes. Horseback riding is available (along the beach, if you like). Miles of bicycling paths and jogging and walking trails lace the resort. Children have their own island playground, with a treehouse, pirate ships, fishing ponds, and a complete program of organized activities during summer and major school holiday periods. The lagoons on the property have been stocked with bream and redfish; there's bass fishing in the Intracoastal Waterway; and deep-sea charters are available for tarpon and kingfish.

▶ *Gestalt*

Few beach resorts can match Amelia Island Plantation's natural beauty. Like Sea Pines Plantation on Hilton Head Island, it belongs to that early generation of environmentally sensitive developments. Its 1,250 acres look like a landscape collage pieced together from strips of Atlantic-washed beach, sand dunes, live-oak and palmetto forests, and tidal salt marsh. The roadways and bicycle paths that lace it connect houses, villas, and mid-rise condominiums with golf courses, tennis courts, equestrian centers, and, of course, the beach. It is as peaceful and tranquil a destination as you could hope for.

Its Racquet Park is surrounded by a forest of moss-bearded live-oak trees and landscaped with palms, sweetgums, water oak, and the occasional magnolia tree. Most of those courts have been laid out sin-

A resort playground, Amelia Island Plantation has 25 tennis courts—one of them a stadium—and rock-solid All American Sports programs.

gly or in pairs among the trees. Thus, a few are shaded—a definite asset during the sweltering summer. A maintenance crew uses a blower to clear leafy debris every morning.

All American Sports runs a rock-solid clinic program, the goal of which is not to change your game but to "send you home making fewer mistakes" (see "The Designer Labels" for an in-depth discussion of AAS's basic philosophy and format). Maureen Rankine, who heads up the camp program from mid-September through May, is an astute and knowledgeable teaching pro. Irrepressibly good-humored, she has that rare ability to get you to work hard and to make it fun.

Amelia gets rave reviews for its instruction, but when it comes to the all-important quality of tennis atmosphere, the resort has as many personalities as Sybil. The crux of the problem is that enrollment in its AAS camps varies greatly from season to season and even from week to week. A clinic with only three people may be rewarding because of all the personal attention you get, but it can never generate the same social atmosphere and opportunities for competition as a larger turnout. If you're a passionate player looking for a week of nonstop tennis, you have to be very careful about when you come.

The best time to be at Amelia is during one of its special weeks. AAS has run a 40s Plus week in March and a singles week over Memorial Day weekend. Both tend to get larger-than-usual turnouts and are thus the optimal weeks to attend if you crave a lively social atmosphere on and off the court.

A typical singles week draws 25 people, most in their thirties and forties, all of whom seem to come with the idea of having fun as well as improving their tennis. During one of those weeks, the organized activities continue off court, as the AAS staff throws cocktail parties (often at one of the pro's condos), gives exhibitions (during which spectators are encouraged to be rowdy and partisan), and organizes road trips into Fernandina Beach for dinner. AAS does not offer a discount to men, though maybe they should since during singles weeks women often outnumber them two to one. All in all, it's a very good time.

The 40s weeks also have organized off-court activities. They tend to be a little more subdued than the singles weeks but still attract a crowd bent on enjoying themselves. You don't have to be over 40 to enroll.

The dates for these special weeks vary from year to year, so check with AAS to see what they have scheduled and when.

Summer. Summer is traditionally a season for families on Amelia, many of whom come from the inland South. Not only does the resort run a superb children's program to entertain kids aged 3 to 12 from 8 A.M. to 4:30 P.M., but the tennis staff also adds a two-hour junior clinic to the daily calendar. All American's adult clinics tend to be small. Hot, humid weather and off-season prices obtain.

Winter. This is the quietest season on Amelia. Daytime temperatures are typically in the 50s and 60s—which is fine for tennis in warmups or golf but is hardly an invitation to sunning on the beach. All American's clinics are almost always small, and there may be a few weeks without any participants at all.

Spring. High season on Amelia runs from roughly mid-March to mid-May, when the weather is ideal. The Atlantic may still be chilly, but daytime temperatures rise into the 70s and 80s. Summer's stifling humidity usually holds off until June.

The azaleas and the AAS clinics bloom at about the same time. During the spring, enrollment typically runs from twelve to 20 students every week. The tennis atmosphere is further enhanced by weekly exhibitions by the teaching pros and more than the usual number of social round-robin tournaments.

Fall. Autumn, on the other hand, is off-season as far as prices go, despite the fact that the weather borders on the ideal and the Atlantic is still warm. The enrollment in All American's clinics, however, varies unpredictably from week to week. A good turnout in the fall is nine to thirteen; at times it drops to three or fewer.

The bottom line on Amelia is to check with AAS first for an estimate of how many campers they expect during the week you're thinking of visiting, and to make your plans accordingly. I don't at all want to discourage you from going during a week when enrollment is small; for some people the personal attention far outweighs the impoverished social atmosphere. For strong intermediates and above, however, the weeks with large turnouts improve the chances of encountering other players at your level.

Amelia is sometimes a bit livelier after dark during weeks with large turnouts, though only if campers themselves get together to try to conjure up some excitement. Otherwise, once the clinics are over, everyone is on his or her own for dinner and entertainment. Except during singles weeks and 40s Plus weeks, the people who come alone find it hard to get through the week without good books or a *TV Guide*.

TRAVEL INSTRUCTIONS: The nearest airport is Jacksonville International, 22 miles away. Rental cars are available there, as is limousine service to Amelia Island (about $30 per person, round trip). Once at the plantation, a shuttle system provides free transportation everywhere within the resort 24 hours a day. Even so, given the generally low prices of rental cars in Florida, it may make sense to rent one, partly to save on limousine transfer fees and partly for the sheer convenience of having your own transportation, which frees you to explore and dine outside the resort.

Boca Raton Resort and Club

· ·

501 E. Camino Real
Boca Raton, FL 33431-0825

(407) 395-3000, (800) 327-0101,
or in Canada (800) 368-1888

SEASON: Year-round, though the main season for the adult camps runs from Thanksgiving into early May.

RATES: *Very Expensive* in high season, from January 1 to April 30; *Expensive* the rest of the year. The Gullikson special clinics include accommodations, three hours of daily clinics, a half-hour private lesson, and unlimited court time.

▶ *Profile*

COURTS: The resort has 29 clay courts in two locations. The main complex, just steps away from the original hotel, consists of 22 courts (2 with lights) laid out in ones, twos, and threes in a grassy park landscaped with red and yellow hibiscus, shrubs, and trees. The remaining 7 courts, all with lights, are a fifteen-minute drive away at the Boca Golf and Tennis Club.

COURT FEES: *Expensive* for the first hour, free after that, and avoidable entirely on tennis packages.

PRO STAFF: The hotel's touring pro is Tim Gullikson, a former international circuit player lately known for his coaching. Unlike most touring pros, who spend as little time as possible at the resort they represent, Gullikson actually lives in Boca Raton, travels little, and thus frequently shows up at the courts. Personable by nature, he is also an exceptionally gifted teacher (something that can be said of very few former touring pros). Gullikson is on call for private lessons and periodically runs his own special tennis clinics.

The Boca Raton Resort features clinics by former international touring pro and current professional coach Tim Gullikson.

The resort's director of tennis is Chuck Gill. A former college player at Carson-Newman College in Tennessee, he began teaching for All American in 1977. He came to Boca Raton late in 1988 after six years as the director at Topnotch at Stowe. If Gill seems to move from one prestigious property to another, it's because he's one of the best in the business, a sharp-eyed student of the game who cares deeply about seeing campers improve. He heads a staff of four to five pros, each of whom not only has solid teaching skills but sees himself or herself, says Gill, "as a host," with all that that implies of making the stay enjoyable.

INSTRUCTIONAL PROGRAMS: The resort's daily calendar includes a stroke-of-the-day clinic followed by an optional hour of drills on the same stroke. That alone would not merit the resort's inclusion in this book; however, several times a year former international touring pro

Tim Gullikson runs his own five-day clinics. Those consist of three hours of drills each morning followed by two hours of supervised match play in the afternoon. In all cases the student-pro ratio never exceeds 4:1.

SPECIAL FEATURES: In addition to its clinic staff, the resort has a tennis concierge whose job it is to help you work out an individualized program, to set up games or lessons, and in general to make sure you have a good time.

LODGING AND FOOD: Altogether there are nearly 1,000 rooms at the resort. The original Moorish-style hotel, The Cloister, dates from 1926. It is the work of the eccentric architect Addison Mizner, who invested its 433 rooms and its loggias, courtyards, promenades, and public spaces with hand-crafted moldings, fountains, antiques, Spanish tile, and Old World elegance. The Cloister's rooms are closest to the courts.

The rooms in the 27-story Tower, by contrast, are more contemporary—at once larger and more tropical than the original chambers in the Cloister, and notable for their aerial views of the Gold Coast. The villas, which border the golf course, offer more privacy, kitchens, and room enough for families or foursomes. The most appealing—and priciest—accommodations are the 212 rooms in the Boca Beach Club, right on the beach across the Intracoastal Waterway from the main hotel (and its tennis courts). Free land and water shuttles connect the two, but that still puts them inconveniently distant from the courts.

The resort has nine restaurants, ranging from the informal cafe Chauncey's Court (not far from the tennis courts) to the *table d'hote* and *dégustation* menus of the Top of the Tower, with its 27th-floor views of the Gold Coast.

OTHER RECREATIONAL AMENITIES: Located right on the Atlantic, the hotel has its own half-mile-long stretch of sandy beach running past the Beach Club, which is on an island across the Intracoastal Waterway from the main hotel complex. The beach site also has two swimming pools, a watersports center, and a very small health club with an aerobics room, saunas, whirlpools, and massages.

The mainland has two more swimming pools; two 18-hole golf courses, one of them designed by Robert Trent Jones; a marina where you can book deep-sea charter fishing, sunset cruises, and scuba and snorkeling outings; a croquet lawn, a Parcourse jogging trail, bicycle rentals, and volleyball and badminton courts. The clubhouse of the

Boca Golf and Tennis Club contains a large fitness center with Paramount and Universal equipment, Lifecycles, rowing machines, aerobics classes, saunas, and steam and massage rooms; racquetball courts; a small gym; and a restaurant, but there is otherwise little reason for a non-golfing hotel guest to go there.

▶ *Gestalt*

When the madcap architect Addison Mizner set about building the Cloister Inn in 1926, he envisioned the coral-pink Moorish hotel as the first structure in a dream city. The demise of the Florida land boom ended Mizner's grandiose vision, but his hotel survives as the centerpiece of the Boca Raton Resort and Club, a 550-acre playground on Florida's Gold Coast.

The tennis complex spreads northward from immediately behind the original hotel. Its 22 clay courts have been laid out in clusters in a parklike setting landscaped with bottlebrush, red and yellow hibiscus, live oaks, and other subtropical flowers and trees. A two-story clubhouse overlooks the action from a vantage point among the trees at one end. It has a sun-drenched patio outside and another awning-covered viewing area upstairs. Smaller patios, shaded by coral-striped awnings, anchor each bank of courts. Finally, there are cold-water fountains between each pair of courts and strategically placed telephones with direct lines to the pro shop.

The only access to the courts is through the pro shop, which gives the tennis concierge her first chance of the day to ask whether she can do anything for you. To her credit, she never waits to be asked. Not a day goes by that she doesn't approach every camper—usually several times—to offer to set up singles, doubles, or mixed doubles matches, either with other hotel guests or local members (among the latter are some strong, very competitive players). No one leaves the resort complaining of not getting enough hours on the courts.

The Gullikson clinics run four to six times a year, usually during April, May, October, and November. Those typically take place on the last bank of courts, which border one of the golf fairways. That location gives campers a little more privacy and the freedom to make mistakes without an audience of spectators. The sessions run three hours, with periodic breaks for water or, midway through, fresh fruit. After each break the focus shifts to a different stroke or concept and the pros rotate to another court and a different group of campers. Just before lunch, when attention typically begins to flag, the drills get more competitive, with the pros challenging students to win points. The intensity of the drills varies with the caliber of players on each court. In

Beds of flowers, hedges of red and yellow hibiscus, and stands of magnolias and live oaks border the resort's clay courts.

short, this is very much a classic station-to-station format, with each successive day's instruction building on what has gone before.

But Gullikson's presence suffuses these clinics with a rare electricity. They are everything you could hope for in a session with a big-name pro but all too rarely get. There is plenty of fluff, as Gullikson poses for photos with the campers and plays a point with each, asking "Which serve do you want: smoky or twisty?" But ultimately it is the substance of the clinics that everyone remembers.

Despite his own athletic talent and success on the tour, Gullikson has a rare ability to tailor his teaching to the needs of club players. More astonishing still, he actually seems to feel he has an obligation to help everyone who comes to his clinics make noticeable progress. He is an exceptionally gifted teacher, with a keen eye for the crucial flaw in a stroke and a dogged determination to do something about it.

Gullikson remains on court throughout the morning clinics. He introduces each session's topic, beginning with groundstrokes and continuing on through strategy and tactics. He then teaches on one of the courts, which means that everyone gets him as an instructor at least once each day. This is a model of the way a big-name clinic ought to be run.

Gullikson's philosophy is not to make major changes in strokes but to build on what the students have. The working method is positive reinforcement and good-natured humor whenever possible. There is never a hint of condescension, especially on courts with beginners. Assisting Gullikson is a staff of pros who have obviously been hired not only for their teaching skills but for their personalities as well.

Among those who often help out is Chuck Gill, who also directs the operation at Boca. He has put together a staff "who like working with people." Gill himself sets the tone with his easygoing demeanor and complete lack of pretentiousness. At the same time, he is a genuine student of the game, a masterful teacher who takes obvious pleasure in seeing people improve.

Gill has more than a decade of experience with the types of instructional clinics run at Boca, but he and his staff are still feeling their way through the two-hour supervised match play sessions being offered in the afternoon. The resort includes those as part of the Gullikson weeks in order to ensure that campers get their fill of tennis. During the week I visited, those sessions were still only months old and virtually all of the people who had signed up for the morning clinics opted to spend the afternoon at the beach or the swimming pool or playing singles matches. Not only do the hotel's other facilities provide stiff competition for the match-play clinics but so, ironically, does the zealous match-making tennis concierge.

Because the match-play clinics are designed to be flexible, it is virtually impossible to predict what may take place during any given week. It will depend not only on how many people sign up but also on their level of play. Anything from playing singles or doubles with a pro to a round-robin tournament is possible. Chuck Gill and his staff clearly have no fixed agenda for the afternoon program and instead make one up depending on how large a turnout they got.

Since the program is new, it is difficult to predict with accuracy just how many people will turn up each week. The first Gullikson clinic drew twelve campers. With more advance publicity, the numbers may go higher.

So far, most of the campers have been coming out of the Northeast and the Midwest. The vast majority are intermediates, though occasionally beginners or advanced players also turn up. Couples predominate, most in their thirties, forties, or fifties.

After the clinics, campers disperse, and the resort is large enough that you may or may not run into them later. Everyone is on his own for meals. All American has a cocktail party at least once a week, and occasionally puts together special excursions, like an evening at a professional women's tournament held nearby. But most of the time very little happens at the resort in the evenings. So coming with a spouse or friend (or better still a group of friends) makes sense.

TRAVEL INSTRUCTIONS: The nearest airports are Ft. Lauderdale (24 miles), West Palm Beach (30 miles), and Miami International (45 miles). All of them have limousine and bus transfers to the hotel and rental cars.

LATE NEWS: As this book goes to press, several Tim Gullikson clinics are planned at the resort for early 1990; however, he has yet to negotiate a new contract or otherwise work out an arrangement for future clinics. So check with the resort for the latest word about his involvement.

Nick Bollettieri
Tennis Academy

5500 34th St. W.
Bradenton, FL 34210
(813) 755-1000 or (800) USA-NICK

SEASON: Year-round, but the adult camps are busiest from November through May.

RATES: *Inexpensive* during the September-to-May high season; *Very Inexpensive* from June through August. Rates include accommodations, full board, all tennis instruction, court time, and transportation to and from the Sarasota/Bradenton airport. Full-week packages run Sunday to Saturday; weekend packages, Friday evening to Sunday noon. Non-boarding packages are also offered.

▶ *Profile*

COURTS: There are 46 tennis courts in all: 7 clay and 35 hard outdoors and 4 carpet indoors. Nine have lights that you can turn on yourself at any hour of the night. The general landscaping is red hibiscus, oleander, palm trees—the stuff that seems to grow wild in Florida—and the odd bit of croton.

COURT FEES: None.

PRO STAFF: Nick Bollettieri (see "The Designer Labels") is a fixture at the academy except during major international tournaments such as the Italian Open, the French Open, Wimbledon, and the U.S. Open. The more significant presence for adults, however, is Butch Young. Young is a former college player whose forte is coaching. He has more than a decade of teaching experience, half of that at Bollettieri's. He has traveled with several of the young professionals to come out of the academy, including Andrea Temesvari and Terry Phelps. He oversees a staff of six pros, several of whom have come through the Bollettieri system and all of whom, says Bollettieri, "treat people as individuals."

INSTRUCTIONAL PROGRAMS: At Bollettieri's you can expect to spend four-and-a-half to five hours a day on court doing drills and another 30 to 45 minutes a day in the video room looking at tapes or listening to lectures on mental toughness, match strategy, movement, and physical fitness. The first two days are devoted to a review of all the strokes, including specialty shots like lobs, drop shots, and overheads. Midweek mixes drills and videotaping with some singles play. And the program finishes with competitive drills and tournament play (with books, t-shirts, and a tennis racquet as prizes). The weekend program condenses the same format into two days. For all sessions, the student-pro ratio rarely exceeds 4:1. Bollettieri's uses the station-to-station format, with campers changing pros roughly every 35 to 40 minutes.

Relatively new at Bollettieri's is a program of "Specialty Weeks," which take place roughly once a month from September through May. More narrowly focused than the normal adult clinics, these sessions concentrate on particular themes, like stroke production, singles strategies, doubles strategies, and mental toughness.

Bollettieri made his reputation through his junior program, which has turned out such nationally ranked players as Andre Agassi, Monica Seles, Jim Courier, Tim Mayotte, Aaron Krickstein, Jimmy Arias, Carling Bassett-Seguso, and Lisa Bonder, to name only a few. His most intensive junior program has some 150 students from more than 30 countries living at the academy and studying in local private schools. Daily and weekly sessions for juniors can be booked year-round.

SPECIAL FEATURES: Videotape is a significant thread in the fabric of all the Bollettieri adult camps. Not only does his staff tape campers three times a week, but there are numerous videotaped lectures—most by sports psychologist Dr. Jim Loehr—on such topics as mental toughness, movement, and even the role of music videos in match preparation. Occasionally, there are on-court demonstrations of how pulse monitors can help you play better in matches. Computerized match charting is available for an extra charge.

PRO SHOP: The camp has everything you need in the way of equipment, clothing, accessories, and restringing services. The merchandise is sold from behind a counter, which means you have to ask for everything you want to inspect, whether it's a racquet, a tennis shoe, or a t-shirt.

LODGING AND FOOD: All of the accommodations, for adults as well as juniors, are in two-bedroom/two-bath air-conditioned townhouses in two-story buildings clustered around the courts. The adult rooms have fully equipped kitchens, televisions, a sparsely furnished living room with one small sofa, and a dining table with four or five chairs. There's a pay phone on the wall. All are just a few steps from the courts. At the end of one of the buildings is a laundry room with free washers and dryers (soap can be purchased in the pro shop).

Three meals a day are served to adults who opt to board at Bollettieri's—and it's really the only sensible thing to do. Breakfast consists of many brands of cereal, toast and bagels, fresh fruit, and hot entrees like eggs, bacon, hash browns, plus orange juice and coffee. Lunch has more fruit, tossed salad, cold cuts and cheese for sandwiches, and some kind of hot dish (lasagna, tortellini, hot dogs, Steak-umms). At dinner there is more salad and fresh fruit, along with steak, chicken, fish, pork roast, canned vegetables, and potatoes or other carbohydrates, none of it memorable. Lite beer and wine are available free to adults (who are otherwise asked to confine their drinking to their rooms so as not to have a negative influence on kids living at the academy).

OTHER RECREATIONAL AMENITIES: Between the adult townhouses and the dining room is a small—make that tiny—swimming pool and a whirlpool. Next to the indoor courts is a Fitness Center, newly expanded to include not only Nautilus equipment and free weights but numerous exercycles, rowing machines, treadmills, and climbing stairs. There is a game room with ping-pong tables, video games, and pinball machines.

▶ *Gestalt*

Wearing nylon jogging shorts and sunglasses but no shirt, Nick Bollettieri fed tennis balls rapid-fire to a fourteen-year-old girl on one court and at the same time chastised another junior two courts away for laziness. A group of adults, taking a water-and-lemonade break from their own program, stood beside his court watching him work. To see the ex-Marine put his junior recruits through their paces makes it clear how Bollettieri's got the reputation for being a tennis boot camp.

Many of the adults standing beside that fence naturally thought they were in for a similarly hard-driving program. That is, after all, what the brochure promises: "Our world-famous Academy offers you the same program which has produced so many tennis stars like Agassi, Arias, Krickstein, Bassett, etc." But in fact the adult program is carpentered together out of softer wood.

Bollettieri himself says the basic philosophy governing the adult sessions is "fun." "Fun" at Bollettieri's means two things: not undertaking major changes in the strokes you arrive with and incorporating more than the usual amount of actual play into the week's clinic hours. Rather than change a stroke, says Bollettieri, his pros look for ways to simplify its mechanics and thus make it more efficient. They'll pay special attention to footwork and movement. Throughout it all, as long as your fundamentals are good, the pros are content to leave your style intact.

A typical day begins at 8:30 A.M. with ten minutes of warmup and stretching. Almost two hours of on-court drills follow, interrupted by periodic breaks for water or lemonade. At 11:30 the group heads indoors either to attend a half-hour lecture/discussion on such topics as strategy and percentage tennis, or to watch and have analyzed the videotapes of their strokes. The afternoon session, following a two-hour lunch break, begins with a fifteen-minute video on some aspect of mental toughness. Then it's back to the courts for another two hours of drill and play.

Bollettieri's direct participation in these adult clinics varies from minimal to none. Although he tries to make at least one appearance to teach on the adult courts each week, he does not, in practice, always succeed. Your closest contact with the man who launched the careers of Andre Agassi, Jimmy Arias, Carling Bassett, and others may be standing at the side of his court watching him at work with the juniors and occasionally a big-name pro. Though he sometimes turns up at lunch, it is usually for business discussions with the pros rather than to socialize with the campers. His priorities obviously lie elsewhere.

The real responsibility for the adult camp rests with Butch Young. Campers rave about his ability to pinpoint the crucial flaw in a stroke. His minor adjustments inevitably produce major improvement.

During the adult sessions, he typically moves from court to court, supervising the instruction and intervening to interject his expertise. More than anyone, he's responsible for giving these clinics continuity and coherence. Unfortunately, he is sometimes called away to travel with one or more of the juniors.

Though moderately demanding, Bollettieri's adult program does not remotely approach the rigorousness of Hopman's at Saddlebrook, nor is it as tough as the All American Sports program at Amherst. On the other hand, it is one of the rare camps to make mental toughness an integral part of the weekly curriculum. Its indoor courts give it a distinct advantage over most other Florida facilities when it rains. Having juniors on the next court whaling the ball motivates adults to work harder. And there is always a chance of seeing a superstar like Agassi.

Like most camps, attendance at Bollettieri's fluctuates. The busiest

87

adult clinics—those with 30 or so participants—are likely to occur from Thanksgiving through New Year's and during March and April. The rest of the year gets 10 to 12 weekly; in summer many of the adults come from South America. Women, I'm told, usually outnumber men. Informality reigns.

Beginners there often get a great deal of individual help, particularly during weeks when attendance is light. Even so, they sometimes feel left out later in the week when the emphasis shifts to matches. At the other end of the spectrum, a player who is much, much stronger than the rest of the week's campers may be given the choice of joining an appropriately strong junior clinic.

Socially, Bollettieri's has a typical tennis camp atmosphere, in which everyone gets to know everybody else quickly and easily. The whole crowd—including the pros—eats in the adult dining room and hangs out at the same swimming pool. From 7:30 P.M. on, however, there is nothing much to do except feed quarters into the pinball machines. There's no bar on the property and none within walking distance. In fact, Bollettieri's is so isolated that there's really nothing within easy walking distance: not a pub, grocery store, movie theater, or shopping mall. Though virtually everyone is too tired to stay up late, no one is ready to go to bed at 8 P.M. The best advice is to befriend anyone with a car.

TRAVEL INSTRUCTIONS: The nearest airport is Sarasota/Bradenton, about a ten-minute drive from the academy. Free transportation from there is included in the package. The alternative is Tampa International, roughly 45 miles north.

Colony Beach & Tennis Resort

1620 Gulf of Mexico Dr.
Longboat Key, FL 34228
(813) 383-6464, (800) 237-9443,
or in Florida (800) 282-1138

SEASON: Year-round, but busiest over Christmas week and from February to April.

RATES: *Expensive* in summer and fall; *Very Expensive* in winter and spring. Rates include accommodations in a one-bedroom suite, Continental breakfast, two hours of daily clinics, free court time, and one fitness or aerobics class.

▶ Profile

COURTS: The Colony has 21 courts in all, which comes out to more than one per acre. Of those, 11 are hard and 10 are clay, the latter engineered to be watered from below. Two have lights. No room is very far from a court. A peculiarity of the complex, however, is that 13 of the courts—including the showcase Number 1 court—run north-south as is customary, while the remaining eight run east-west. The latter layout makes the sun a distinct factor on one side, especially during the winter, when it's low in the sky.

COURT FEES: None.

PRO STAFF: The director of tennis is Joe Simonetta, a former Penn State University player and USPTA pro with fifteen years of teaching experience. He oversees a staff of five to six teaching pros, most all of whom are themselves USPTA certified. His senior pro, Sammy Aviles, began his tennis career at age seven as a camper at Nick Bollettieri's Tennis Academy and has been on court in one way or another in the more than quarter century since. An astute and knowledgeable instructor, Aviles is quick to zero in on pivotal flaws in strokes. His warmth

89

and good nature make him a favorite of the kids in the Colony's junior program.

INSTRUCTIONAL PROGRAMS: The major clinic for adults, the "Tennis Plus" package, integrates a daily two-hour morning clinic with a tennis-to-music warmup, videotape analysis, and afternoon round robins and exhibitions. In addition, the Colony runs a junior academy and a "Tiny Tots" program.

SPECIAL FEATURES: The Colony guarantees its match-play service in the sincerest way possible: by promising to provide a pro free of charge if the staff can't find anyone else.

SEASONAL TENNIS EVENTS: Early each December the Colony hosts the Hackers Open, a week-long amateur tournament for A, B, and C players. Bud Collins, the television commentator known for his flamboyant language and clothes, directs the round-robin competition. There are singles, doubles, and mixed doubles events in four divisions: 30 and under, 40 and under, 50 and under, and over 50. The tournament is long on prizes, fun, and social events, none of which prevent participants from taking the competition seriously—which is to say that entrants play to *win*.

LODGING AND FOOD: The Colony has 232 one- and two-bedroom condominiums in two-story clusters. Little separates one building from the next but a patchwork of open spaces and the narrow roads that lace the property. Eighteen acres is not much to work with, and in places the Colony feels as though everything has been shoehorned in.

Each unit has a small but fully equipped kitchen, a large deck or balcony, comfortable furniture, and a cable television. The long, narrow bedroom contains two double beds and a second, smaller television. Two more beds fold down out of closets in the living room. The bathroom is finished in travertine marble and has a tub/shower with a built-in whirlpool; an adjacent vanity area has a second washbasin and large mirror. Each cluster of condominiums has a coin-operated washer and dryer on the main level.

The Colony is that rare resort to have a restaurant you might eat in even if you were staying somewhere else. The Colony Restaurant, which overlooks the Gulf of Mexico, has won awards not only for its cuisine but also for its 20,000-bottle cellar stocked with some 600 wines. Its diverse menu, part American, part Continental, features local seafood along with steaks, duck, chicken, and pasta. Many of the dishes can be prepared low in salt and cholesterol.

In addition to that formal dining room (jackets for men), the Colony has Windows for classic home cooking (shepherd's pie, pot roast, that sort of thing). If you'd rather eat in, there is Tastebuds, a gourmet market and deli.

OTHER RECREATIONAL AMENITIES: The Colony borders the twelve-mile-long white-sand beach that lines the Gulf of Mexico side of Longboat Key. It has a watersports center that rents sailboats, windsurfers, and other watersports equipment. Just behind the beach is a swimming pool. In the building adjacent to Court Number 1, there are separate men's and women's health clubs with saunas, steam rooms, whirlpools, and massage rooms. The fitness center is separate; it has aerobics classes, treadmills, rowing machines, exercycles, Stairmaster, free weights, and several pieces of specially designed resistance equipment. Bicycles are available for rent.

▶ *Gestalt*

Small, friendly, and right on the beach, the Colony is a luxury resort with a long reputation as a haven for tennis players. Its 21 courts constitute a very large complex given that there are only 232 rooms. Court time is free, game matching attentive. And during the busy winter season social tennis activities abound.

But what makes the Colony extraordinary is that it looms so large in the minds of tennis players—despite the fact that in recent years it has sought to diversify its image by placing more emphasis on its fitness and aerobics programs, its Gulf of Mexico beach and watersports center, and its fine dining and extensive wine cellar. Such is the power of its tennis mystique that the resort continues to attract a solid contingent of players, even though its tennis programs are neither so intensive nor so vigorous as they were a decade ago.

The principal clinic is a two-hour-a-day session geared to intermediates. The best part about them is a tennis-to-music warmup, a kind of aerobics session with tennis racquets. In it, you use a lot of the same footwork and hand movements that come into play in tennis. It's a clever way to begin.

The clinic itself is cut from old cloth. Each pro has up to six students (rather than the optimal four) and seems to have pretty much free reign in deciding what to teach. If there is an underlying methodology, it doesn't show. All in all, this is an exceptionally lightweight program to find at a resort with the Colony's reputation. Where is its usual willingness to experiment?

To be fair, what I saw was a very new program, one that had not yet been tested in high season. I only hope that it changes, because if that were all I had to go on, I'd be hard pressed to rate its programs among the world's best. The fact that the Colony *can* run a more sub-91 stantial program is evident from its junior academy, a day camp for kids living in the area. Their three-hour workouts are much more demanding—and frankly a lot more fun—than the regular adult clinics. Fortunately, when stronger adults come along, the Colony has been willing to feed them in with the juniors. So if the regular clinic is too easy, don't be shy about letting the staff know you're interested in something more demanding.

That same, almost inadvertent catering to stronger players shows up again at the fitness center. Its resistance equipment is the sort you'd find in a sports clinic or rehabilitation center rather than in your local health club. The staff who show you how to use it understand exactly what specific routines tennis players ought to be doing to improve performance and prevent injury. They even have workouts using racquet handles attached to giant rubber bands that simulate actual stroke production. This is stuff for active players, so again it's surprising not to find more on-court programs for them.

When the Colony is busy—over Christmas week and from February to April—the morning clinics may fill up (they can take 24 people) and the afternoon calendar includes both competitive and social tennis events. That, plus the matches the staff sets up, means you're certain to get as much tennis as you can handle.

The rest of the year is dicier, however. Summers bring families (the Colony has an excellent "Kidding Around" program to entertain children and daily "Tiny Tots" clinics). In late spring and early fall you may find blocks of rooms occupied by conference groups (if you break out in a rash around people wearing name tags, then ask before you book).

The winter crowd seems to have jetted in straight from cold northern cities like New York and Chicago. Couples far outnumber singles. The small size of the resort means that you're almost certain to bump into the people you meet on the court at the beach, pool, or bar.

And you're almost certain to spot Dr. M. J. "Murf" Klauber. A former dentist, Klauber bought the Colony in 1970 and personally presides over its day-to-day operations with the attentiveness of an innkeeper. You'll find him doing aerobics in the morning and looking in on the restaurant at night. His presence, like the resort's tennis mystique, is one of the Colony's impalpable assets.

TRAVEL INSTRUCTIONS: The nearest airport is Sarasota/Bradenton, about 20 minutes away by car. Tampa International is roughly an hour's drive.

Harry Hopman/ Saddlebrook International Tennis

....

100 Saddlebrook Way
Wesley Chapel, FL 34249

(813) 973-1111, (800) 237-7519,
or in Florida (800) 282-4654

SEASON: Year-round, but busiest from January through March.

RATES: *Moderate* overall but with seasonal fluctuations. Low-season rates apply from late May to mid-September, high season from mid-January to the end of April. The Hopman package includes accommodations, five hours of clinics daily, matches with instructors, free court time, and fitness and agility exercises. Separate clinic-only packages are available; there are several inexpensive motels within easy driving distance of the courts.

▶ *Profile*

COURTS: If courts alone were the measure of a great tennis resort, then Saddlebrook would rank near the top. It has 37 courts altogether and plans to build at least two grass, which would give the resort all three of the Grand Slam-tournament surfaces.

The major complex is near the center of the resort in a section called the "Walking Village," which is also where the pro shop and Hopman office are located. That complex consists of 17 hard and clay courts, 5 with lights. A few minutes' drive away in Lakeside Village are 14 additional hard and clay courts.

All of the courts are laid out in pairs with an awning-covered patio in between with chairs and a refrigerated water fountain. Just outside the fences there are trees and neatly tended beds of flowers and shrubbery. Pros sweep the lines before every session and the grounds-crew maintains the courts in first-rate condition.

COURT FEES: Expensive, but complimentary on Hopman packages.

PRO STAFF: Although Harry Hopman, the legendary Australian Davis Cup coach, died in 1985 (see "The Designer Labels"), the organization he built survives, headed now by two of his former staff, Howard Moore and Tommy Thompson. Moore is the tennis coordinator, Thompson the head professional. A third important member of the team is Dr. Jack Groppel, whose title is Director of Player Development. He heads a complete fitness, nutrition, and sports medicine program at the resort.

Thompson is a former circuit player who joined the Hopman organization in the mid-1970s. During his career, he has worked with more than 200 pros, traveling with Vitas Gerulaitis, Jimmy Brown, Yannick Noah, and Heinz Gunthardt, among others. He heads a staff of 36 instructors, among them noted coaches Alvaro Betancur and Roland Jaeger and a handful of others who have, like Thompson, traveled with touring pros. One measure of the overall quality of the staff is that the typical instructor has been with the Hopman organization for an average of six years.

Hopman's puts its new instructors through an apprenticeship program. Among the most important skills they have to learn is the ability to work four people very hard while giving each individual attention. The nature of the program means that instructors must have not only solid tennis skills but, says Thompson, "enthusiasm" as well.

INSTRUCTIONAL PROGRAMS: Two separate programs go on simultaneously at Hopman's: one for adults, another for juniors.

The adult program consists of five hours of daily drills supplemented several afternoons each week by a match with one of the teaching pros. The maximum student-pro ratio is 4:1. All levels can be accommodated, from rank beginners to international touring pros.

There are really two junior programs: a live-in program with students enrolled in the Palmer Academy, a private school within Saddlebrook; and summer and school-holiday programs for beginners, intermediates, and advanced players. Normally juniors have to be at least 9 years old to be accepted, though on occasion those as young as 7½ have been allowed to attend.

SPECIAL FEATURES: High-quality videotaping takes place at least once each week and is followed immediately by a thoughtful critique (see the "Gestalt" section below for how video meshes with the overall Hopman philosophy). Ball machines are available, but only the incurably masochistic can even think of hitting more tennis balls once the sessions and clinics end.

For those genuinely serious about their game or their fitness, Hopman's also offers a menu of supplementary programs under Dr. Groppel. These include a computerized fitness evaluation, tailor-made fitness programs, nutritional profiles, competitive psychological profiles, and a special high-tech "shuttered video analysis" of your game. Though not part of the regular clinic, all of these programs are offered to clinic participants at reduced cost.

Early in the week Hopman's arranges transportation for those who want to go grocery shopping. Dr. Groppel gives a talk on some aspect of tennis fitness, nutrition, or mental toughness one night a week. And one night a week there is an excursion to the mall to shop or catch a movie.

LODGING AND FOOD: Guests on Hopman packages have a choice of two types of accommodations: hotel rooms with two double beds and a patio, or very spacious one- or two-bedroom suites with patios and complete kitchens. All have cable TV. Location varies: some are near the Superpool, restaurants, courts, and fitness center in the Walking Village; others are near the pool and courts in Lakeside Village. Hopman's adult clinics typically take place on the Walking Village courts in winter, in which case it makes sense to book a room there. But during the rest of the year the clinics are likely to be held at Lakeside, raising the dilemma of having to choose to be near the courts or near the restaurants. There is a free shuttle between the two, which are about a ten-minute walk apart.

Like many resorts, Saddlebrook subscribes to the Captive Audience Theory of Inflated Restaurant Pricing. Eating there is expensive, especially at breakfast, which makes booking one of the large suites with kitchen facilities look like an act of fiscal responsibility. It's that or rent a car. The one compensation is that the food at both the pricier jackets-for-men Cypress Room and the informal Little Club is very good. Both have salads and sandwiches at lunch and fresh fish and pasta dishes every night. In addition, for the nutrition-conscious, the Cypress Room also has limited spa menu.

OTHER RECREATIONAL AMENITIES: Besides tennis, Saddlebrook has two Arnold Palmer–designed golf courses bordered by pines and cypress and riddled with lagoons and other water hazards. However, the centerpiece of the resort is its half-million-gallon, amoeba-shaped Superpool. At 270 feet long, it is vast enough to contain a 25-meter lap pool, water volleyball and water basketball courts, and a diving area. Around it are children's wading pools and heated whirlpools. Nearby is the Jockey Club Fitness Center, which contains Nautilus equipment, free weights, exercycles, climbing stairs, aerobics classes, massage rooms, and a health bar, as well as the usual saunas, steambaths, and whirlpools. There is another, smaller swimming pool and (hotter) whirlpool near the courts at the Lakeside Village complex.

▷ *To Note:* The demands of the Hopman program make it imperative to start getting in shape weeks or months before you show up. Jog, do windsprints, bicycle, climb stairs, do aerobics—whatever you have time for. You're not likely to be able to do enough, but even a little bit helps.

▶ *Gestalt*

Saddlebrook, where Harry Hopman International Tennis makes its home, is a 480-acre, award-winning resort/residential development 25 miles north of Tampa. Its very design is unique. At the core of the resort is a compact Walking Village whose centerpiece is a huge free-form pool. Arrayed around the pool's perimeter are restaurants, a conference center, golf and tennis pro shops, a fitness center, the major tennis complex, and clusters of two-story buildings containing the rooms and suites. The golf courses and jogging and bicycle trails radiate from there.

I was staying in the Walking Village at a time when the clinics were taking place at Lakeside, so I caught a shuttle to arrive in time for the 8:45 A.M. warm-up exercises. It was one of the few times the week's campers were all together. At 9:00 everyone split into their assigned groups and headed for the courts with their pro, who would stay with them throughout the week.

There were only three campers in my group: a man in his early twenties who was living at Saddlebrook in the hope, probably vain, of eventually making it to the circuit; a fiftyish German doctor, back with his wife for his annual four-week stint at Hopman's, and me. All three of us had arrived knowing that this was without question the most demanding tennis regimen for adults anywhere in the world. For five hours a day I ran and hit, ran and hit, ran and hit, scrambling from one side of the court to the other or up to the net and back until I was out of breath, wobbly-legged, and convinced that I couldn't get to another ball, except that just then Neil, the pro, would say, "Only five more. You can do it. Go, go," and somehow I'd get to five more balls, or almost, before finally being excused to drink water, towel off, and gather up balls while one of the other guys went through the same drill.

Harry Hopman did not get to be the winningest Davis Cup coach ever by pampering his players. He believed in physical conditioning and in pushing people to their limits and then beyond. Hopman died in 1985 but his notions live on in the Saddlebrook program. "Our philosophy is to challenge the player," says head pro Tommy Thompson. "Our feeds are a little bit harder, a little bit faster, and a little bit farther away than they're used to." It isn't boot camp exactly—the pros are not sadistic drill sergeants whose every other word is an insult—but it *is* grueling. "Fun" is not a word in the Hopman vocabulary.

Hopman's is for the hard-core. It hardly qualifies as a vacation unless your idea of a good time is five hours of drop-dead drills. Astonishingly, a few beginners do come and often get special attention in smaller-than-usual classes. But by its very nature this is a program for people who've already had some instruction and experience. The instructors focus on results rather than on the intricacies of strokes. "We want people to think about what they're going to do with the ball, not how they're going to do it," says Thompson. Dr. Groppel puts it another way: "What we deal with here at Hopman is getting your feet in the right place at the right time and your racquet in the right place at the right time." If you want lots of technical instruction, go somewhere else.

After five hours of this kind of work, most people are ready for the whirlpool—or bed. But, come midweek, the drills are followed by a match with one of the instructors. "He will play you, and beat you, and tell you why you lost," says Thompson.

The Hopman camp remains a place where you'll occasionally see international touring pros like Scott Davis, Ramesh Krishnan, John Frawley, Peter Doohan, Kathy Rinaldi, Jaime Yzaga, and Kathleen Horvath working out. In addition, Saddlebrook is one of the U.S. Tennis Association's National Training Centers, which means that some of the nation's most promising juniors are there from time to time honing their skills.

All of that gives Hopman's an international reputation and it shows in the clientele the clinics attract. They come from all over the world—especially Europe, South America, and Japan. They range in age from their mid-twenties to sixty and above. Men outnumber women, but only slightly. The largest turnout occurs from January through March, when there may be 40 to 60 adults and 80 to 90 juniors in the clinics. The smallest adult clinics take place during August, when a typical session might have ten to fifteen campers.

It is hard to find serious fault with anything that goes on on court at Hopman's, but when it comes to bringing campers together socially off court, the program fails absolutely. Meeting other people, which is normally easy, is unnecessarily difficult there. You are never introduced to anyone but the two or three other players who make up your group. Everyone goes his or her separate way for breakfast, lunch, and dinner. There is no central place for campers to gather. The only quasi-social event comes late in the week when they take a busload of people to the mall to shop or see movies. There needs to be a cocktail party on the first or second night—or immediately following the first afternoon's session—so people can get to know one another and the other pros. With so little time between the morning and afternoon sessions, it would even make sense to add lunch to the package and serve it at the courts, which would have the added benefit of bringing campers together socially. One thing is certain: something has to be done to ensure that the people who've come alone don't have to have dinner alone. It is a shame that Hopman's attracts people from all over the world who share a passion for tennis and then does nothing—nothing!—to bring them together. The hard-driving, merciless regimen is fine on court and is unquestionably one of the Hopman program's major assets, but that's no reason to make campers work hard at making social contact with one another once the clinics are over.

TRAVEL INSTRUCTIONS: Saddlebrook is 25 miles north of Tampa International Airport. Transfers can be arranged through the resort. However, given Saddlebrook's isolation and the generally low cost of rental cars in Florida, it makes economic sense to rent one. You'll have no problems parking next to your room in Lakeside Village, but that is not possible in the Walking Village. You may be tempted to leave your car with valet parking—despite its larcenous prices—especially since they'll tell you that the only option is to park miles away. Don't believe them. The Hopman staff can suggest ways around it.

Sea Pines Plantation

P.O. Box 7000
Hilton Head Island, SC 29938
(803) 785-3333 or (800) 845-6131

SEASON: Year-round, but busiest from May to Labor Day.

RATES: *Moderate–Expensive,* depending on the accommodations and time of year. The rates are highest in March and April and from late August through the end of October; lowest from November through February. The basic package includes accommodations, three hours a day of instruction, and unlimited court time. Clinic-only packages are also available.

▶ *Profile*

COURTS: There are 65 courts within Sea Pines Plantation, enough to make it the largest tennis resort in the nation. Most of the tennis activity takes place amid the tall pines and live oaks at the Sea Pines Racquet Club, an attractively landscaped complex with 24 clay courts, one of them a stadium, and 5 lighted hard courts. The lower-numbered courts bear the names of women who've won the annual Family Circle Cup tennis tournaments: Steffi Graf, Chris Evert, Martina Navratilova, Tracy Austin, and Evonne Goolagong.

COURT FEES: *Expensive,* but Sea Pines Resort packages include two complimentary hours.

PRO STAFF: Sea Pines' touring pro is former U.S. Open and Wimbledon champion Stan Smith. He developed the resort's tennis programs and personally conducts two four-day camps each year and gives two exhibitions. The day-to-day operations are handled by director of tennis Bunny Williams, a former tennis coach with a national ranking in the women's 35s. The head pro is Missy Malool, a former tour player and coach. All of the remaining staff of six pros are certified, often by both the USPTA and USPTR. "We look for people-oriented people," says Williams. "First and foremost they are teachers. They have an abil-

Sea Pines Plantation has more courts than any resort in the nation, and lays them out amid the native pines and live oaks.

ity to communicate and verbalize on the court and have a critical eye for the student. It's also important that they be good players, because they represent us when they're playing tournaments and exhibitions."

INSTRUCTIONAL PROGRAMS: Sea Pines not only has more courts than any other resort in the country but more clinics as well. Two of these, the Stan Smith Davis Cup Camps, amount to special events. Scheduled twice a year, usually in April and October or November, the four-day camp covers stroke production, strategy, drills, and exercises, with Smith personally involved on two of the four days.

100

Most of the clinics take place at the Sea Pines Racquet Club, a 29-court enclave near Harbour Town and site of the annual Family Circle Cup.

Chief among the year-round programs are: a four-day "Tennis Academy," which is a series of three-hour-a-day midweek clinics that cover the fundamentals of strokes and strategy; and a midweek "Davis Cup Drill Clinic," which stresses footwork, court coverage, strategy, and shot selection for intermediate to advanced players. Beyond that there are short clinics for beginners, Tiny Tots (ages 5-8), and juniors (ages 9-16; available during vacation weeks), and popular weekend clinics with videotape analysis.

SPECIAL FEATURES: Many of the clinics at Sea Pines include video-tape analysis and ball-machine drills, the stock fare of any good resort,

101

but it stands out for the depth and commitment of its player services. To enhance the social atmosphere, the racquet club stages mixed-doubles round-robins, exhibitions, and happy hours once or twice a week during the March-to-October high season. Events planning even goes so far as to include a complimentary NTRP evaluation and an equipment seminar.

SEASONAL TENNIS EVENTS: The Family Circle Magazine Cup takes place every April on the clay courts at Sea Pines. A nationally telecast event, it typically draws several of the world's best women players. Also on the yearly calendar are a sanctioned amateur senior tournament in May and a junior tournament over Labor Day Weekend.

LODGING AND FOOD: There are no hotels at Sea Pines, so basic accommodations consist instead of one-, two-, and three-bedroom villas. Prices vary according to locations and views. The Sea Pines Racquet Club, the hub of tennis activity at the plantation, is in Harbour Town within easy walking distance of more than half a dozen villa complexes, a few with their own separate bank of courts. Staying there puts you on the opposite site of the island from the beach, though a free shuttle and bicycle paths make it easy to get around the 4,500-acre property. All villas have fully equipped kitchens, living/dining areas, and patios or porches.

Dining options within Sea Pines Plantation are varied enough for you to eat out every night of the week and still not exhaust the possibilities. There are also supermarkets, bakeries, and delis with gourmet take-out. Moreover, if you're willing to leave the plantation, you'll find scores of additional restaurants strewn across the island.

OTHER RECREATIONAL AMENITIES: Five miles of dune-backed beach fringe the entire eastern edge of the plantation. Behind it are three 18-hole golf courses, including the Pete Dye/Jack Nicklaus-designed Harbour Town Links, one of the top 50 in the nation and the site of the PGA's annual MCI Heritage Classic. In addition, there is an equestrian center, two marinas (with charter fishing fleets), lagoon fishing, crabbing, a 605-acre forest preserve, and miles of biking and jogging trails.

▶ *Gestalt*

Hilton Head Island is often referred to as a "civilized wilderness." The 42-square-mile parcel of Low Country real estate, roughly 35 miles north of Savannah, Georgia, is the ultimate American resort destina-

102

tion, rich in tennis courts and golf courses, marinas and stables, bicycle paths, and children's playgrounds. During the busy April-to-September high season, its population swells to over 70,000, as vacationers and second-home owners come down to join the people who live there year-round. Together they share 12 miles of Atlantic-washed beach, forests of live oaks and pine trees, marshes, and tupelo swamps with more than 260 species of birds, an estimated 200 alligators, and uncounted deer, raccoons, turtles, and bobcats.

Sea Pines Plantation occupies the entire southern tip of the island, from Calibogue Sound on the Intracoastal Waterway eastward to the Atlantic. It is a model of brilliant planning and environmental sensitivity. The road from the main gate winds past a forest preserve, the pine-post fences of Lawton Stables, and the individual vegetable gardens at Heritage Farm. Villas cluster unobtrusively behind giant moss-bearded trees and native shrubbery. Stop signs are green; so are fire hydrants. There's a village of sorts, called Harbour Town, near the red-and-white-striped lighthouse that is a virtual symbol of Hilton Head. But the opposite side of the island holds something even more precious: a five-mile-long beach bordered by little more than dunes and forest. Only the boardwalks leading inland suggest that anything lies beyond. And there isn't a hotel for miles.

Sea Pines is no less impressive as a tennis destination. Its 65 courts make it the largest resort complex in the country, which is impressive in itself. But Sea Pines takes the grandeur a step beyond by scheduling a wealth of weekly tennis clinics and activities for every level of player, from tiny tots to tournament competitors.

The major instructional program in its weekly arsenal is the Stan Smith Tennis Academy, which takes place at the 29-court Sea Pines Racquet Club near Harbour Town. Stan Smith himself runs the academy only twice a year; the rest of the time it's in the hands of former touring pro Missy Malool. The twelve hours of instruction follow a standard progression from groundstrokes to strategy and playing situations, but among the aspects that distinguish this clinic are Malool's technical orientation, a result of the training and work she's done with Vic Braden (see "The Designer Labels").

"We use video equipment as probably the most important part of our week," says Malool. "I think seeing is believing, and I have a tendency to be very technical. I'm visual, so I seem to teach in that manner."

As a Braden protegée her first choice is to teach a looping topspin forehand and backhand, but unlike Braden she doesn't insist that it's the only correct way to hit a ball. "If they're satisfied with what they're doing, then I'm not going to try to change it," she says. "I'm here for them, they're not here for me. I try to get into what they want."

That personal attention is one of the major assets of the academy. To foster it, she deliberately keeps student-pro ratios low—never more than the industry standard of 4:1. The groups then get pushed at whatever pace they can handle.

Malool is serious about her teaching and expects her staff to be too. Campers mostly rave about the quality of the instruction. What's missing, some say, is the jovial, make-the-drills-fun approach typical of some other programs. A no-nonsense attitude runs through these clinics, not because the pros lack a sense of fun but because they're intently focused on what they're trying to accomplish.

Beginners and intermediates make up the largest contingent in these clinics (stronger players tend to opt for the afternoon drill sessions). Most are couples, aged anywhere from 35 to 65, mainly out of the Midwest, Northeast, and Canada.

Once the clinics end at noon each day, everyone scatters to pursue whatever other interests lured them to Hilton Head to begin with. There are mixed-doubles round-robins two afternoons a week and an exhibition/happy hour on another, but the orientation of the racquet club is toward teaching and matches more than socializing.

TRAVEL INSTRUCTIONS: The nearest major airport is in Savannah, Georgia, about 45 minutes away. It is served by most of the major airlines. Even closer, however, is the small commercial airport on the northern end of Hilton Head Island, which is served by a couple of commuter airlines. Both airports have taxi and limousine service to the tennis center, as well as car-rental agencies.

Van der Meer Tennis Center

. . . .

P.O. Box 5902
Hilton Head Island, SC 29938
(803) 785-8388 or (800) 845-6138

SEASON: Year-round, though in summer the major clinics take place at Sweet Briar College.

RATES: *Inexpensive–Moderate,* depending on the time of year and on whether or not Van der Meer himself runs the clinic. The basic package includes accommodations, tennis instruction, unlimited court time, and access to the facilities of the health club. It is also possible to book just the instruction.

No tennis teaching facility in the world can match the breadth of instructional programs offered at the Van der Meer Tennis Center.

▶ *Profile*

COURTS: The center has 24 courts in all, 21 of them hard, the other 3 clay. Eight have lights; 4 are covered. The courts surround a full-service pro shop with classroom facilities.

COURT FEES: None.

PRO STAFF: Dennis Van der Meer (see "The Designer Labels") heads a staff of some 18 teaching pros, all of whom have been certified by the United States Professional Tennis Registry (USPTR), whose international headquarters are on Hilton Head Island. Among the senior support staff who participate in various of the clinics are sports psychologist Dr. Jim Loehr and former Czechoslovakian Davis Cup player Dr. Louie Gap.

INSTRUCTIONAL PROGRAMS: No tennis teaching facility in the world can match the breadth of instructional programs offered at the Van der Meer center. In any given week there is likely to be everything from half-hour "Munchkin" sessions (for kids aged 3 to 6) to five-hour-a-day adult clinics, often personally conducted by Van der Meer himself. I've reviewed the Van der Meer adult clinic in the Gestalt section below, but here's a breakdown of the various programs offered for adults and juniors.

Adult programs. The mainstay for adults is a three-day weekend or five-day midweek clinic consisting of five hours a day of instruction and drills. These are open to players of any level, including novices. Periodically the center also schedules special "Advanced Adult Clinics" for players with NTRP ratings of 4.0 or above. Rather than concentrate on strokes, those advanced sessions focus on such topics as stroke selection, developing an attacking game, tactics and tournament preparation. Intermediate and advanced players also have the option of signing up for fast-paced "Match-play Drill Clinics," designed to sharpen strokes and improve reactions. Also on the calendar are occasional "Seniors Clinics" for players 45 and older, mental toughness programs (called TennisUniversity II), and various teacher-training courses for those interested in becoming certified teaching pros. Besides these longer programs, the center offers hour-long stroke-of-the-day clinics and two-hour drill sessions on either a daily or weekly basis.

Junior programs. As it does for adults, the center runs three- and five-day junior clinics for boys and girls ages 9 to 16. Van der Meer personally conducts some of these clinics; others are under the direction of senior staff. For tournament-level players ages 12 to 18, the center runs a "World-Class Training Program." These one-, two-, or four-week sessions take place from March through August (excluding May). In addition there are hour-long junior clinics (for kids aged 9 and up) and half-hour "Munchkin" clinics (for kids ages 3 to 6) available on a daily basis several times each week.

SPECIAL FEATURES: An in-depth videotape analysis is part of the regular clinic at the center, though it can also be done in conjunction with a private lesson. Potentially more useful is the computerized charting of singles matches. Ball machines are available for rent.

SEASONAL TENNIS EVENTS: The Tennis Center hosts two big adult USTA-sanctioned tournaments, the Van der Meer Classic in June and the We've Got You Covered event in December. Both have Open, 35s, and 45s divisions, singles and doubles, for men and women, and typically get more than 100 entries.

LODGING AND FOOD: The basic package at the Van der Meer center is for instruction only, leaving you free to stay anywhere you like on Hilton Head Island. The center does have its own accommodations available, however, in the Beach Arbor Villas just across the street from the courts and offers discounts to clinic participants. The villa lodging ranges in size from tiny, rather spartan but very inexpensive rooms with twin beds and a refrigerator to suites with fully equipped kitchens.

There is one restaurant and bar on the property, the Player's Club, an oak-and-brass fern bar that caters to tennis players by serving pasta, seafood, pizzas, salads, and sandwiches. Several others are within walking distance.

OTHER RECREATIONAL AMENITIES: The beach is roughly a block away from the courts. Those staying at the Beach Arbor Villas get a temporary membership in the health club, which has indoor and outdoor swimming pools, whirlpools, a sauna, racquetball courts, Nautilus weight-training equipment, and exercise rooms.

▶ *Gestalt*

An hour into the clinic, Dennis Van der Meer already knows every camper's name and the peculiarities of his or her strokes. He proves it later during the analysis of the videotape. Standing with his back to the television monitor, he asks for the name of the person hitting the ball, finds him or her in the crowd, and still without looking at the screen demonstrates what's wrong with the stroke, giving it a goofy name and exaggerating its flaws for comic effect. He then shows what needs to be done to correct it and moves on to the next person, never once having to glance at the screen, even if there are more than forty people in the clinic.

That kind of personal attention is central to Van der Meer's camps. The brochures for his Tennis Center clearly indicate which clinics he will personally run. And for Van der Meer, running a clinic means being there on court during every minute of the three-day or five-day sessions. He introduces each new topic, analyzes the videotapes, and roves from court to court, making sure to help everyone individually. Wearing a tiny microphone in his shirt, he sometimes shouts instructions at campers three courts away, calling them by name and leaving everyone with the sense that he notices absolutely everything that goes on on every court.

He seems not only to be ubiquitous but also to have an aura of irrepressible enthusiasm and good humor. He teases everyone. When they seem to take him seriously he quickly recants, saying "I'm just kidding you" and always, always calling them by name. He laughs at his own, often silly jokes, and campers laugh with him because they can't help it. Like a performer on stage, Van der Meer seems never to be more alive than on the court in front of an audience.

At the same time, he genuinely seems to care deeply about helping his students improve. Everyone gets his personal attention, not just once but several times a day. What's more, he often spends a little extra time with the people having the most trouble.

Underpinning his teaching is his own Official Standard Method of Instruction. What he has done is break down each stroke into its component elements and then establish a step-by-step process for teaching it. He calls it "simple tennis based on sound biomechanics." All of his pros teach in exactly the same way, so as you move from court to court during the clinic you'll never have one pro telling you one thing, another another.

His teaching method embraces all the various ways to hit each stroke. Thus, although he personally believes in the value of a classical style, he's not going to force you into his mold. What he does do, however, is look for ways to expand campers' repertoires. "Take the guy who has heavy topspin and that's the only stroke he has," says Van der Meer. "If he comes to a Van der Meer camp, I would add a slice approach, for instance. I wouldn't take away his topspin, I'd just give him more versatility."

In the course of a three-day or five-day clinic, he covers all the strokes, including topspin lobs, drop shots, and spin serves. From there he moves on to work on consistency, footwork, and mobility. Toward the end he introduces strategy and tactics. Along the way, he usually finds time to weave in some basic principles of mental toughness, to help campers overcome problems of tension, choking, and faulty concentration.

The basic adult camp at the tennis center is not as rigorous as its six-hour-a-day format suggests. One reason is that the 6:1 student-pro ratio, which is high by industry standards, means you hit fewer balls during the course of the drill sessions. Another is that you get to rest while Van der Meer talks—or performs—which he loves to do. (The Tennis Center conducts other, more demanding clinics for advanced players who want a vigorous workout at the same time they're honing skills.)

That helps to explain why there are people still eager to play once the clinics are over. In an effort to beef up the Center's social atmosphere and encourage more people to stay in the Beach Arbor Villas, Van der Meer has added an exhibition with free beer on Sunday evenings, and round-robins four times a week (which doesn't stop some people from heading straight for the beach, swimming pool, or Player's Club bar). Whereas once as many as 90 percent of the campers stayed somewhere else on the island, lately more than half book rooms at the center. It's easier than ever to hook up with a group headed to dinner, if not at the Player's Club then at one of the other nearby restaurants.

Virtually all of the clinics personally conducted by Van der Meer fill to their 42-student capacity, no matter what time of year they're scheduled. In general, the center draws heavily from Ohio, Georgia, and the Northeast, in that order. Women outnumber men three to two. The crowd consists of a mixture of couples, friends traveling together, and a few singles. Most are 35 and over. All are serious enough about their tennis not to be out very late at night.

But then the tennis is the real lure of the Van der Meer center. No other big-name pro spends as much time on the court with club players as Van der Meer.

TRAVEL INSTRUCTIONS: The nearest major airport is in Savannah, Georgia, about 45 minutes away. It is served by most of the major airlines. Even closer, however, is the small commercial airport on the northern end of Hilton Head Island, which is served by a couple of commuter airlines. Both airports have taxi and limousine service to the tennis center, as well as car-rental agencies.

Wild Dunes Beach & Racquet Club

P.O. Box 1410
Charleston, SC 29402-1410
(803) 886-6000 or (800) 845-8880

SEASON: Year-round, but the clinics draw their largest number of participants in the spring.

RATES: *Moderate–Expensive,* depending on the time of year and type of accommodations. The clinic package consists of accommodations, five hours of daily clinics, free court time, and free use of ball machines, swimming pools, saunas, and bicycles.

▶ Profile

COURTS: The Racquet Club has 19 courts in all, 8 with lights, including a 500-seat permanent stadium. Except for one hard court used mainly for teaching, all are clay laid out in pairs and separated by walkways and a few odd palm trees. Here and there patios with tables and chairs provide places to hang out before and after matches. There are more tables and chairs on the deck of the two-story clubhouse, half-hidden in a grove of trees. Besides a full-service pro shop, it contains lockers and showers, classrooms for the clinics, and a bicycle-rental outlet.

COURT FEES: *Expensive,* but complimentary on packages.

PRO STAFF: Director of tennis Randy Chamberlain is a former junior and college player from Texas with two decades of teaching experience. He heads a staff of six pros, many of whom have been there since the mid-1980s or earlier. "We've made a point of getting good pros and retaining them," notes Chamberlain.

INSTRUCTIONAL PROGRAMS: Wild Dunes has a lengthy menu of tennis instruction for both adults and juniors. The programs range from stroke-of-the-day clinics to intensive two- and five-day camps.

Those intensive sessions, geared to intermediate and advanced players, run five hours a day, enough time to progress beyond stroke production into strategy, conditioning, improving reflexes, and even mental toughness. The curriculum includes one or more sessions of videotape analysis. The student-pro ratio is 4:1. Once the clinics are over, campers get free additional court time and complimentary use of ball machines.

The sessions for juniors range from hour-long introductions to tennis to five-day live-in camps during selected weeks in the summer.

SPECIAL FEATURES: Few resorts take as eclectic an approach to tennis instruction as Wild Dunes. State-of-the-art video and ball machines are not enough: the Racquet Club also has EYESPAN, a device for testing and improving hand-eye coordination and peripheral vision; and computerized match charting. In addition, there is a Programming Coordinator who sets up matches and feeds guests into the weekly round-robins and other social tennis events.

SEASONAL TENNIS EVENTS: Early each May Wild Dunes hosts the U.S. Clay Court Championships, a men's professional event that has drawn players like Michael Chang, Brad Gilbert, Kevin Curren, and Robert Seguso.

LODGING AND FOOD: Where you opt to stay in Wild Dunes depends on your priorities and your pocketbook. The least expensive option is to book a Lagoon Room (actually a villa bedroom with a private entrance), which has two double beds, private bath, and a small refrigerator. Those rooms are located just a short walk from the courts but more than two blocks from the ocean. Two- and three-bedroom villas with fully equipped kitchens and washers and dryers are available in the same location.

By far the loveliest accommodations—short of renting an entire house—are the villas that rise just behind the dunes lining the Atlantic-washed beach. Well-appointed and spacious, they have fully equipped kitchens, washers and dryers, and anywhere from one to four bedrooms. Staying in one of those means you are within steps of the beach but face hopping on a bike or catching a free shuttle to get to the courts.

There are two restaurants at Wild Dunes, both of them informal. Island House, just across the road from the Racquet Club, specializes in Low Country dishes and fresh local seafood, while the Club in the golf clubhouse serves prime cuts of mesquite-grilled beef. That's a limited choice, but Charleston and its culinary abundance are only fifteen miles away.

111

OTHER RECREATIONAL AMENITIES: Two-and-a-half miles of hard-packed sandy beach fringe Wild Dunes's Atlantic shore. The newest addition to the shorefront is a large Beach Pavilion with three swimming pools, broad decks, and additional conference facilities. Windsurfers and sailboats can also be rented. When it comes to golf, Wild Dunes ranks among the finest resorts in the nation. It has two 18-hole courses, both designed by Tom Fazio. The newer of the two is the 6,709-yard Harbor Course, whose narrow fairways and marsh hazards demand pinpoint accuracy. But it's the older, 6,715-yard Links Course, at once difficult and uncommonly lovely, that established Wild Dunes's national reputation. Wild Dunes also has a Yacht Harbor and Marina for deep-sea fishing charters and harbor cruises. It's possible to fish in the surf, creeks, or freshwater lagoons. The Swim Center near the Racquet Club has an Olympic-size pool and aquafit and aerobics classes. And from Memorial Day to Labor Day there are children's activity programs that take children as young as age 3.

▶ *Gestalt*

Hilton Head's deserved reputation as the ultimate resort destination in the country so overshadows the other barrier-island developments along South Carolina's coast that it is easy to overlook even as extraordinary a property as Wild Dunes. The family-oriented 1,500-acre resort occupies the northern end of the Isle of Palms, a scant fifteen miles from the magnificent historical district of Charleston. Staying at Wild Dunes means having a full complement of resort activities all within easy access of that Southern city's architecture, culture, sightseeing attractions, shops, restaurants, and nightlife.

Unfortunately, being near Charleston in the fall of 1989 also meant being in the path of Hurricane Hugo. Wild Dunes bore the brunt of the storm's fury, losing trees, dunes, and its marina. Many of the houses and villas were badly damaged. Yet the two-story tennis clubhouse escaped almost unscathed, some say because a member of the staff had the presence of mind to tape a vibration-damper to the door before evacuating the island. The water level reached 5½ feet, but the pro shop on the second floor suffered only a cracked skylight.

Wild Dunes expects to be operating as a resort again by May of 1990. Very little needs to be done to get the tennis center ready. Falling trees crushed the fences and broke off one stairway leading to the stadium seating, but damage to the courts themselves was minimal.

The programs I saw obviously took place before the hurricane. I have no way of knowing how quickly Wild Dunes's tennis clinics can recover from that natural disaster. At the same time, given its stellar tennis operation in the past I'm reluctant to drop it from the book, especially since I know that Randy Chamberlain is doing everything he can to re-establish his programs and may in fact have some of them going again by May 1990. Thus I have left this review much as I wrote it before the storm. But phone the pro shop before you book to ascertain exactly how far along the resort is in its recovery and exactly what you can expect as a tennis player during the week you're planning to visit.

The Racquet Club stands on a patch of level ground near the center of the development. What remains of huge trees shade its two-story cypress clubhouse, whose second-floor covered deck overlooks the stadium and the courts beyond.

Depending on which way you come in, you may pass the strange-looking EYESPAN panel. It is the first clue to the Racquet Club's irrepressible curiosity and desire to experiment. Computerized match-charting is available as well.

Except for videotaping, the technological orientation does not carry over into the clinics. What animates them is the pros' enthusiasm, and that is no accident. Director of tennis Randy Chamberlain wants that love of tennis to rub off because, he says, "The basic thing that will make players good is if they keep enjoying the game."

Maybe that's what gives an edge to the Wild Dunes clinics. The most ambitious is an intensive five-hour-a-day program. "It is not just a drill camp," insists Chamberlain. "It's not just something where we do a thousand drills a day. And it's not just a mechanical and technical camp."

It is instead a comprehensive seminar on everything from technique to strategy, notable for its abundance of personal attention. The camp begins with a few skill tests (like seeing how fast you can run around the court) and an evaluation of stroking consistency. Part of the object is to give you a benchmark against which to measure your progress. They're dedicated to having students set goals at Wild Dunes.

Beyond that, the pros adapt their teaching methods to the personalities of the students. "There are some people who are used to and only accept drill-sergeant techniques," notes Chamberlain. "We have different pros who are more adept at that sort of teaching. We have other pros who are more technically oriented and others who are just more fun-and-games oriented."

The bottom line for him is: "Our philosophy is to make sure that they're having fun. They're there five hours a day; they're going to burn out unless they're progressing."

113

To make sure that everyone gets that personal attention, the clinics never have more than four students to a pro. The intensive programs typically have from twelve to sixteen students during the busy part of the year, from March through July. They tend to range from solid intermediates to low advanced. Singles make up about 20 percent of the business. It is hot and humid at Wild Dunes in the summer, which slightly depresses the numbers of people in the intensive clinics but raises the playing level. Otherwise, summer brings an expansion of their junior clinics. The crowd at Wild Dunes comes partly from Atlanta and Charlotte and partly from the Midwest and Northeast.

There are social round-robins three times a week for everyone staying at Wild Dunes, and an exhibition with free beer and soft drinks, but there is nothing specifically scheduled for the campers. In practice, though, the pros and students are together so much of the day that informal pizza parties and other gatherings tend to happen spontaneously. There is virtually no nightlife on the property other than a lounge which occasionally has live music. But then Charleston and all it offers is only a half-hour's drive away.

TRAVEL INSTRUCTIONS: The nearest airport is in Charleston, about 15 miles away. Rental cars, limousines, and taxis are available.

Van der Meer Summer Camps

Sweet Briar College
Sweet Briar, VA 24595

or

Information: Van der Meer Tennis Center
P.O. Box 5902
Hilton Head Island, SC 29938
(803) 785-8388 or (800) 845-6138

SEASON: Early June through early August.

RATES: *Inexpensive–Moderate.* The package includes dormitory accommodations, all meals, tennis instruction, and unlimited court time. Clinic-only packages are also available.

▶ *Profile*

COURTS: The campus has 14 tennis courts, all of them hard. Two have lights.

COURT FEES: None.

PRO STAFF: Dennis Van der Meer (see "The Designer Labels") heads a staff of as many as 20 teaching pros, all of them certified by Van der Meer's U.S. Professional Tennis Registry.

INSTRUCTIONAL PROGRAMS: Adults have a choice of four programs at Sweet Briar: (1) an adult clinic, open to anyone, including novices; (2) an advanced clinic, open to players with NTRP ratings of at least 4.0; (3) TennisUniversity I, for those who want to learn how to teach using the Van der Meer's Official Standard Method of Instruction; and (4) TennisUniversity II, for intermediates and above who want to work on mental toughness. These clinics range from two to five days in length, and generally have you on court from five to six hours a day. Van der Meer personally teaches some but by no means all (the schedule clearly indicates which ones he will conduct; senior staff members take over in Van der Meer's absence). The student-pro ratio never exceeds 6:1.

For juniors, there are several five-day clinics for boys and girls aged 10 to 16 and a special summer circuit program, which runs from two to five weeks, that is open to a limited number of qualified advanced juniors aged 12 to 18.

SPECIAL FEATURES: The clinic includes at least one session of videotaping. Ball machines are available for use after class.

PRO SHOP: Surprising as it may seem, there is a full-service pro shop on campus selling everything from balls and accessories to clothing, racquets, and shoes.

LODGING AND FOOD: The only accommodations on campus are the dorms, which have twin beds and student desks. Linens are provided but not towels or soap. There's a laundromat nearby.

The meals, which are served in the main cafeteria, break with usual dormitory fare by including fresh vegetables grown in the area, homemade yoghurt, lots of fruits and salads, and a variety of entrees, among them eggplant parmesan, fried chicken, and ham. The kitchen has no trouble accommodating vegetarians.

OTHER RECREATIONAL AMENITIES: The college has an indoor swimming pool, a large gymnasium, squash and platform tennis courts, two theaters for tennis films, and lakes for swimming, boating, and fishing.

▶ *Gestalt*

The campus of Sweet Briar College covers 3,300 acres of meadows, woodlands, and lakes in the eastern foothills of the Blue Ridge Mountains. The 650 women who attend during the academic year are gone during the summer months, replaced by a changing guard of tennis players, who come for Van der Meer's clinics and find themselves with this gorgeous campus all to themselves.

Van der Meer himself spends most of June and July at Sweet Briar, teaching most, but not all, of the clinics. The programs offered at Sweet Briar are exactly the same as their counterparts at the Hilton Head Island center, and Van der Meer is every bit the charismatic showman in the Blue Ridge Mountains as he is in South Carolina (see the review of the Van der Meer Tennis Center in South Carolina for details about a Van der Meer training session).

What's different is the social atmosphere. At Sweet Briar, almost everyone stays on campus and eats in the cafeteria. You can't help but meet most of the other campers because the entire crew is on the same schedule, beginning with breakfast and ending with an optional—and never very late—stop at the on-campus pub. Genuine nightlife does not exist at Sweet Briar, but at least there is a place to gather after dinner. An easygoing camaraderie animates the camp from beginning to end.

Like all campus programs, Sweet Briar is very informal. T-shirts and shorts are just as acceptable in the cafeteria as they are on the courts. Tennis is what lures the crowds.

The crowd at Sweet Briar tends to come from Ohio and the Mid-Atlantic states. A typical midweek session gets about 40 campers, while on weekends the attendance may reach 60 or more. There are usually about the same number of men as women, mainly in their late thirties or early forties. As a group they seem to have much in common. After all, given Sweet Briar's seclusion the only reason for coming is the tennis, and thus the Van der Meer program tends to get players relatively serious about their games. Moreover, the statistics Van der Meer has compiled on their income suggests that they can afford more luxurious digs but evidently prefer Sweet Briar and its complete lack of pretention to a posh resort.

These clinics are not so rigorous as their five-hour-a-day format suggests. That's due partly to the high student-pro ratio (6:1) and partly to Van der Meer's performances, during which you get to rest. But five hours a day in the summer sun is still a lot of tennis, enough to have the whole camp in bed asleep by 10 P.M. In any case, Van der Meer's intention is not to run you into the ground, but to give you the benefit of his expertise.

TRAVEL INSTRUCTIONS: The nearest airport is in Lynchburg, Virginia, 12 miles from campus. Taxi and limousine service is available from there to the college (transportation is provided in packages for juniors). There is also bus service to Lynchburg and to the town of Amherst, which is three miles north of Sweet Briar.

MIDWEST, WEST, AND SOUTHWEST

....

Arizona
▶ John Gardiner's Tennis Ranch on Camelback, Scottsdale
▶ The Wickenburg Inn Tennis & Guest Ranch, Wickenburg

California
▶ Vic Braden Tennis College at Coto de Caza
▶ John Gardiner's Tennis Ranch, Carmel Valley
▶ Rancho Bernardo Inn, Rancho Bernardo
▶ Reed Anderson Tennis School, Palm Springs

Missouri
▶ The Lodge of Four Seasons, Lake Ozark

Nevada
▶ Reed Anderson Tennis School, Incline Village

Texas
▶ John Newcombe's Tennis Ranch, New Braunfels

John Gardiner's Tennis Ranch on Camelback

5700 E. McDonald Dr.
Scottsdale, AZ 85253
(602) 948-2100 or (800) 245-2051

SEASON: October to early May (or perhaps as late as Memorial Day), with highest rates in effect from Christmas to mid-April.

RATES: *Very Expensive.* Gardiner's offers three-day and weeklong packages that include accommodations, all meals, three hours of daily tennis clinics, and complimentary court time. The full-week package adds optional afternoon tennis tournaments and two half-hour massages.

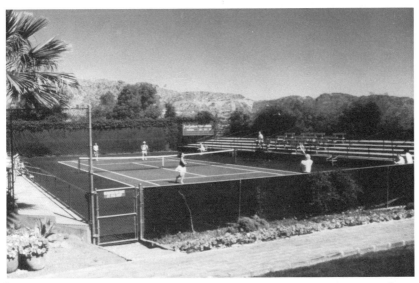

The stadium court at the "Tiffany's of Tennis": John Gardiner's Tennis Ranch on Camelback in Scottsdale, Arizona.

▶ *Profile*

COURTS: This Gardiner complex consists of 22 hard and 3 artificial-grass courts laid out on terraces in the side of Camelback Mountain. One is a permanent stadium. Orange trees and beds of desert foliage border the fences. Planters and hanging baskets of flowers are everywhere.

COURT FEES: None.

PRO STAFF: Director of Tennis Billy van Diense has been with the Gardiner organization since the early 1970s. He heads up a staff of 25 pros, ranging in age from their early twenties to a few seniors ranked in the 55s and 65s.

INSTRUCTIONAL PROGRAMS: The basic Gardiner session consists of 3½ hours of instruction and drills each morning. During the early part of the week these focus on the various strokes, but as players improve the emphasis shifts to drills that simulate points and finally to strategy and playing situations. The student-pro ratio never exceeds 4:1 and is often lower.

Each day begins with a warmup session that lasts half an hour. That is longer than most, but Gardiner's has found it helps reduce injuries. The last half hour of each morning is a "Go Where You Like" session in which one court is designated for each of the strokes (including drop shots and lobs); you head for whichever court is working on the stroke you want additional help with. Once the regular session finishes, there is a supplemental half hour for the hard core who still crave more. A long lunch follows. Afternoons are given over to a variety of tournaments and social tennis activities.

SPECIAL FEATURES: Two courts at the ranch have what amount to indefatigable, unerring opponents in the form of self-feeding computerized ball machines. The pros use them as automatic feeders during the clinics; campers can use them after class to drill. The basic clinic also includes videotape analysis, which is done at least once during each camp; and from time to time, when the group seems to need it, the pros hand-chart matches looking for patterns of mistakes.

SEASONAL TENNIS EVENTS: In mid-January, Gardiner's stages the Senators Cup, a charity tournament whose players are U.S. senators and heads of companies like Motorola and Time Warner. The money raised goes to fund the Hospice of the Valley.

LODGING AND FOOD: When it comes to providing food and lodging, Gardiner's philosophy is that people who go on a tennis vacation "don't want to live worse than they would at home." Thus, "ranch" does not in any sense mean rustic. The basic unit of accommodation is a *casita,* which is a spacious two-bedroom/two-bath condominium individually decorated according to the tastes of the owner. Each has a full kitchen, a large beamed living room with a fireplace, and patios off both bedrooms. The second bedroom has a private entrance and can be locked off from the living quarters to create a simple room for two. The master bedroom, kitchen, and living room, which has a fireplace, rent as a one-bedroom suite. Two couples or a family can take the entire casita themselves.

All of the casitas are within walking distance of the clubhouse and restaurant. Higher on the mountain stand several three- or four-bedroom houses, some with their own tennis courts, swimming pools, saunas, and whirlpools.

Freshly squeezed orange juice and a newspaper are delivered to the doorstep of each room early in the morning (there is coffee and a coffee maker in each room already). For breakfast, guests head down to the restaurant in the clubhouse for a lavish buffet of fresh fruits, cereals, pastries, and maybe eggs Benedict, supplemented by a menu of made-to-order hot items. Lunch is another groaning-board buffet, sometimes served outside around the pool. It's likely to consist of cold soup, cold cuts, salads, marinated vegetables, fresh fruit, and a variety of hot dishes.

At night, the view from the dining room of the lights of Paradise Valley is breathtaking; but dinner is, to be blunt, disappointing. Not only are the entrees served from chafing dishes rather than prepared to order—which is inexcusable at these prices—but the menu leans to preparations in vogue a generation ago: rack of lamb, beef Wellington, chicken or veal piccata, and fresh fish swimming in butter sauce. Their suspect nutrition aside, these dishes fail to leave any lasting culinary impression. That, too, is inexcusable at these prices.

OTHER RECREATIONAL AMENITIES: Besides courts the ranch has a large swimming pool at the clubhouse and several smaller pools scattered around the condominiums. There are whirlpools in the clubhouse locker rooms. Joggers can take off on desert trails in and near the ranch. Golf privileges at many of the greater Phoenix courses can be arranged.

▶ *Gestalt*

Not long after Gardiner's Camelback ranch opened in 1968 it came to be known as "Tiffany's of Tennis," which meant that it both epitomized luxury in a tennis vacation and charged deluxe prices for it.

123

In the spring the air at the Camelback ranch smells of orange blossoms, and fresh fruit is as close as the back fence.

From the outset it promised solid tennis instruction coupled with fine food and supremely comfortable accommodations. Gardiner coddled his clientele by delivering fresh-squeezed orange juice and newspapers to their doors every morning and providing complimentary massages as part of the clinic package. An unreconstructed traditionalist, he dressed his pros in tennis whites and until the early 1980s insisted that his guests do likewise. He required (and still requires) jackets and ties for gentlemen after 7 P.M. All in all, he sought to re-create the atmosphere of an exclusive private club: elitist, a little stuffy, and closed to those unprepared to write a hefty check for a few days or a week of privileges.

That formula has served Gardiner well. More than two decades later, the Scottsdale ranch is still the first one most people think of when conversation turns to posh tennis camps. It is, after all, one of only nine or ten resorts that exist primarily to cater to the passions of tennis players. And of those, only three others—Gardiner's ranches in Carmel Valley and the new one at Rancho Santa Fe and the Inn and Tennis Club at Manitou in Canada—do so with as much attention to the off-court amenities as to the on-court programs.

The paradox of a place like Gardiner's is that if you come hoping to elevate your tennis game, you will eventually have to wean yourself from all that coddling, put on your best designer tennis outfit, and submit to a regimen of running, drilling, and sweating (see "The Designer Labels" for a more thorough discussion of the Gardiner philosophy and method). No Gardiner pro is going to subject you to the indignity of drop-dead drills, but the clinic's primary goal is to give you a good physical workout (how else would you know you got your money's worth?). By midweek a complimentary massage may seem less like a perk than a necessity.

Gardiner's makes good use of its ball-machine courts and videotapes everyone at least once a week, but if there is one routine that epitomizes the Ranch's approach to tennis it is "two up, two back." This is, as the name suggests, a doubles drill in which two players are at the net, two at the baseline. The team at the baseline puts the ball in play by attempting to lob over the team at the net. From then on the point is played out as it would be in a regular game. What it does is take away the serve as a weapon and force both teams to rely instead on strategy and tactics—especially the lob and the importance of having both players at the net. So intrinsic is this drill to a Gardiner clinic that the main tournament of the week is played as "two up, two back," rather than as normal doubles.

The Scottsdale ranch devotes a lot of time to doubles, partly because that's what most people play, partly because it's more social. To help players overcome their discomfort of venturing to net, the pros do a series of drills on deep volleys and angle volleys and supplement it with work on approach shots—how and when to hit them and what to do once you have. The philosophy is to make the net less intimidating.

If that sounds like an approach geared to the intermediate player, it is. They make up the core of any Gardiner clinic. Most are between

45 and 60 years old, though in the last few years, I am told, Gardiner's has "recognized a trend to either a little younger, or at least a little younger-looking, and perhaps a little more fit." Roughly 60 percent of them are women.

In any given week you're likely to find at least 35 people in the clinics, and during the Christmas holidays and the months of February and March attendance soars above 50. Over the major holidays—Thanksgiving, Christmas, Spring Break, and Easter—families make up a large segment of the clientele, and the ranch responds by adding special tennis programs for juniors.

At any time, the clublike atmosphere encourages socializing. Between a welcoming cocktail party on Sunday and round-robin mixers on Monday and Tuesday (open even to those who opt not to take the clinics), you get to know virtually everyone. Whether you choose to eat with them or not is up to you; there's no forced camaraderie, and the couple who prefer a table for two can always have one.

The restaurant and bar overlook Paradise Valley, which at night is a gorgeous sea of tiny lights. Everyone gathers at the bar for drinks—gentlemen in coats and ties, of course—before dinner. Afterwards on weekends a few linger to dance the night away until the wee hour of, say, 10:30 P.M.

TRAVEL INSTRUCTIONS: Phoenix's Sky Harbor Airport is 6 miles away.

The Wickenburg Inn Tennis & Guest Ranch

P.O. Box P
Wickenburg, AZ 85358
(602) 684-7811 or (800) 528-4227

SEASON: The inn is open year-round, even during the wilting heat of the desert summer; however, anyone packing a tennis racquet should confine his or her visit to the period between early October and May 1.

RATES: *Moderate.* That rate category is based on a package consisting of accommodations, three meals a day, three hours of daily tennis clinics, complimentary horseback riding and court time, nature programs, and arts and crafts instruction (but not materials).

▶ Profile

COURTS: There are 11 hard courts in all, none of them lighted. Two are next to the lodge in a virtual botanical garden of desert foliage, but the main tennis complex sprawls along the bed of a dry wash known as the Casita Valley for the adobe *casitas* on the knoll just above. Ramadas in various locations among the courts shade chairs and water coolers. The clubhouse is an air-conditioned double-wide trailer containing restrooms, showers, a sitting room with a television, and the pro shop, which has a limited selection of clothing and gear. Overnight restringing is available. During high season, buffet lunches are sometimes served right at the courts.

COURT FEES: None.

PRO STAFF: The inn's director of tennis is Ed Granger. A young, personable, enthusiastic teaching pro, he spent one of his college summers instructing at the John Newcombe Tennis Ranch in Texas before coming to Wickenburg in June of 1987 right out of Washington State University, where he was captain of the tennis team and broke all of the school's singles and doubles records. His staff consists of a USPTA-certified assistant pro and a local college player.

INSTRUCTIONAL PROGRAMS: Clinics at the inn run three hours a day and come in either three-day or five-day packages. They begin with the basic strokes and progress into more intensive drills and the basics of strategy and tactics. Videotaping may be done once or twice each session. Granger keeps the teaching ratio to 4:1.

SPECIAL FEATURES: Wickenburg offers a game-matching service pitting guests against other guests, hotel staff, or local members; unfortunately, the inn seems to take that responsibility lightly. Several guests complained to me that the pro-shop staff not only failed to find them games but, worse, hardly seemed to make any effort. If there were round-robins or other social tennis events where you could meet other players, the problem would be less severe, but none take place, except over the major winter holidays. Unless the staff decides to make this a priority, you'll either have to keep after them until they succeed or check the sign-up sheet and make the calls yourself. If all else fails, you can always rent the ball machine.

LODGING AND FOOD: The inn has two types of accommodations: standard hotel rooms and casitas. All ten of the basic rooms are in the lodge. They have the advantages of being in the same building as the dining room and near the swimming pool, but are otherwise small and undistinguished. The casitas are not only richer in character but vastly more comfortable. Built of adobe brick, all have wood-beam ceilings, fireplaces, a scattering of antiques, Spanish-tile accents, large walk-in closets, wet bars, and private patios. With couches that convert to beds, the casitas can easily sleep four. They come in two sizes, studios and deluxe suites, the latter with a separate living room, private sundeck, and, in a few cases, a bathtub-cum-whirlpool. Perched atop a knoll and landscaped with desert foliage, the casitas seem to comprise a tiny village laced with dirt pathways. In the same area is an outdoor hot tub, the arts and crafts center, an observatory for stargazing, and a free self-service laundry.

Dining at the inn is about what you'd expect; that is, homestyle rather than haute cuisine. All the meals are self-service, from the salad bar to the chafing dishes of fish, chicken, beef, and pasta. Count on ice cream, pies, and cakes for dessert. On Saturday nights, rather than eat in the dining room, you can go on a trail ride (for all levels of riders) to Eagle Flats for an outdoor steak barbecue. Box lunches are available any day at no extra charge.

Dinner, like everything else about the inn, is blue-jeans informal.

But there is something peculiar, it seems to me, about the dining arrangements. When you arrive a waitress seats your party at its own table. That's fine for couples and families who want to eat together but miserable for people who come alone and haven't yet made friends. It would be easy enough to have a large table for those who'd prefer company—not only singles, but couples too—and would add immensely to the social atmosphere.

OTHER RECREATIONAL AMENITIES: Tennis may get top billing, but the Wickenburg Inn is first and foremost a guest ranch. There are free horseback rides into the desert every day for all levels of equestrian skill, as well as weekend cookouts. Lessons and longer rides can also be booked at extra cost. In addition there is a small swimming pool, an outdoor hot tub, an arts and crafts center (for lessons in weaving and in making belts, pocketbooks, moccasins, and pottery), a stargazing observatory, and a nature center, whose naturalist takes guests into the desert for an introduction to its flora and fauna. Special children's programs are added over the Thanksgiving, Christmas, Spring Break, and Easter holidays.

▶ *Gestalt*

The sign for the Wickenburg Inn points to a dirt road running due east off U.S. 89 through a gap in a barbed-wire fence into the desert. The gravel track, called Bobwhite Lane, has the texture of a washboard, which makes exceeding the posted 20-mile-per-hour speed limit almost impossible. Birds flit among the branches of the palo verde and mesquite trees. A cottontail rabbit, startled by the car, scampers through the cactus and wildflowers looking for a place to hide. After a mile and a half of snaking through this landscape, the road swings around a hill and drops down into a hardpan parking lot just steps away from the main lodge.

All around is desert—not a lifeless Saharan landscape but one that contains more than 300 different plant species. The ranch itself covers 4,700 acres and butts up against other large spreads stretching away toward the jagged purple mountains rising in the distance. There is a grandeur in such desert settings and a seductive beauty that is all the more powerful for being totally unexpected.

But then, who would imagine that a dude ranch would have more than one tennis court for every five of its rooms, a general manager who plays senior tournaments, a strong teaching pro, and three-hour-a-day instruction clinics? Yet the first thing you notice when you arrive is not the stables but two beautifully laid-out tennis courts in a virtual desert botanical garden directly in front of the lodge. And when you check into your adobe casita, you soon find that the footpaths leading down into a dry wash end at a complex of nine additional courts and a pro shop.

You may also find a note on one of the tables about the Wickenburg's tennis clinics. The three-day and five-day sessions cost extra, so you would expect the inn to encourage guests to sign up; yet neither the people who check you in nor the staff in the pro shop broaches the subject.

"Obviously we want to have as many clinics as possible," says Ed Granger, the director of tennis. They do, he adds, run them whenever anyone signs up, but he admits that Wickenburg could do more to create that demand. "I think we should be having clinics going here every day, but that's something we need to do in terms of marketing and promotion to get those people here."

When the clinics do come off, Granger does a superb job of making them both fun and demanding. The sessions typically begin with a mini-tennis warm-up, and the next three hours are characterized by varied drills, thoughtful instruction, and a lot of joking and kidding. The three-day sessions cover all the major strokes; the five-day programs add singles and doubles strategy and a review session, going back over everything Granger has touched on while adding new drills. His philosophy throughout is to emphasize fun.

The campers are a diverse group from all over the country, most in their thirties, forties, or fifties. Couples and families far outnumber singles.

Because of the limited teaching staff, the clinics at Wickenburg are necessarily small—four to eight people on average. That means you get a lot of personal attention and have much more say in what you work on, provided the others in the group agree. The drawback is that you may not meet many other tennis players at your level. The era of large clinics at Wickenburg ended in the mid-1980s in part because the inn quit pushing them. Today clinics run only when there is demand for them, which may not be every day of the week—or, for that matter, every week.

That poses a logistical problem for anyone who wants to attend a clinic during his or her stay. Signing up for one at the same time you make your reservation guarantees you'll get instruction. But a full-scale clinic will come off only if others sign up too. If no one does, you'll be given the option of private or semiprivate lessons instead or of dropping your request entirely.

Fall is typically very slow at the inn, despite magnificent weather. Your best chances of catching a clinic in session are from mid-January to the end of April. During that period, clinics generally take place five or six days a week, with anywhere from four to six participants. Only rarely do as many as a dozen people enroll. Over the major winter holidays—Thanksgiving, Christmas, Spring Break, and Easter—you'll also find special children's programs, on and off court, to cater to the many families that come during those periods.

There is so much I love about the Wickenburg Inn—its desert setting, its homey casitas, and its guest-ranch informality—that I wish they'd do more to enhance the tennis atmosphere. The staff has to make a stronger commitment to game-matching and ought to schedule at least one social round-robin every week. The decision to offer clinics is meaningless unless they also make a concerted effort to get people to turn out every week.

Maybe I am unrealistic for wanting tennis to be as strong a reason for coming to the inn as horseback riding. But to come back to my casita after breakfast on a clear, comfortable March morning and see only a couple of courts in use makes me crazy. It isn't enough that no other dude ranch has as much to offer tennis players. I see those empty courts and talk to people who never found an opponent and all I can think of is the untapped potential.

TRAVEL INSTRUCTIONS: The nearest airport is in Phoenix, 70 miles to the south. Arrangements for transportation can be made through the inn, provided you give 48 hours' notice. Otherwise, rental cars are abundant. The drive takes about 90 minutes.

Vic Braden Tennis College at Coto de Caza

....

1 Coto de Caza Dr.
Coto de Caza, CA 92679

(714) 581-2990, (800) 42-COURT,
or in California (800) CALL-VIC

SEASON: Year-round.

RATES: *Expensive.* There are so few rooms for rent at the college that Braden markets lodging and instruction separately. He does occasion-

The Vic Braden Tennis College is a western institution, known for its charismatic founder and its scientific research into tennis's "physical laws."

The college has 17 hitting lanes, each capable of feeding up to 900 balls an hour.

ally put together packages over holiday periods, however, so check when you make your booking.

▶ *Profile*

COURTS: The college has 17 hard courts, 14 of them with lights, in several locations around the clubhouse, and a three-story observation tower. The three main teaching courts, each with its own ball machine, have been painted with targets, X's, and dotted lines to facilitate teaching angles. Braden supplements the courts with 17 hitting lanes, each with a ball machine capable of feeding 900 tennis balls an hour.

COURT FEES: None.

PRO STAFF: Vic Braden himself (see "The Designer Labels") heads a staff of as many as nine teaching pros, a few of whom have been with him for more than a decade. Asked what he looks for in a teaching pro, Braden says, "People who like people, who genuinely like them and want to help." Teaching them his teaching methods is easier, Braden insists, than finding pros who have "an internalized feeling about the value of the human being."

INSTRUCTIONAL PROGRAMS: Braden's programs run two, three, or five days. Each day's teaching session lasts a minimum of six hours,

133

with the option of more on-court work and unlimited access to the hitting lanes. Braden estimates that you'll hit at least a thousand balls a day—more if you have the stamina. That helps to compensate for the rather high student-pro ratio of 6:1, which is well beyond the optimal standard of 4:1. There is, however, the option of additional work in the evening for those who don't feel they've had enough. By any standard, Braden's is a rigorous program.

SPECIAL FEATURES: Braden's is the most high-tech tennis-teaching facility in the world. In addition to those 17 hitting lanes, he makes extensive use of videotape, showing and analyzing the tapes immediately after they're shot in courtside viewing rooms. He has a modern classroom equipped with four videotape viewing screens where he introduces (sometimes in person, often on tape) the various topics.

LODGING AND FOOD: The college itself owns ten rooms at Coto de Caza. They are situated just below the college, less than a hundred yards from the courts. Larger than typical hotel rooms, they have beamed cathedral ceilings, wet bars, small refrigerators, standard bathrooms with a second sink outside, an outdoor deck, and a tiny hearthless fireplace. These are currently being gutted and refurbished, and Braden is contemplating adding skylights (the rooms are dark now) and mini-kitchens with microwaves. The college is also negotiating to rent some of the privately owned one- and two-bedroom condominiums near the courts, but just how many, if any, they will have is at the moment uncertain. Check when you call to make a booking.

There is one restaurant at the college. Its lunch menu includes burgers, steak sandwiches, marinated chicken breast, steamed vegetable platter, and "create-your-own" pizzas, while dinner choices run to fish, chicken, steak, and pasta. The prices are moderate, the cuisine unmemorable.

OTHER RECREATIONAL AMENITIES: The college has an Olympic-size outdoor swimming pool and Jacuzzi, a basketball court that doubles as an aerobics room, and a small fitness center with workout equipment. The Coto de Caza development has an equestrian center and superb golf course, though at this writing it is uncertain whether Braden's students will have access to those facilities.

▶ Gestalt

I've had to hedge about certain aspects of the Vic Braden Tennis College because Vic and Melody Braden have just completed negotiations to buy the college. The good news is that the facility is now theirs and they're planning to revitalize the program. The bad news is that I have

134

no way of critically reviewing what has yet to be introduced, and Braden has a number of new ideas about how he wants to reorient his clinics. In what follows, I'll keep Braden's plans separate from his established methods.

With his beaver smile, incurable euphoria, and comic patter, Vic Braden became the best-known tennis teacher in the nation in the late 1970s and early '80s when he had a syndicated television series called *Vic Braden's Tennis For the Future*. He proved himself a master of making fun of tennis players' quirks and foibles. He singlehandedly popularized phrases like "Give your opponent a fuzz sandwich" and maxims like "Learn to hit the same old boring shot; you'll never get tired of winning." His jokes often touched psychological chords, but his instruction was rooted in extensive biomechanical research into the physical laws that govern tennis. What Braden discovered through that research was a kind of Platonic ideal: the best possible way to hit each of the various strokes.

As a result, no one who attends his college in the foothills of the Saddleback Mountains of Southern California can escape getting a vigorous dose of the Braden Doctrine. Of all the schools reviewed in this book, none takes as dogmatic an approach to tennis instruction as his college. It is crucial, therefore, to know what Braden advocates and, if you come, to be prepared to try it. Specifically, you should know that Braden is going to teach you a looping swing to generate topspin on both the forehand and backhand, and he's going to teach you his way even if you have decades of experience hitting it another.

Braden is very explicit. "I hear people say, 'It's just to take my natural talent and improve upon it.' But physical laws dictate what happens to a tennis ball—not natural talent—so you can't violate physical laws. . . . If somebody says, 'I don't want to change,' I understand that, but I don't understand why they're here."

He is dumbfounded by pros who advocate taking the strokes you already have and simply trying to make them better or more efficient. "I don't want to ever tell a person that I'll give them one-fourth efficiency levels," insists Braden, "because to make a ball do a certain thing you have to hit it in a precise manner, no ifs, ands, or buts about it."

So, the first rule in coming to Braden's is *Be prepared to change.*

The second is that you should expect to spend your time on strokes rather than playing. There is only a minimal introduction to tactics, strategy, and percentages because, says Braden, "Most of the people who come here really aren't good enough to do that."

Though the name "college" suggests an institute of higher tennis learning, Braden insists that beginners and intermediates stand to benefit most from his methods. "If I had my druthers," he says, "I'd take

135

7,000 people a year who'd never hit a ball in their life. We'd do more for them. We'd develop the electrical signature for muscle contractions better. But, of all things, people think our school is for advanced players. It's just the reverse. We tell people: 'If you're an A player, don't come here. It's not going to help.'"

A day in the life of a Braden camper is likely to begin in the classroom with a Braden lecture, usually on videotape though once or twice a week Braden appears in person. After the lecture, you go out with your group—all of whom play at about the same level—for on-court instruction and drills, interrupted periodically by workouts on the hitting lanes. You can also look forward to being videoed several times, and having the results analyzed immediately in one of the courtside viewing rooms. If after six hours of that you still want more, you can continue the instruction and workouts on into the evening. What you won't get, and this is crucial to note, is personal help on court from Braden himself.

That, however, is one of the things Braden contemplates changing, now that he owns the college. "My goal is to take fewer people and do a better job," he says. "I'd like to have more contact with the people who are learning."

He's also thinking about having people fill out a learning-style inventory when they arrive in order to find out how each of them learns most easily. That way the pros would know to demonstrate strokes to visual learners and to explain force vectors and biomechanics to the analytical learners. It's a method he's used at his ski college in Aspen and wants to use at his tennis college as well. He feels that he will then be able to start guaranteeing his program.

What's more, he wants to focus on combating the fears and anxieties that inhibit learning something new. "It's very uncomfortable making a change," notes Braden, "and, for most people, the pain they suffer in making a change is greater than the pain they suffer in losing to people. That's why the majority of people in this world go back to their old ways. Even though they take lessons, they still play the same way they played twenty years ago." He believes that his job as a coach is to find a means to do something about that.

Other plans, like starting an evening program with seminars on a variety of topics not necessarily related to tennis, will depend on how many people he can accommodate at the college itself. As it stands, with only ten rooms available, most of his students must stay elsewhere, and leave once the clinics end. In part because there are so few rooms for overnight guests, a substantial portion of his campers come from cities in the Los Angeles-San Diego corridor, so there are few people around to socialize with after class and nightlife is all but non-existent.

The turnout during the day, however, has been running 40 to 60 on weekends, and smaller during the week. The crowd is generally half men, half women, and often comprised of couples or small groups of friends. The atmosphere is very low key; t-shirts and running shorts far outnumber designer outfits. Sweat suits are fine in the restaurant and bar at night.

That post-clinic atmosphere is not likely to change much unless Braden gets access to more accommodations, but most people attend the college for its classes rather than its social life. Just how the daily program will evolve remains unclear, but Braden's goal is to turn it into a "learning enjoyment center." He sees tennis instruction as having a wider context. "We change lives—not just forehands."

TRAVEL INSTRUCTIONS: The nearest airport is Orange County, roughly 30 miles away. From Los Angeles International, figure on roughly 90 minutes by car.

John Gardiner's Tennis Ranch

Box 228
Carmel Valley, CA 93924
(408) 659-2207

SEASON: Late March to late November.

RATES: *Very Expensive.* The Carmel Valley ranch offers five-day (Sunday-to-Friday) and two-day weekend packages that include accommodations, all meals, nightly cocktail parties, tennis instruction, and unlimited court time.

▶ Profile

COURTS: The ranch has 14 hard courts, none with lights. Two have their own computerized ball machines. Ivy covers many of the fences, which are supported by cypress rather than metal posts, the better to blend in to the hillsides of oak, live oak, and eucalyptus.

COURT FEES: None.

PRO STAFF: Director of tennis Rick Manning and head pro Jeff Stewart have both been with the Gardiner organization (see "The Designer Labels") for more than a decade. They head a staff of six pros, most of whom are in their early twenties, all of whom are dedicated to providing personal and personable service.

INSTRUCTIONAL PROGRAMS: The basic clinic runs four hours a day. That is supplemented, however, by two optional half-hour special sessions and as much social tennis as you can handle beyond that. How much time you put in on the courts at Carmel Valley depends more than anything else on your own stamina.

A typical day begins with a fifteen-minute warmup at 9:15 followed by two-and-a-half hours of group instruction interrupted at midmorning by a break for juice and fresh fruit. At noon, there is a pro available for an optional half hour of additional instruction. After lunch, there is another optional session from 2:30 to 3:00, during which you can work on anything you want, usually in the company of no more than one other player. From 3:00 to 4:30 the regular clinic turns its attention to strategy and movement drills. At 4:30, the pros are around to supervise (and sometimes play in) matches, providing advice if you ask for it.

As the week progresses the emphasis shifts early on from straight stroke production to strategy, tactics, and playing situations, with by far the heaviest emphasis on doubles. Gardiner estimates that the typical camper hits 1,000 balls a day.

During the summer, the ranch also runs three-week-long live-in junior camps at Carmel Valley, using dormitories and a separate dining room at one end of the ranch. Children aged 9 to 16 of any ability level may enroll. They spend five-and-a-half to seven hours a day on the courts and are expected to behave like young ladies and gentlemen.

SPECIAL FEATURES: Videotaping is done once a week and extensive use is made of the two ball-machine courts.

LODGING AND FOOD: There are only fourteen deluxe rooms at the Carmel Valley ranch, all of them just steps away from the courts. Built of rough-cut redwood and covered with ivy or wisteria so that they nearly disappear, all have cable televisions, private patios, individual coffee makers, blow-dryers, and his-and-hers (white and pink) terry-cloth bathrobes. The smaller Center Court Cottages house one couple in a comfortable bedroom with its own fireplace, while the Pool Lanais have two bedrooms, each with private bath, on either side of a sitting room with a fireplace. There are several larger two-bedroom houses as well—Forest Hills, Wimbledon House, and Grand Slam—with spacious fireplace-equipped living rooms, kitchens, and private patios; most of the houses also have their own outdoor whirlpools.

The sybaritic comfort that begins in the cottages reaches its zenith in the dining room. Three times a day guests sit down to a feast. Breakfast is served in a glass-walled sun porch. Off to one side is a table laden with fresh fruit—raspberries, strawberries, melon—that serves as an appetizer to the main course of made-to-order eggs Benedict, pancakes, or omelets accompanied by ham, Canadian bacon, sausage, croissants, and sourdough bread. For lunch, which, weather permitting, takes place outside on the terrace alongside the pool, the kitchen prepares homemade soup, some kind of souffle (a Ranch trademark); numerous salads and vegetable dishes; a salmon or caviar mousse perhaps; hot dishes like lamb curry with condiments, chicken crepes with mushrooms, or just a barbecued hamburger on sourdough; and a choice of several desserts, like a fresh fruit cobbler or fruit souffle.

Ultimately, however, it is the dinners that account for the Ranch's culinary reputation. There are always two entrees, a fish and a meat; accompanied by a souffle of, say, mushroom, artichoke, or corn; salad; fresh vegetables; and a dessert souffle, often chocolate, lemon, or almond. Butterflied leg of lamb is a Gardiner specialty. Beef Wellington might share the sideboard with red snapper or petrale sole, served in a lemon and caper sauce. Well-chosen American wines accompany the dinners.

OTHER RECREATIONAL AMENITIES: With one court for each room, tennis is the real business of the ranch; however, there are also two heated swimming pools, an outdoor whirlpool, and men's and women's saunas. Arrangements can be made to play at any of the dozen golf courses on the Monterey Peninsula.

▶ *Gestalt*

A tiny sign on a fencepost along Carmel Valley Road is all there is to mark the entrance to John Gardiner's Tennis Ranch in Carmel Valley. It gives no clue whatsoever that nestled in the wooded ravine below lies not only the most sybaritic of all tennis camps in the U.S. but also the oldest. A one-time apricot orchard (hence the name "ranch") has been transformed into an enchanted garden. Sycamores and eucalyptus, magnolias and live oaks shade broad patches of lawn, while a profusion of flowers—roses, fuchsia, mock orange, violets, primroses, chrysanthemums, and carnations—splashes color into every nook and cranny.

This was the first American tennis camp. Gardiner had been teaching at the Lodge at Pebble Beach when he had the radical notion of opening a facility that catered to tennis players. He was convinced that people would take a vacation during which they spent the better part of their waking hours on the tennis court. Originally, his clinics were for women, but it wasn't long before they began asking to bring their husbands, too. Then Gardiner added a tennis camp for kids and the six-room operation that lost $19,000 in its first year of operation began to turn a profit. Gardiner's success eventually led others to follow his lead, but the cradle of the modern tennis vacation is that 25-acre ranch in Carmel Valley.

More than three decades later, the ranch that once went begging for clients has become the most exclusive tennis resort in the nation. It has a mere fourteen rooms, one for each court, which severely limits the number of guests it can accommodate. Gardiner himself lives there with his wife Monique during much of the March-to-November season, and he is in many ways as selective about whom he lets into his adult camps as you would be about the people you let stay in your home. Thus, he gives first preference to people he knows and to their friends. He also looks favorably on those who've attended one of his other camps—Scottsdale especially—and made the right impression on its staff. Complete unknowns who can't so much as drop the name of a member or former guest may find that the ranch is full, except perhaps during the first and last weeks of the season.

The intimacy of the Carmel Valley ranch and its sometime clientele of Hollywood celebrities, politicians, and corporate executives underlies Gardiner's quest for socially compatible guests. After all, they'll not only be thrown together on the courts but at meals as well. Socially the ranch feels like a posh summer house, where guests may not know each other but share an acquaintance with the host, a love of tennis, and often memories of having seen Bill Tilden, Don Budge, or Jack Kramer play. Except for two weeks a year when the ranch runs special "Ladies Only" sessions, couples predominate. The rather starchy social atmosphere, emphasis on doubles, and above all the hefty price tag (more than $640 a day for two people) tend to have far greater appeal for the over-50 crowd than the younger generations.

Traditional to the core, Gardiner dresses his pros in tennis whites and requests that guests stick to predominantly white attire on court as well. Not all do. It goes without saying, however, that everyone dresses for dinner, men in coats and ties, women in cocktail dresses. The nightly ritual begins at 7 P.M. with cocktails and hors d'oeuvres around the fireplace in the clubhouse. An hour later the crowd strolls into the dining room to take places at any of the family-sized tables for six or eight.

You serve yourself from a sideboard heaped with the evening's fare. The food is very good, drawing on the rich bounty of fruits and vegetables grown in that part of California and on the fresh seafood taken in Pacific waters. Lamb is a specialty, as are souffles. The menus, like Gardiner's insistence that his pros wear tennis whites, hark back to an earlier era, when the good life could be pursued without a thought to salt, fat, and cholesterol. If you're concerned you can let the kitchen know when you arrive. By having the fish without the rich sauces and skipping the souffles you can manage quite well. His determination to meet his guests' needs makes Gardiner obliging.

Attention to service suffuses the ranch. Early each morning, fresh orange juice and newspapers are discreetly delivered to each of the cottages (there are coffee makers and coffee in the rooms). The daily clinics never have more than four people to a pro. Instructors only make

141

major changes in strokes that are not working; otherwise, the focus is on helping you to become more efficient and consistent with what you already have.

Despite the group-lesson format, every effort is made to individualize the instruction. The pros get together between sessions to discuss among themselves how best to approach each player's game. To make sure you get enough personal attention the clinics include two optional half-hour sessions for anyone who wants more work. As the week progresses, there are more "Go Where You Like" sessions, which let you decide which part of your game to get extra help with. The small size of the camp allows the staff the luxury of adapting the program to each individual.

After the clinics, there are social events, like mixed doubles tournaments that have you changing partners often. The week concludes with a "two up, two back" tournament played before an audience of other campers. That's followed by a graduation ceremony with champagne, prizes, diplomas, and a copy of Gardiner's own tennis clinic workbook that reviews everything you've been taught. Many will be back again.

(See Canada's Inn & Tennis Club at Manitou for a comparison of Gardiner's Carmel Valley Ranch with another luxury tennis facility.)

TRAVEL INSTRUCTIONS: The Carmel Valley Ranch is just over eleven miles east of Route 1 on Carmel Valley Road. The closest gateway is the Monterey Peninsula Airport, fourteen miles away. The Ranch will arrange to pick you up and drop you off there. The other options are San Jose Airport (90 miles away) or San Francisco International (130 miles away), either of which necessitates renting a car.

Rancho Bernardo Inn

....

17550 Bernardo Oaks Dr.
San Diego, CA 92128
(619) 487-1611, (800) 854-1065, or in
California (800) 542-6096

SEASON: Year-round, with lower rates from June 1 to September 30.

RATES: *Expensive.* Rates include accommodations, breakfast and dinner, three hours of daily clinics, unlimited free court time, transfers from the airport, a cocktail party, and a gift pack.

▶ *Profile*

COURTS: The Inn has 12 hard courts, 4 with lights, in a pleasant setting at the base of a grassy slope. Between the pairs of courts there are shaded patios with wooden-slat benches forged from wrought iron. A small, ivy-covered clubhouse with a red-tile roof sits partway up the hill. Inside is the pro shop and videotape viewing room. Outside is a flagstone patio with tables and chairs and a series of stair-stepped terraces that provide an amphitheater-like seating for the two show courts.

COURT FEES: *Moderate,* but complimentary on packages.

PRO STAFF: The Inn has a touring pro in Ros Fairbank, one of the world's top 50 women and twice winner of the French Open doubles. Though her schedule is unpredictable, she is on site periodically throughout the year to help with special doubles and mixed doubles clinics.

Paul Navratil heads the permanent staff, which consists of five very experienced USPTA-certified pros. Born in Czechoslovakia, Navratil played tennis for the University of Southern California and taught in Venezuela before coming to the Inn in the mid-1970s.

INSTRUCTIONAL PROGRAMS: Other facilities have tennis complexes; the Inn has a Tennis College. In one sense the name is mislead-

143

ing: the ivy-covered walls notwithstanding, this is by no means a hoary academic institution with a lengthy syllabus of tennis courses. It does, however, have one of the more thoughtful programs in the country and extremely high-quality instruction.

The programs are moderately intense, with three to four hours of on-court instruction and drills. Two-, four-, and five-day packages are available.

There are two short courses. "Stroke and Strategy," which is geared to all levels of player, spends the first day analyzing and critiquing your basic strokes and the second putting them into practice, while working on the fundamental principles of strategy for singles and doubles. The sessions combine straight instruction with movement drills and extensive videotape analysis. "Drill and Play" combines play situations, in which the pro functions as a coach, with high-intensity drills; it is intended for experienced players.

Campers looking to stay longer can opt for a four-day "Mixer," which combines the two short courses, or a comprehensive "Five-Day Set," which begins with stroke development before progressing into strategy and supervised play. There are also future plans for clinics that will combine tennis instruction and drills with workouts at the new fitness center.

SPECIAL FEATURES: Top-quality color videotaping is included in all the basic clinics, and extensive and creative use of ball machines takes place in the "Drill and Play" sessions.

Finding an opponent during busy holiday periods is never a problem, since two staff members do little else but put together matches between guests. At other times, tennis-playing guests may be in short supply (or tied up in conferences), but the staff can then draw on the resort's local membership. Navratil has made this a priority, saying "We've gotten to the point where if we can't satisfy them we'll just put on an instructor to hit with them." Social events, like round-robins or challenge courts, are scheduled only during periods when there are numerous social guests (as opposed to conventioneers) in house: over major holiday weekends or during the Ros Fairbank clinics.

SEASONAL TENNIS EVENTS: Apart from the Ros Fairbank doubles clinics (dates vary, so check with the resort), the major annual event is a USTA-sanctioned senior tournament that draws approximately 250 entrants. There are men's and women's singles and doubles sections for every five-year age group from 35 to 70. Among the past participants are Pancho Gonzalez, Whitney Reed, and Dodo Cheney. The weekend event usually takes place in early December.

144

LODGING AND FOOD: Decorated in early California ranch style, the Inn's 287 spacious rooms come warmly appointed in antiques, pottery-and-brass lamps, dark-wood trim, and a color scheme borrowed from the desert. Each has a patio or balcony. All are in low structures, no taller than three stories, in various locations around the central ranch-house and its restaurants and pools.

Its two restaurants complement each other. The finer of the two is El Bizcocho, which consistently ranks among the best in San Diego County. The cuisine is nouvellish French—broiled swordfish with dijon mustard sauce, roast duckling with apples in a green peppercorn sauce, and pheasant with cabbage and juniper berries suggest the range. Every night, however, there is one special *cuisine minceur* meal that totals less than 900 calories even with dessert. These special meals change but run to fresh marinated scallops with mustard-and-dill sauce, sauteed lamb with mint and goat cheese, or a broiled veal chop with red bell pepper. Jackets are required.

Lighter dining is available all day at the Veranda, a casual indoor/outdoor restaurant that specializes in American fare and fresh seafood.

Tea is served every afternoon, along with sherry, port, finger sandwiches, and assorted French pastries.

OTHER RECREATIONAL AMENITIES: Besides tennis, the inn has an 18-hole golf course and three 9-hole executive courses. There are two beautifully situated outdoor swimming pools, one in a garden off the lobby, the other in a courtyard. Both have whirlpool spas. During August and over Christmas and Easter weeks there are free children's camps, for kids aged 4 to 17. The newest amenity is a 5,000-square-foot fitness center with exercise equipment, steam, saunas, whirlpools, massage rooms, a racquetball court (which can be used for aerobics), and a juice bar.

▶ *Gestalt*

Set in the San Pasqual Mountains 25 miles north of San Diego, the Rancho Bernardo Inn occupies land that was once part of a 17,000-acre ranch. Red-tile-roofed houses have replaced cattle as the dominant feature on the green, rolling hills, but the Inn itself hints at an earlier era in its California ranch architecture. The lobby manages to be both elegant and homey, with its wood-beam ceilings, terra cotta tile floors, and rough-hewn antique furnishings. Beyond it lie hacienda-like courtyards containing swimming pools and sculpture gardens.

This is by no means an ordinary hotel nor does it have an ordinary tennis center. Director of tennis Paul Navratil, who came to the Inn's

The Rancho Bernardo Inn looks like an old California ranch but features sumptuous cuisine and a well-run Tennis College.

Tennis College in 1976, has been there an eternity by resort standards, long enough to have had more than 30,000 students pass through his programs. A couple of his pros have themselves been on staff for more than a decade. All of that experience and an extraordinary sensitivity to the changing needs of today's tennis players makes this one of the most outstanding clinic programs anywhere.

Under those circumstances it is entirely disconcerting to arrive at the inn to find the courts almost empty and only a couple of members hanging out on the patio alongside the ivy-covered college. The club-like atmosphere generated whenever there are dozens of people anxious to play tennis is sadly missing at Rancho Bernardo, except over the major holidays, because convention groups make up a substantial percentage of the resort's clientele. The friendliness of the staff goes a long way toward making up for the missing camaraderie. And once the clinic starts any misgivings vanish.

Pinpointing exactly what makes this program so impressive is not easy. Partly it is the pros' abilities to spot the essential flaw in a stroke. Partly it is the way a ball machine is used to free the pro to teach rather than always having to feed. And partly it is unusual drills: like working on the various ways to return serve by using not only groundstrokes but also lobs, chips, and dinks. But mainly it is the pros' enthusiasm and sense of fun that makes the time go very quickly.

If there is one program that demonstrates Navratil's keen sense of what today's club player needs it is the "Drill and Play" clinic. Developed for experienced players, these clinics start out with advanced drills that simulate points or develop quick reactions and then move on to actual playing situations during which the pro functions as coach, helping you to scout opponents' weaknesses or adjust to their strengths and in general critiquing all the players' performances.

"The essential philosophy is to try to help people with their tennis at the same time they are having a good time," says Navratil. "I'm definitely not a Harry Hopman. We try to be somewhere in between the complete luxury and the complete militaristic type of camp." Neither is he a dogmatic teacher wedded to one particular style of play. Instead he takes a pragmatic approach of trying to improve the skills people already have.

The solidity of this program, the caliber of the pros teaching it, and the ability to make drilling fun ought to make the Rancho Bernardo Inn one of the most popular tennis destinations in the West. It deserves to be, particularly given the warmth and character of the hotel and the superb food in El Bizcocho. Yet the number of tennis vacationers in these clinics remains small, running five to six people in fall and winter, twice that in spring and summer. What suffers in that situation is not the instruction, which if anything is more personal, but the tennis atmosphere. Social events like round-robins take place only when there are enough social guests in house to warrant it.

The reason for the sparse turnout is that convention groups often fill so many of the rooms that the hotel has little reason to heavily promote its tennis programs. But the clinics there are so good that it would be a shame to let that keep you away. Instead, when you phone to make reservations ask how many others have signed up for the particular clinic you're thinking of attending (if reservations cannot give you an answer, get in touch with Navratil at the Tennis College: (619) 487-2413. Check on the dates for the Ros Fairbank clinics, since those typically get a larger-than-usual turnout. If you're planning to go for only a few days, book a weekend rather than a midweek reservation. But, one way or another, keep the Rancho Bernardo Inn high on your list of western tennis resorts.

TRAVEL INSTRUCTIONS: San Diego International Airport is 25 miles away. The hotel will arrange transportation if given 24 hours' notice.

Reed Anderson
Tennis School

. . . .

Winter campus

Gene Autry Hotel
4200 E. Palm Canyon Dr.
Palm Springs, CA 92264
(619) 328-1171 or (800) 288-1171

SEASON: October 1 to May 15, with highest rates from January 1 to May 15.

RATES: *Inexpensive* in low season, *Moderate* in high. The basic package includes accommodations, Continental breakfast, three hours of daily clinics, and unlimited court time. Separate clinic-only packages are also available.

▶ *Profile*

COURTS: The hotel has 6 hard courts, none of them lighted, laid out in pairs with umbrella tables in the middle and lawns all around. Palm trees and flowers border one side, while oleander hedges screen the courts from the wind and neighboring property. There is a swimming pool next to the courts and a tiny stucco hut that functions not so much as a pro shop as a staging area for guests booking court reservations. It has balls for sale and racquets to rent but little else. Overnight restringing can, however, be arranged.

COURT FEES: None.

PRO STAFF: Reed Anderson is not a household name, even in houses full of tennis players, but he has been competing since he was a child and teaching for almost two decades. Regionally ranked as a junior, he went on to play tennis for San Diego State and then spent six years on and off the satellite tour before losing his competitive drive and opting to teach full-time. He already had considerable clinic experience, hav-

148

ing worked for the Billie Jean King/Dennis Van der Meer Tennis-America program at Lake Tahoe in the mid-1970s. He started his school at the Gene Autry Hotel in 1982 and then added a summer version in Lake Tahoe in 1988 (see under "Nevada"). He has a staff of two assistants, both of whom honed their teaching skills under Anderson's tutelage.

INSTRUCTIONAL PROGRAMS: Clinics at the Tennis School run three hours a day and come packaged either in five-day midweek or two-day weekend versions. They include at least one session of videotape analysis and extensive use of ball machines. The student-pro ratio never exceeds 5:1.

"Tennis School I" takes players of any level, evaluates problems they may be having with their strokes, and strives to upgrade their entire game by focusing on basic footwork, shot selection, court positioning, and strategy. "Tennis School II" is designed for graduates of School I and players with NTRP ratings of 4.0 or higher. It spends less time on stroke production and instead concentrates on advanced drills, serve and volley, return of serve, strategy, tactics, and mental conditioning.

SPECIAL FEATURES: Tennis School I includes an in-depth videotape analysis of each student's game. Both schools make extensive use of ball machines, employing them to do most of the feeding and thus freeing the instructor to work directly with the campers on the same side of the court.

LODGING AND FOOD: In Palm Springs, where every new resort is more lavish—and often more expensive—than anything that had gone before, the Gene Autry Hotel stands as a monument to unpretentiousness. The 186-room hotel rises at the edge of Palm Springs, about a 10-minute drive from the shops on East Palm Canyon Drive. It is owned, as the name suggests, by the famous movie and television cowboy. Autry memorabilia decorates the lobby, the most stunning example being a saddle trimmed in silver and gold. The service throughout is low key and very friendly, in the best tradition of western hospitality.

No one would describe the rooms as posh but they are comfortable and newly redecorated in what might be called contemporary ranch style. Most are not in the main building but in several two-story structures strung out along the property. Virtually all have patios or balconies. In addition, there are a dozen one-bedroom bungalows, huge in size, with refrigerators, coffee makers, and secluded patios.

As for dining, the Sombrero Room is as unpretentious as the rooms, with its Continental and Mexican specials and a huge Sunday buffet.

OTHER RECREATIONAL AMENITIES: There are three outdoor swimming pools on the property and two outdoor whirlpools.

▶ *Gestalt*

Palm Springs has been a feature on the tennis landscape since the 1930s, when Charles Farrell and Ralph Bellamy built the Racquet Club of Palm Springs and invited their Hollywood friends—Clark Gable, Carole Lombard, Kirk Douglas, Humphrey Bogart, William Powell, and the Marx brothers, among others—to come play or just hang out at the bar. Today, greater Palm Springs is one of the tennis capitals of the world, with an estimated 500 courts in its parks, country clubs, and numerous resorts. That would seem to make it fertile ground for tennis programs as well, yet few have taken root. It's as though people still come mainly to play—and to stargaze—rather than to take clinics.

The exception is the Reed Anderson Tennis School. The school's motto is "We teach individuals, not systems." Anderson is not about to make major changes in anyone's strokes, unless an inherent flaw could cause injury, and he plans the program from day to day, or even hour to hour, modifying it to suit whatever that particular group of students needs or wants.

Anderson himself is on court teaching throughout every one of his clinics, and that personal attention is what makes these clinics special. He deliberately limits attendance, rarely taking more than 15 people so he can get to know everyone's background, expectations, and needs.

Underpinning his approach is a steadfast commitment to the fundamentals: "The older I get," says Anderson, "the more I realize you have to do certain things to hit the ball right."

The clinics, which run from 9 A.M. to noon, attract not only guests of the Gene Autry but visitors staying elsewhere in the desert and even occasional locals. Once the clinics are over, however, the hotel's tennis activity plummets. Don't expect to find dozens of people hanging around the courtside pool waiting for their chance to hit a few balls. Although Anderson's school may be the best instructional program in the desert, the Gene Autry Hotel itself hardly has enough tennis atmosphere to measure. The clinics attract enthusiastic players and, if you're lucky, some of them may be staying in the hotel and thus be available for matches in the afternoons, but don't count on it. The

150

hotel does not in general attract a tennis crowd nor does it have local tennis members. Anderson's staff will try to help set up matches, sometimes recruiting from nearby resorts, but they don't always succeed. If you're hoping to spend your vacation on the courts, stay at one of the desert resorts known for its tennis atmosphere (like the historic Racquet Club of Palm Springs, the low-key Shadow Mountain Resort, or the posh La Quinta Golf and Tennis Resort) and book Anderson's clinic separately.

His clinics attract the largest turnout during the period from Christmas to New Year's (when he's had as many as 25 students) and again in March (when the turnout runs from 12 to 15 each week). Otherwise, he typically has eight to 10 enrolled. Most of those are couples aged 35 to 55 (he gets very few families), about 60 percent of whom stay in the hotel. During the winter, some of the players are likely to come from the Northwest, western Canada, and the Chicago area, but the clinics are otherwise made up primarily of Californians.

Baseball enthusiasts may want to plan their vacation for March, when the California Angels come to the desert for spring training and have been staying at the Gene Autry Hotel. Besides, says Anderson, "March is the best month in the desert."

TRAVEL INSTRUCTIONS: The hotel is only a few miles from the Palm Springs airport. Courtesy transfers are available.

The Lodge of Four Seasons

Lake Road HH
Lake Ozark, MO 65049-0215
(314) 365-3000 or (800) THE-LAKE

SEASON: February to late October.

RATES: *Moderate.* Packages include accommodations in the Lodge, ten hours of instruction, unlimited additional court time, and access to the Racquet Club's facilities. The Four Seasons also accepts clinic-only bookings.

▶ *Profile*

COURTS: There are 23 courts altogether, a large complex by any standard but particularly impressive for the Midwest, which tends to be regarded as a tennis-resort wasteland. The lakefront Lodge itself has 6 courts, 4 of them outdoors, the remaining 2 in a multifunction gym. However, the clinics and the real tennis activity take place at the Racquet Club, atop a hill roughly a mile away. Besides 4 hard courts indoors, the club has a 4,000-seat amphitheater-like stadium court carved into a hillside and an additional dozen courts (9 hard, 3 clay) in a clearing beyond an outdoor swimming pool. Each of those courts is individually fenced and widely separated from its neighbor, a generous layout that leaves room for sidewalks, beds of flowers, and even covered patios in between.

COURT FEES: *Moderate,* but complimentary on packages.

PRO STAFF: The Racquet Club is the midwestern headquarters for the Dennis Van der Meer's tennis operation (see "The Designer Labels"). Van der Meer supplies the teaching staff and makes personal appearances a few times each year to give clinics. The current director of tennis is Mike Lowdermilk, who has spent more than a decade teaching and coaching tennis, both in the U.S. and in India. He heads a staff of from two to four full-time pros, all of them certified by Van der Meer's United States Professional Tennis Registry.

152

INSTRUCTIONAL PROGRAMS: From late winter into late autumn, the Racquet Club runs ten-hour clinics over three days, beginning either Monday or Friday. Adopting a station-to-station format and a 6:1 student-pro ratio, these sessions cover all the basics from stroke production to tactics and strategy and elementary mental toughness. Videotape analysis is also done.

A few times a year, Dennis Van der Meer himself shows up to personally conduct special twelve-hour adults clinics (usually once in May, once in August), an eighteen-hour Mini TennisUniversity for would-be tennis teachers (also in May), and a twelve-hour junior clinic (usually in February).

SPECIAL FEATURES: The Racquet Club staff sets up matches, either with other resort guests or with local tennis members; rents ball machines; and arranges match charting, which shows where you're winning points, where losing. Videotaping is a regular part of the clinics.

SEASONAL TENNIS EVENTS: During the summer months, the Racquet Club stages numerous competitive events including member-guest tournaments (over the Fourth of July and Labor Day weekends) and USTA-sanctioned adult and junior tournaments.

LODGING AND FOOD: The resort has two types of accommodations: hotel rooms and condominiums. The hotel is the rambling 300-room Lodge of Four Seasons along the shore of the lake. It was thoroughly refurbished in European style for its 25th anniversary celebrations in 1989. Rooms in the newer Atrium wing have two double beds, a large sitting area, spiffy appointments, and oblique views of the lake, while those in the older section have antique-like furniture, a bit more character, and, in some cases, balconies facing the lake.

The condominiums are roughly a mile away on a hilltop slightly back from the lake but just steps away from the ultra-luxurious Racquet Club and the main complex of tennis courts. Built in Mediterranean style, the two- and three-bedroom condos have two baths, fully equipped kitchens, fireplaces, screened-in porches, and washer/dryers. Some are huge. Note, however, that the packages combining tennis clinics with condominium accommodations are based on four people to a condo, so you'll need to bring along a few friends.

Putting aside the differences in accommodations, the condominiums have the advantage of being right next to the courts and the extraordinary amenities of the Racquet Club. The Lodge, on the other hand, has a desirable lakefront location and it is much the livelier place to be, with more activities, more nightlife, and all but two of the resort's eight food outlets. Those range from a sidewalk pizza place to the Continental and American cuisine of the Toledo Room, a restaurant Mobil awards four stars. The two restaurants not at the Lodge are a steakhouse at the golf course and the culinarily eclectic Wingfield's (pastas, salads, "Grand Slam" burgers) overlooking the indoor courts at the Racquet Club. The latter is open only for lunch and dinner, but not every day.

OTHER RECREATIONAL AMENITIES: When it comes to sports, the Four Seasons is one of the foremost resorts in the Midwest. It has a private beach on the lake, a marina, a sailing school, waterskiing, boat rentals, and guide services. Golfers can look forward to an 18-hole Robert Trent Jones course, a 9-hole executive course, and a driving range. There are riding stables, trap and skeet shooting, basketball and volleyball courts, bicycle rentals, a bowling alley, a movie theater, and a video arcade. And that's just down at the Lodge. The Racquet Club is an impressive 110,000-square-foot palace with Italian marble floors and designer interiors. It contains not only four indoor tennis courts but a state-of-the-art fitness center with a spa (for everything from massages and facials to hair care and skin treatments), aerobics rooms, a health club (with Nautilus and David equipment, treadmills, computerized exercycles, and rowing machines), a 25-meter indoor lap pool, squash and racquetball courts, indoor golf practice cages, pool tables, and a pro shop. Its staff can also do complete cardiovascular, fitness, and nutrition evaluations.

▶ Gestalt

The construction of Bagnell Dam in the 1930s backed up the Osage River to create 60,000-acre Lake Ozark in west-central Missouri. Almost immediately it became a favorite summer retreat, for people in St. Louis and Kansas City in particular. Long, narrow, and fringed with coves, the huge lake has more than 1,300 miles of shoreline bordered by low hills forested in oaks and maples and dotted with second homes.

The town of Lake Ozark, near the dam, has a much-too-familiar strip of t-shirt shops, all-you-can-eat restaurants, mom-and-pop motels, fakey Old West architecture, riverboat cruise docks, carnival rides, ice-cream shops, miniature golf courses, skeeball arcades, and go-kart tracks. It's a kind of black hole of carnivalism and gimcrackery, a period piece of tourist-trap architecture.

The Four Seasons may have an address in Lake Ozark but it is miles distant geographically and esthetically. The resort occupies 200 acres of the wooded Horseshoe Bend peninsula. The 300-room lakefront Lodge was originally built in 1954 and refurbished in European style for its 25th anniversary. The elegant Racquet Club and its 160 condominiums, which date from the mid-1980s, occupy the top of a knoll with views of the lake in two directions.

The Racquet Club seems bent on becoming the tennis capital of the Midwest. The staff works with area juniors to build grass-roots interest in the sport, and the resort tries to stage some kind of amateur tournament or spectator tennis event roughly every other weekend throughout the summer. All of that helps contribute to the elusive "tennis atmosphere" that ultimately distinguishes a great tennis resort from a merely good one.

The clinics add one more stone to that tennis foundation. The basic program runs for ten hours over three days and manages to cover an extraordinary amount of ground. Serves, groundstrokes, volleys, and overheads get special attention. Videotaping is done on each of the first two days and shown and analyzed almost immediately. Periodically, the clinic introduces what they call "station training." In that format, each pro teaches something different—lobs on one court, serve and volley on another, doubles strategy and communication on a third. Campers change courts every fifteen minutes or so and thus get introduced to a variety of strokes and playing situations. If the group is strong enough to merit it, those stations might include return of serve, topspin lobs, or half volleys.

In general, the stronger the campers, the more sophisticated and demanding the drills. Van der Meer's progressive teaching methods apply throughout, so every pro teaches the same way. Lowdermilk seeks to maintain a light tone. Besides improving strokes, he likes to introduce practical tips for warming up (he has a ten-minute routine) or using practice time to best advantage. He also passes out fliers that outline basic doubles tactics. He even reviews the videotapes after campers leave and a few weeks later sends some follow-up suggestions for what they should be working on.

The turnout at the clinics has been increasing annually. During the spring and fall, a dozen people typically show up for the midweek sessions, eighteen on weekends; summer sessions get twelve to eighteen midweek and as many as twenty-four on weekends (the most they can handle with four pros).

Several times a year Van der Meer himself comes to the Racquet Club to personally conduct special twelve-hour clinics (see the review of the Van der Meer Tennis Center in South Carolina for a summary of the Van der Meer method). Enrollment in his clinics often reaches 40.

The crowd at the Racquet Club comes mainly from St. Louis and

Kansas City, the two major cities within driving distance, with occasional campers from Chicago, Detroit, and the greater Midwest. It's a mix of couples, groups of friends, and fragments of tennis teams, most of them in the 35-to-45 age range.

There is a tendency for the people who come together to stay together. The staff does stage a beer-and-soft-drinks orientation session on the first evening, but that's about the extent of the organized social activities. The three-day/two-night sessions simply don't afford much time to pursue new acquaintances. Nevertheless, the combination of solid instruction, the magnificent Racquet Club, and the recreation on the lake makes the Four Seasons easily the finest tennis destination in the entire Midwest.

TRAVEL INSTRUCTIONS: The airports in Columbia and Springfield are each roughly 75 miles from the resort, but the drive from Columbia is faster. Flying in to either Kansas City or St. Louis leaves you with about a 150-mile drive.

Reed Anderson Tennis School

· ·

Summer Campus

Lakeside Tennis Club
977 Tahoe Blvd.
P.O. Box 5576
Incline Village, NV 89450
(702) 831-5258 or (800) 222-2612

SEASON: Mid-May to mid-September, but busiest July and August.

RATES: *Moderate.* The basic package includes accommodations, three hours of daily clinics, and unlimited court time. Anderson also markets the school separately, without accommodations.

▶ *Profile*

COURTS: The club has 9 hard courts, none lighted, clustered around a large pro shop, bar, and cafe. Ponderosa pines are the backdrop for the complex, whose layout is more than usually spacious. The cafe has outdoor tables, shaded by umbrellas, with courtside views of the action. When needed, the club has access to 3 additional courts next door.

COURT FEES: None.

PRO STAFF: Reed Anderson brings the staff from the school's winter campus in Palm Springs to Lakeside in the summer (see the review of the Reed Anderson Tennis School in California for background on Anderson and his teaching staff). He also brings Owen Gillen, who holds a ranking in California in the 45s, to run the shop and when necessary help with the instruction.

INSTRUCTIONAL PROGRAMS: This is essentially the same program Anderson runs at his school's winter campus in Palm Springs. One major difference is the addition of a two-hour junior program each afternoon for kids who've come with their parents.

157

SPECIAL FEATURES: The club is situated at 6,000 feet above sea level, and playing tennis at that altitude takes some getting used to. You'll notice the lack of oxygen and the tendency of even high-altitude balls to rocket through the thin air. Sand has been mixed into the Lay-kold top dressing to give the courts more texture and thus slow the balls down, but that does nothing to counter every lowlander's tendency to hit long, at least at first.

Nor does it diminish the danger of sunburn, which is far more extreme in this thin air than at sea level. Take or buy at least a number-15 waterproof sunblock and plan to use it. One way or another you're likely to spend most of the day outdoors, on or off the courts.

Clinics run in the morning, but Anderson schedules optional events on several of the afternoons, including a weekly potluck doubles round-robin, ladies' and men's days, and a monthly social round-robin intended mainly for the members but open to guests. There is also a hostess to arrange games, often drawing on the small but enthusiastic local membership. Videotaping is done as part of the clinic, and there are ball machines for use afterwards.

LODGING AND FOOD: For a club with only 36 units to rent, Lakeside has an unusual variety of accommodations. The options range from studios to three-bedroom cottages. All of them have kitchens, balconies, and televisions; most have fireplaces. There's also a coin-operated laundry on the premises.

The Courtside Cafe is open for breakfast, lunch, and snacks, but not dinner. Its menu seems to change from year to year. At present it serves Chinese food. More to the point, it has a bar, which makes it a gathering place before and after matches.

OTHER RECREATIONAL AMENITIES: The club itself has only a very small pool and Jacuzzi, but guests get access to two private beaches along the shores of Lake Tahoe. There is a massage therapist, who, when not kneading sore muscles, conducts nature walks and seminars on New Age philosophy.

▶ *Gestalt*

The club was built in 1972 by Billie Jean King and Dennis Van der Meer as part of their TennisAmerica string of camps. That scheme foundered on the rocky economy of the 1970s. Thereafter it had five owners in five years, and then a series of managers, but seems finally to have stabilized.

In the early 1980s it was often the site of celebrity tournaments, with film stars like Clint Eastwood, Lloyd Bridges, Gene Hackman, and Cathy Lee Crosby (a former teaching pro) battling it out on court.

Anderson taught here during those days, left to found his own school, and then came back in the summer of 1988, bringing his school and staff with him.

Lake Tahoe can be magnificent in the summer—deep blue in places, emerald green in others. The air smells of pine. There are good biking routes near the club and stables where you can book trail rides.

Anderson's clinics, which run in the mornings, leave plenty of time free for the other activities that lure visitors to Lake Tahoe in the summer. As in Palm Springs, Anderson follows a general plan, subject to constant and capricious revision depending on the needs of a particular group of campers. The week-long program begins with instruction on all the major strokes, moves on to drills, and ends with playing situations. Videotaping is done twice, once early in the week, once at the end. Anderson makes extensive use of ball machines—he has four new ones with remote controls—and often joins in the drills himself, not only telling you what he wants you to do but showing you.

His *ad hoc* methods give the impression that he's making up the program as he goes along, and to some degree that's true. Anderson's motto is "We teach individuals, not systems." Thus no two clinics are alike because no two groups of campers are alike. He and his pros are very receptive to suggestions. By the same token, he does not advocate one particular way of hitting the ball. He works to improve what you already can do.

The sessions run roughly three hours a day, enough to provide a workout, but they stop well short of being grueling. Diehards can always play more in the afternoon.

During July and August, the clinics often fill to their fifteen-student maximum. The crowd, which comes mainly from the San Francisco Bay Area, is typically a mixed group of professionals ages 35 to 55, some singles, some couples, some families.

Lakeside's layout, with its restaurant and bar overlooking the courts, gives it the feel and social atmosphere of a small tennis club. Everyone gathers in one place before and after the clinics or matches.

After dark, anyone intending to eat must either whip up something in his or her room or leave, since the restaurant at the club does not serve dinner (though that may change). Ask the staff or local members for suggestions about where to eat in the area. Nightlife, on the other hand, is as close as the casinos and shows at Hyatt Lake Tahoe, which is within walking distance.

TRAVEL INSTRUCTIONS: The nearest airport is in Reno, 35 miles away.

John Newcombe's Tennis Ranch

. . . .

P.O. Box 310469
New Braunfels, TX 78131-0469

(512) 625-9105, (800) 444-6204 or in Texas
(800) 292-7080

SEASON: Year-round, but busiest in the spring and fall.

RATES: *Inexpensive–Moderate*. Rates include accommodations, all meals, six hours of daily clinics, unlimited court time and ball machine use, and entertainment.

John Newcombe's Tennis Ranch in the Texas hill country combines solid instruction on court with a devotion to having fun off court.

▶ *Profile*

COURTS: The Ranch has 28 hard courts, 8 with lights and 4 under cover in an open-sided building. All are laid out in banks of four or eight, bordered by a scruffy lawn and a few live oak and cedar trees.

COURT FEES: None.

PRO STAFF: The director of tennis for the adult program is Jeremy Fieldsend—a.k.a. "Jungle Jeremy"—who coached and played college tennis in his native Zimbabwe, where he also earned a master's degree in exercise physiology. He heads a staff of seven to ten pros in the adult program. Most are college or state-ranked players chosen for their enjoyment of people and then trained in the Ranch's teaching methods.

INSTRUCTIONAL PROGRAMS: Like most dedicated teaching facilities, the Ranch runs everything from weekend clinics for adults to live-in programs for promising juniors. All are basically six-hour-a-day sessions with student-pro ratios of no more than 5:1. The Ranch uses a station-to-station format, which has campers moving on to a different set of drills and a different pro every 45 minutes or so during the clinic.

There are three levels of adult programming. The most basic is the "Adult" clinic, for players who want to work on stroke production and singles and doubles strategy. It comes in both two-day weekend and five-day midweek packages, available almost every week of the year. The "Advanced" clinic, for upper-intermediate and advanced players, consists of intensity drills, combination ball drills, court movement, and singles and doubles play. Finally there is a "Championship" program for tournament-caliber players—that is, those with NTRP ratings of 5.0 or above—who already have all the strokes but want to hone their competitive skills. These last two advanced sessions only take place during selected weeks of the year, mainly during spring and fall.

Periodically the Ranch hosts special celebrity clinics personally conducted by the likes of John Newcombe, Fred Stolle, and Dick Stockton. These essentially follow the same format as the regular adult clinics, except that the celebrity pro introduces the day's program and roves from court to court making suggestions. The staff tries to ensure that everyone in the clinic gets to hit at least once with the star.

Juniors also have a choice of programs. Over holiday weekends there are family packages that provide separate adult and junior instruction. From March through the end of August the Ranch runs one-and two-week junior camps, putting the kids up in dorms and providing plenty of supervision. Finally, there is a "Competitive Edge" program, which is open only to English-speaking high school juniors and seniors with state or national rankings. Students live at the Ranch, attend the local high school, work on tennis and fitness, and play tournaments, though the emphasis is not only on tennis but also on education and social development.

SPECIAL FEATURES: The day begins at the Ranch with a half-hour "Tips on Tennis," which are light-hearted lectures or videotape presentations on such topics as mental toughness or the frustrations of learning new strokes. Color videotaping is done often enough to cover all the major strokes, usually early in the program. Packages also include unlimited free use of the ball machines after class.

SEASONAL TENNIS EVENTS: The biggest event on their tennis calendar is the Clarence Mabry Senior Open in January. A men's and women's event, it has competition in singles, doubles, and mixed doubles in all the senior levels from 35s to 75s. In the fall, the Ranch has been hosting a special (and premium-priced) "Legends Week" for men who are rated 3.5 or higher. Newcombe, Owen Davidson, and other tennis greats give clinics, coach, eat, and socialize for the entire five days. A similar program for women is planned for the spring.

LODGING AND FOOD: Accommodations at the Ranch range from small motel-like rooms to spacious one- and two-bedroom condominiums with complete kitchens, fireplaces, balconies or patios, and washer/dryers. Most are in one- or two-story buildings just steps away from the courts and the communal dining rooms in the 1960s-era lodge.

The kitchen at Newcombe's continues the ranch metaphor by serving up western fare such as prime rib, barbecue, chicken, shrimp, trout, and a nightly pasta dish. There is a good salad bar with lots of fresh fruits and vegetables.

OTHER RECREATIONAL AMENITIES: There is a small swimming pool and heated outdoor whirlpool.

▶ Gestalt

The road to the Newcombe ranch rises and falls as it follows the rolling contours of the Texas hill country. The main features of the landscape are trees, cedars and live oaks mostly, and billboards that advertise *biergartens* and sausage houses. That may seem like an odd combination, but New Braunfels was founded by a German prince and, within months, 5,000 of his countrymen had joined him. More than a century later, the legacy of its German origins survives in smokehouses, beer gardens, and a fall Wurstfest.

The Newcombe tennis facility, on the other hand, was originally a dude ranch. John Newcombe, the U.S. Open and Wimbledon Champion and Australian Davis Cupper, and Clarence Mabry, the eminent tennis coach of Trinity University, bought it in 1968, "upholstered" it, and turned it into a year-round tennis camp (see "The Designer Labels").

The programs naturally evolved from the techniques Mabry was using at Trinity. He had led the university to national intercollegiate championships and turned out several top-ten players, among them Dick Stockton, Brian Gottfried, and Chuck McKinley. From the beginning he thus had a clear idea of the approach he wanted to take. "We have always been sticklers for two things," he says, "establishing and teaching the basics and having fun while we do it."

The emphasis on fun does not mean that the Ranch's programs are lightweight. This is one of the nation's rock-solid teaching facilities. Mabry's influence and Fieldsend's training program for the pros mean that there really is a tested methodology underpinning everything that happens on court. The pros know what to look for, or, as one camper puts it: "You don't get one pro telling you one thing and another telling you something else." It helps too that Fieldsend gets personally involved, roving from court to court helping individual campers or taking over the drills.

The program is intensive but, unlike Harry Hopman's International in Florida, for example, the emphasis is on teaching strokes rather than on conditioning. The sessions thus begin slowly, with careful attention to proper hitting techniques. Only as students progress do the drills become more demanding and aerobic, culminating in that most dreaded of all Ranch routines: the Bucket of Balls Drill.

The BOBD is one of the family of so-called "drop-dead drills" designed to develop quickness and endurance. Instead of hitting only a few balls at a stretch, each camper hits a series of dozens and dozens, racing to one side for a forehand, then to the other for a backhand, up to the net to cover a drop shot, and then back to the baseline to chase down a lob. Since there is no set pattern, reacting quickly to the ball coming off the pro's racquet becomes paramount. Not until the pro's bucket (or basket) of balls is empty does the camper get to quit. Groups at the Ranch have been known to make up t-shirts that read "NO BUCKET OF BALLS DRILL, MATE."

The joking that goes on between pros and campers on court sometimes continues right through dinner and into the night at the bar. The socializing off court is as much a part of the Ranch atmosphere as the clinics on. John Newcombe himself may be there only rarely, and the teaching staff is as likely to come from Texas, Oklahoma, or Michigan as from Down Under, but the camaraderie at the Ranch is nonetheless Australian. Campers and pros eat in the same dining room.

Many evenings have some kind of entertainment, ranging from an exhibition to song-and-dance routines starring the pros. Each session closes with a banquet during which Fieldsend shows an edited candid-camera videotape of the week's events. On Saturday nights the Ranch brings in its staff guitarist, who backs up anyone who wants to perform and sings popular country-and-western songs, plus a few of his own, such as "Oh no, here comes an overhead." On any night formal attire is a pair of jeans.

The regular adult clinics run year-round but attendance trails off during July and August, when daytime temperatures can reach the 90s. Otherwise a typical weekend session in fall or spring gets 60 to 80 participants, often pushing the student-pro ratio up to 5:1; midweek sessions tend to be somewhat smaller—fifteen to 30 on average— which means the student-pro ratio rarely exceeds 4:1 and you get more personal attention. During the summer, by contrast, there are rarely more than 20 adults in the midweek camp, while in winter midweek attendance plummets to as few as five or six.

Texans account for the largest percentage of campers, though in spring they're likely to be joined by snowbirds out of Canada and the Great Lakes. Weekends have more couples than the midweek sessions, though there is always a mixture. The longer midweek sessions, by their very nature, attract more serious players and sometimes entire tennis teams or groups of players from particular clubs.

All in all, the Ranch's staff works harder than anyone's to make sure you have fun on and off the court and still come away with the tools to improve your game. At the end of a session Fieldsend gives a farewell speech, saying, "We've given you a bunch of things to work on because that's our job. But now you've got to decide what you want to use and still have a good time playing." They never forget that tennis is a game.

TRAVEL INSTRUCTIONS: The nearest airport is San Antonio International, 30 miles south. Given 48 hours' notice, the ranch will arrange economical limousine service between the San Antonio airport and the Newcombe property.

BAHAMAS, CARIBBEAN, AND MEXICO

▶ Club Med–Paradise Island, Bahamas
▶ Club Med–Sonora Bay, Mexico
▶ Palmas del Mar/All American Sports Clinics, Puerto Rico

Club Med–Paradise Island

P.O. Box N 7137
Paradise Island, Bahamas

(809) 326-2640

c/o

Club Med Sales Inc.
7975 N. Hayden Rd.
Scottsdale, AZ 85258

(212) 750-1687 or (800) CLUB MED

SEASON: Year-round.

RATES: *Inexpensive* in summer, *Moderate* in winter, *Expensive* at Christmas. Rates include accommodations, all meals, tennis clinics, free court time, all the rest of the club's sporting activities, and nightly entertainment. No children under 12 are permitted.

▶ Profile

COURTS: This club has 20 clay courts, 8 of them with lights. Built on the harbor side of the island facing Nassau, the courts fan out from a clump of tropical trees and flowers containing a tiny, wood-frame tennis center, which functions as a staging area for the intensive clinics. The lighting is old-fashioned and dim but free and available at the push of a button at any hour of the night.

COURT FEES: None.

PRO STAFF: Like all Club Meds, the tennis-teaching staff at Paradise Island changes every six months. A chief of tennis—or *chef de tennis*—oversees the program, assisted by eight to ten pros (see "The Designer Labels" for a more thorough discussion of Club Med teaching in general).

As the flagship for Club Med's version of an intensive tennis clinic, the Paradise Island club is virtually a synonym for tennis.

INSTRUCTIONAL PROGRAMS: Along with Sonora Bay in Mexico (discussed later in this book), Paradise Island is one of the flagships of what Club Med calls its intensive tennis program. "Intensive" to habitues of tennis camps conjures up images of five hours a day of rigorous drills, but *chez* Club Med it is a relative term: it means longer sessions and more emphasis on social competition than you'd get at an ordinary Club. The basic format of their intensive program calls for two-and-a-half hours a day of instruction and drills supplemented almost every afternoon by tournaments, social round-robins, exhibitions, challenge-the-pro events, and the like. One videotaping session is included in each week's program.

SPECIAL FEATURES: Besides videotape equipment, Paradise Island has a ball machine, and encourages its use by setting it up adjacent to the Tennis Center on the one court in the entire complex that is individually fenced. That same court also has a backboard.

For those who'd rather watch tennis than hit, the Club runs videos of recent matches throughout the day at the tennis center.

SEASONAL TENNIS EVENTS: From time to time Club Med–Paradise Island hosts such special events as clinics by big-name pros, tennis festivals, and mixed doubles tournaments, occasionally giving away major prizes like trips for two to Club Meds in Tahiti or Bali. The dates vary, so before you book ask whether anything is scheduled for around the time you want to travel.

PRO SHOP: Nonexistent. The tennis center does have racquets available for use free of charge, but nothing else—not even balls. Those can be purchased at the Bazaar (a boutique near the theater) at two to three times the price you'd pay in the U.S. Overnight restringing, though not done at the Club, can be arranged.

LODGING AND FOOD: The Club has 310 rooms in eleven buildings. All of them are situated on a rise above the main beach to either side of Grayleath, a lovely old estate mansion with a swimming pool. Inside is a restaurant and bar, a fitness center, a game room, an arts and crafts center, and a laundry room with free washers and dryers.

Following a multi-million-dollar refurbishing in 1988, which included eliminating the Baby and Mini clubs, the Paradise Island facility looks superb. The accommodations are vastly improved. Somewhat smaller than the average hotel room, each has two twin beds, a private bath with a large tiled shower, air conditioning, two safes, and locks on the doors; none has a phone or television. At Club Med, a room is a way station that provides a place to sleep and change clothes without encouraging you to linger.

Meals, on the other hand, do. Not only is the food abundant and extremely good, but the tables for eight in the main Porcupine Restaurant encourage meeting new people every time you sit down to eat. Breakfast and lunch are hot and cold buffets long on wonderful breads, pastries, fresh fruits, salads, and cheeses. Dinner begins with a similar self-service buffet of soup, salads, and breads, but the evening's one entree—steak on some nights, chicken or fish on others—is brought

169

to the table. Complimentary (but ordinary) red and white wines flow freely. Both smoking and nonsmoking sections are available.

The other two places to dine, Grayleath and Harbourside, are traditional restaurants with salad bars, table service, and a la carte menus (seafood at Grayleath, Italian at Harbourside). You pay nothing extra to eat there but must make reservations the day before. Tables are for however many there are in your party, from two to 20.

OTHER RECREATIONAL AMENITIES: The 21-acre village fronts a long, lovely public beach on the northern side of the island and a smaller private beach on the southern side facing Nassau Harbor. Together their watersports centers offer sailing, windsurfing, and kayaking. Snorkeling excursions leave daily for an offshore reef. Other facilities include a large freshwater swimming pool, fitness center, aerobics and water aerobics classes, pitch-and-putt greens and golf practice nets, archery, volleyball, water volleyball, and a basketball court. Deep-sea fishing excursions and golf-course privileges are offered at extra cost.

▷ *To Note:* Club Med does not provide tennis balls for its tournaments, so you'll need several cans, both for those events and for any playing you do on your own. Given the prices in the Bahamas, you'd be wise to bring them from home. You may also want to bring a water jug, since the only water cooler at the courts is the one at the tennis center, which is a long walk from the farthest courts.

▶ Gestalt

Paradise Island has the largest clay-court complex in Club Med's American Zone, and it was the first to begin offering the two-and-a-half-hour "intensive" clinics. That emphasis on its on-court programs has virtually made it a synonym for tennis. It consistently attracts the largest number of players of any resort in the Americas. Some weeks there are upwards of 200 racquet-wielding guests in house, which ensures an abundance of opponents and good turnouts for the almost daily tournaments and social tennis events.

At the same time, it can also mean a massive turnout for the clinics. The optimal student-pro ratio of 4:1 is not only unthinkable at a Club Med but probably regarded as suspiciously antisocial. During the busy December-to-April season, ratios of 15:1 and higher occur, at least early in the week, before attrition brought on by sunburn, late nights at the disco, romances, and a desire to take full advantage of the Club's other activities takes effect. Advanced players and strong intermediates generally fare better than weaker players, because their classes are typically somewhat smaller and they are skilled enough to benefit from drilling among themselves. Beginners and low intermediates, who need basic instruction and personal attention, can never get as much out of a Club Med session as they would from one of the better resort programs. On the other hand, the people who choose Club Med over a traditional resort tennis program probably do not regard a dramatically improved backhand as the touchstone of a successful vacation.

Though there are some seasonal variations that I'll explain later, the format is basically one of clinics in the mornings and tournaments and other on-court activities in the late afternoon. The mob that shows up for instruction is divided into groups of roughly equal ability and sent out to the courts with a pro. Though the approach and teaching styles differ from pro to pro, in the course of a week you'll work on all the basic strokes and be introduced to singles and doubles strategy. The advanced groups often shift quickly from stroke production to point-simulation drills and match-play situations.

If the large classes rule out much personal attention, they nonetheless guarantee that you'll meet lots of people who play at roughly your level. It thus becomes easy to set up your own matches. It's worth attending the clinics for a day or two, if only as a way of becoming acquainted with other players.

The tournaments and social tennis events planned for late afternoons are open to all guests, whether they've been taking the clinics or not. Again, the current chief of tennis decides what events to run, but there are always singles and doubles tournaments and some kind of social tennis mixer.

The intensive clinics run year-round but are likely to draw larger crowds in winter than in summer. From fall through early spring the broad crescent of the main beach is battered by Atlantic waves and all but disappears, leaving sun-worshippers to crowd together on the narrow ribbon of sand along Nassau Harbor. Cooler temperatures often prevail, bringing ideal conditions for tennis but discouraging topless sunbathing. The clinics tend to be very large. By April the situation reverses, with the magnificent beach fronting a calm Atlantic ideal for swimming, sailing, and windsurfing. Tennis activity shrinks to the cooler hours of the morning and late afternoon as it tries to avoid the heat and humidity that begin in spring and intensify throughout the summer. Facing stiff competition from the beach and watersports, clinic sizes diminish. Even the most fanatic players avoid the courts between 11 A.M. and 3 or 4 P.M. Such is the tennis mystique of Club Med–Paradise Island, however, that even in midsummer there are likely to be 35 or more people in the clinics. The on-court activity may slow but it never stops.

171

But what may surprise anyone who has never been to a Club Med is the crowd Paradise Island attracts. A substantial proportion are professionals, typically from the Northeast, Midwest, and Canada and ranging in age from their late twenties to their early fifties. Many are single and form romantic attachments, though that doesn't seem to be their primary goal in coming. This is not in any sense a heavy singles scene. The disco, which doesn't open until 11:30 P.M., gets a minimal crowd, many of them the gentle organizers, or G.O.s, who work at the club. Harder to explain is why many of these same professional people love joining in for the silly songs and dances that follow the nightly cabaret show, though the best explanation comes from a high-power lawyer, who told me, "I have so much pressure and responsibility in my job that it's a relief to come here and forget all that and just be silly."

TRAVEL INSTRUCTIONS: The nearest airport is Nassau, about 20 minutes away. Club Med markets its packages both with and without airfare and transfers.

Club Med–Sonora Bay

Playa de los Algodones
Guaymas, Sonora, Mexico

c/o

Club Med Sales Inc.
7975 N. Hayden Rd.
Scottsdale, AZ 85258

(212) 750-1687 or (800) CLUB MED

SEASON: March to November.

RATES: *Inexpensive.*

▶ *Profile*

COURTS: The club has 29 hard courts, 14 with lights, on several terraces landscaped with magenta bougainvillea and oleander. A grand-

The craggy Sierra Madre Mountains backdrop the 29 hard courts at Club Med–Sonora Bay in Mexico.

stand shaded by a wooden ramada separates the Number 1 and Number 2 courts. There are cold water fountains throughout the complex so you're never more than a few courts away from potable water. The lighting at Sonora Bay is of much better quality than that at Paradise Island while still affording the same all-night, self-service convenience.

COURT FEES: None.

PRO STAFF: As is true of all Club Meds, the tennis-teaching staff at Sonora Bay changes every six months. A chief of tennis—or *chef de tennis*—oversees the program, assisted by eight to ten G.O. (gentle organizer) pros (see "The Designer Labels" for a more thorough discussion of Club Med teaching in general).

INSTRUCTIONAL PROGRAMS: Sonora Bay offers Club Med's "intensive tennis program" consisting of two-and-a-half hours a day of clinics supplemented by an almost daily calendar of tournaments, social tennis events, contests, and exhibitions. During the summer, however, when daytime temperatures soar into the 90s, the clinics often get cut back from the advertised two-and-a-half hours daily to less than two because it's hot enough by 10 A.M. to drive off all but the hard core.

SPECIAL FEATURES: Videotaping is routinely done each week as part of the clinic program; the analysis that accompanies it can be variously useful or perfunctory depending on the enthusiasm of the current chief of tennis. The same fluctuation afflicts the ball machine. Though set up daily on one of the grandstand courts, where it's available on demand to anyone interested in using it, it doesn't always work and at times has had too few balls, all of them well past their prime.

SEASONAL TENNIS EVENTS: Like the Paradise Island club, Sonora Bay sometimes hosts such special events as clinics by big-name pros, tennis festivals, and mixed doubles tournaments, and occasionally gives away major prizes, like trips for two to Club Meds in Tahiti or Bali. The dates vary, so, before you book, ask whether anything is scheduled for around the time you want to travel.

PRO SHOP: There is a tiny pro shop, which has free loaner racquets but no merchandise, not even tennis balls (they can be purchased at the sundries shop near the swimming pool, except when the shop runs out, which it has been known to do). The staff can make arrangements for overnight restringing.

LODGING AND FOOD: This club has 375 rooms in stucco buildings whose pueblo-like architecture blends beautifully with the desert and craggy mountain setting. The rooms are small and typically Club Medish in their built-in twin beds, showers without tubs, and minimalist decor. All have air conditioning but lack phones and televisions. A few have private or semiprivate terraces or tiny balconies. Except during holiday periods, single rooms may be available at no extra charge.

There are two restaurants: the main one with tables for eight and huge buffets of fruits, salads, cheeses, breads, and various hot entrees; and the more intimate El Rancho, where you need reservations but dine a la carte at a table for however many are in your party. El Rancho also starts serving breakfast early, which is a boon to tennis players since it's located adjacent to the courts. Beer and wine are free with lunch and dinner.

Overall, the food at Sonora Bay was not as good as that at other clubs I've visited: tasty enough and abundant but nothing to rave about. Most surprising was the limited use made of fresh seafood, despite the fact that over 400 species of fish inhabit the Gulf of California. But like all the staff at a Club Med, chefs change every six months, and the current one may have more enthusiasm for the local marine bounty.

OTHER RECREATIONAL AMENITIES: Few clubs or resorts can match Sonora Bay's for the variety or abundance of its recreation. There are two beaches with watersports centers that offer waterskiing, sailing, and windsurfing, including intensive all-day windsurfing workshops. Its complete dive shop has excursions for certified divers and lessons to novices. An equestrian center has everything from simple trail rides to intensive English and Western riding programs. In addition, there is a fitness center, a large outdoor swimming pool, a golf driving range and hitting nets, and basketball, volleyball, and bocce. Golf on a local 18-hole course can be arranged at extra cost, as can deep-sea fishing.

▷ *To Note:* Club Med does not provide tennis balls for its tournaments, so you'll need several cans for competitive events and for any playing you do on your own. Given the prices in Mexico, you're wise to bring them from home. Moreover, the Club does not supply beach towels, so bring one or more of those as well. Near the tennis courts is a laundry room with free washers and dryers.

▶ *Gestalt*

The road from the airport at Guaymas to Club Med–Sonora Bay winds along the coast through an arid yet strangely alluring landscape of cactus-dotted desert. In the background rise the peaks of the Sierra Madre mountains, a craggy range of stratified rock that is buff-colored

A rustic ramada separates the two grandstand courts, shading players and spectators on hand for the afternoon tournaments.

in some places, dusty plum in others. The desert sweeps down out of those mountains toward the Gulf of California, where it ends in a shoreline of pebbly beaches, cliffs, and rocky outcrops. And in one of those places where desert becomes beach stands the pueblo-like village of Club Med–Sonora Bay.

With its large complex of 29 courts, Sonora Bay obviously hopes to attract hordes of tennis players. Offering an "intensive" tennis program and several special festivals and tournaments is further proof of their dedication to the sport. The irony is that participation in the tennis often gets diluted because of rigorous competition from the numerous other activities that are part of the Club's daily calendar. Lots of people come down for tennis only to be seduced away, for at least part of the time, by horseback riding, windsurfing, scuba diving, or something else.

Yet even during my visit in August, when the heat makes it arguably the worst month for tennis, there were at least 40 people who managed to make it to the shorter-than-usual hour-and-45-minute clinics nearly every morning and to the social round-robins and tournaments in the late afternoons. Many came from Southern California and Arizona, where playing in the heat on hard courts is routine. But even they abandoned the courts between 11 A.M. and 4 P.M.

So the popularity of tennis at Sonora Bay ebbs and flows with the season and the corresponding appeal of other sports, particularly of those associated with the water. The summers at Sonora Bay are hot, with temperatures sometimes rising into the low 90s during the day. When they do, the refreshing Gulf of California looks vastly more appealing than a cement court. Spring and fall hold out the best all-around compromise: warm enough to make the beach appealing but not so torrid as to make playing tennis a wilting experience.

For these reasons, the clinics in the fall and early spring tend to be larger than those during the hottest parts of the year. Sonora Bay does not, however, enjoy the same degree of tennis mystique as Paradise Island, so the student-pro ratio rarely gets out of hand the way it does at the Bahamas club. Even so, it never approaches the optimal 4:1, which means you'll get less personal attention in its clinics than you would at a resort's. On the other hand, during a good week more than 50 people enroll in the program, ensuring a good cross-section of players and big turnouts for the social tennis events and tournaments.

There is a disco at the Club, but the crowd Sonora Bay lures seems far more interested in playing to exhaustion during the day than in dancing away the nights. The tennis programs begin at 8 A.M. during the hot months (early breakfast is served in El Rancho right next to Court Number 1), which is hardly conducive to staying out until the wee hours. The guests as a whole seemed more than usually fit the week I visited, and more interested in white wine and light beer than in brain-numbing tequila concoctions.

The crowd varies. Many of the tennis players seem to come from the Texas-to-California corridor, though the club as a whole attracts people from both coasts. August brings planeloads of French. Beyond that it is a mixture of singles and couples mostly in their twenties, thirties, and forties.

TRAVEL INSTRUCTIONS: The nearest airport is a 20-minute drive away in Guaymas, Mexico, roughly 250 miles south of the Arizona border. Club Med charters leave weekly from Los Angeles and Houston.

Palmas del Mar/All
American Sports Clinics

P.O. Box 2020
Humacao, Puerto Rico 00611
(809) 852-6000 or (800) 221-4874

or

Information: All American Sports
116 Radio Circle Drive
Mt. Kisco, NY 10549
(914) 666-0096 or outside NY (800) 223-2442

SEASON: Year-round, but busiest from December through Easter.

RATES: *Very Expensive* in season, which runs from mid-December to mid-April; *Expensive* the rest of the year. Rates include hotel room, suite, or villa accommodations; three to five hours of tennis instruction, one or more private lessons, and free court time.

▶ *Profile*

COURTS: Palmas has 20 courts in all, which makes it the largest complex in the Caribbean. Of those, 5 are clay (one of which serves as a stadium) and 15 hard. Four have lights, though playing tennis under those lights is a lot like trying to read under a 30-watt bulb.

Reasonable attention has been paid, though, to making the setting attractive, with a huge banyan tree overarching the clubhouse and plenty of bougainvillea, oleander, and other miscellaneous tropical foliage planted about.

COURT FEES: *Expensive,* but complimentary on All American packages.

PRO STAFF: All American Sports maintains a staff of from three to five pros at Palmas, including a director of tennis and, during winter and

The Mediterranean-style Monte del Sol condominiums rise behind the courts at Palmas del Mar, where All American Sports runs clinic programs.

early spring, a camp director. The people in those top positions may change every few years, but they are always drawn from among the more senior and experienced pros in the All American organization. Alex Pakozdi, a personable former Chilean Junior Davis Cup player, currently heads the program.

INSTRUCTIONAL PROGRAMS: All American Sports has three-, four-, five-, and seven-night packages that combine accommodations with tennis instruction. There are basically two types of programs: a three-hour "Top Seed," which consists of group clinics and drills, videotape analysis, and one or more private lessons; and a two-hour "Match Point" clinic, during which the pro functions as a coach, providing tips about strategy and shot selection while you're actually playing matches.

179

You can sign up for one or the other or both. In no case does the student-pro ratio exceed 4:1.

SPECIAL FEATURES: A few weeks after the end of high season, Palmas often schedules a Singles Week, enticing people to come alone by taking 10 percent off the normal single-occupancy rate.

SEASONAL TENNIS EVENTS: The All American clinics run year-round, but during the winter season the staff spices the weekly calendar with such events as doubles clinics, mixed doubles round-robins, strategy and doubles exhibitions, and a Davis Cup competition (which pits teams of hotel guests against teams of local members). Moreover, during Christmas, Presidents Week, and other school vacation periods they also run junior clinics.

LODGING AND FOOD: The All American package gives you the option of staying in a hotel, suite, or villa, depending on the depth of your pocketbook. The least expensive option is the 102-room Candelero Hotel, a few minutes' walk inland from the beach. A mere hundred rooms may sound intimate, but this is a very ordinary hotel whose rather shopworn accommodations see heavy traffic in groups attending meetings in the adjacent conference center. It's separated from the tennis courts by a golf fairway; your choice is either to wait interminably for the free shuttle, walk around the fairway (though don't expect to see signage to help you find the way), or cut across, dodging white spheres and bilingual abuse. For all its drawbacks, that is where most of the AAS campers stay. It has a restaurant, Las Garzas, with a good breakfast buffet and an uninspired, leaning-to-heavy dinner menu. It also has a bar touted as the liveliest place in the resort, which only underscores how much Palmas is about daytime activity and not nightlife.

There is, however, another hotel currently under construction at Palmas: a 475-room Ritz-Carlton, which promises to introduce a level of elegance the Candelero never even dreamed of. Unfortunately, it will not be finished until late 1991. Meanwhile, somewhat posher accommodations are to be found in the 23-suite Palmas Inn, which is next to the casino up on the hill high above the courts. Each of its junior suites has a large patio and views of tropical gardens and the Caribbean.

The last and most spacious option is to book one of the hundreds of villas. You have a choice of locations, including along the beach, golf course, and harbor. For ease of access to tennis, nothing beats Monte Sol Village, on the hill just above the court complex. Each of the one-bedroom villas has a living room, dining room, fully equipped kitchen, and its own washer and dryer. Supplies can be purchased at a general store.

There are more than half a dozen additional restaurants scattered throughout the resort. Perhaps because of the pervasive Mediterranean architecture, several of these restaurants specialize in French cuisine, the best among them Chez Daniel, which is open year-round, and Le Bistrquet, just above the harborside courts, which is open from November through April.

OTHER RECREATIONAL AMENITIES: Palmas is a complete resort of a sort that's rare to find in the Caribbean. Beyond the essential beach— a narrow three-and-half-mile-long strand bordered by palm trees—it has a 6,690-yard Gary Player–designed golf course, horseback riding stables, and a fitness center (with exercise equipment, aerobics classes, and massages). A watersports center rents windsurfers and one- or two-person sailboats and provides lessons in both sports. Its staff also arranges bareboat and crewed charters of larger sailboats and schedules parasailing and waterskiing. Snorkelers and divers can book half-day trips to the island of Vieques, and there are deep-sea fishing boats available for charter. You can also rent bicycles.

▶ *Gestalt*

Palmas del Mar bills itself as "the new American Riviera," and in an unintended sense the phrase is absolutely accurate. Like parts of the Riviera, Palmas is turning into condoland, suffering as it does under the misguided notion that Mediterranean-style architecture is vastly more pleasing to the eye than the subtropical forests that originally blanketed its 2,700 acres. There is a certain irony in barring construction taller than a palm tree only to replace vast tracts of the natural vegetation with villas. Plans call for eventually developing 60 percent of the acreage.

But everything is relative, of course, and Palmas will never become the shoulder-to-shoulder hotel horror that is Miami Beach or, for that matter, the Condado in San Juan. Situated on Puerto Rico's southeast coast, roughly 35 miles from San Juan, it basks in tranquility. It has enough trees and flowers and such an abundance of recreation that many people find it appealing despite its love affair with condominiums.

Not open to debate, though, is what happens on court. Because of All American Sports, Palmas has the finest tennis programs anywhere in the Caribbean. The three-hour morning clinics wed solid instruction with a sense of fun. None of the pros will try to make dramatic changes in your strokes, unless that's what you want. Instead

181

they'll introduce minor adjustments to render what you can already do more effective. The drills are structured to give you a workout without leaving you exhausted.

Even during high season, from December to Easter, the clinics at Palmas have been modest in size, averaging about ten people a week. The exception is Singles Week, which often falls in late April and may get sixteen or more. Summers are dead as far as adult business goes, but the junior programs have a Caribbean following. In the fall, the adult clinics may have five or six campers.

The groups typically include a mixture of couples and singles, except over the Christmas holidays, when All American runs simultaneous junior clinics and thus also gets a smattering of families. The largest contingent originates in the Northeast, with a secondary wave flying down from the upper Midwest.

Until recently, All American offered only a three-hour morning clinic. Now they supplement that with the option of a two-hour supervised play session in the afternoon, which does depend, more so than the instruction, on a larger turnout. All American plans to recruit additional participants from regular hotel guests and Palmas' local tennis members. But as I'm writing this, that new format has not yet had a full winter's trial run, so I don't have any reliable information about how well-attended the match-play sessions will be.

Coming to the Caribbean to play tennis is not the sun-defying act of madness it may seem. The Trade Winds temper the climate. You won't be booking court time between noon and 3 or 4 P.M., but the rest of the day is fine. Pack a good waterproof sunblock, hat or visor, wristbands, and griptape and you'll be fine.

The fact is, you want to play hard during the day because Palmas languishes at night. The brochure's insistence that the bar at Las Garzas is the liveliest place in the resort may be true. It certainly isn't the small and very subdued casino or the discotheque next to it. Maybe the new Ritz-Carlton will infuse some excitement into the Palmas evenings, but for now nightlife ends with dinner.

TRAVEL INSTRUCTIONS: San Juan International Airport is 35 miles away. Van service can be arranged through All American and is less expensive than a taxi.

CANADA

· ·

▶ Gray Rocks Inn, St. Jovite, Quebec
▶ Inn & Tennis Club at Manitou, McKellar, Ontario

Gray Rocks Inn

. . . .

P.O. Box 1000
St. Jovite, Quebec, Canada J0T 2H0
(819) 425-2771 or (800) 567-6767

SEASON: The tennis programs run from late May to mid-September.

COST: *Inexpensive–Moderate,* depending on the type of accommodations chosen; special reduced rates apply during the first few weeks of the season. The basic package includes accommodations, all meals, at least three-and-a-half hours of daily tennis clinics, unlimited free court time, and access to the fitness center.

▶ *Profile*

COURTS: The Inn has 22 clay courts in two locations: 10 adjacent to the hotel and another 12 a short drive away at the golf course. The latter complex is the one used for the tennis schools.

COURT FEES: *Moderate,* but complimentary on packages.

PRO STAFF: The director for the adult programs is Stan Gendron. A Canadian with a master's in sports psychology, he has been part of the inn's summer tennis program since the mid-1970s and serves as a national tester for the USPTR, one of the organizations that certifies teaching pros. He heads a staff of twelve pros chosen for a variety of qualities, among them their commitment to teaching tennis and their enjoyment of people. There are always a few strong players among them as well as several with physiology backgrounds.

INSTRUCTIONAL PROGRAMS: There are two basic programs: a six-day and a weekend. The six-day program begins with an evaluation session Sunday afternoon and runs through Friday. The main instruction and drills take place every morning from 9 A.M. to 12:20 P.M. Two afternoons a week are devoted to competition: singles on one, a doubles team event on another. The remaining three afternoons have round-robins (a social mixer, men's and women's doubles, and a pro-am), which are open to anyone staying at the hotel, whether taking the clinics or not.

185

The weekend clinics specialize in particular aspects of the game. Each keeps to a narrow theme, which differs from week to week. One weekend may schedule work only on serve and return of serve, while another focuses on groundstrokes, a third on drill and match play, or yet another on volleys, volleys, and more volleys. There is also an Initiation to Tennis weekend specifically for novices. Whatever the topic, the clinic runs eight hours in all. Videotaping is a regular element in both the six-day and weekend sessions.

For juniors, Gray Rocks runs two- and four-week coed sessions for kids ages 11 to 17.

SPECIAL FEATURES: On one of the afternoon sessions during the six-day program the staff charts your errors while you play singles matches. In the analysis that follows you learn where most of your mistakes occur and can thus work to improve those parts of your game. Ball machines are available for rent.

SEASONAL TENNIS EVENTS: Dennis Van der Meer (see "The Designer Labels") personally conducts an adult clinic and Tennis-University I, an introduction to tennis teaching, usually in mid to late August.

LODGING AND FOOD: The main lodge is a multi-turreted red-roofed Victorian overlooking Lake Ouimet. The smallest of its 180 rooms are so tiny that one guest complained of "having to go out in the hall to change her mind" and not all have private baths; none are elegant, not even the deluxe rooms with fireplaces. Far nicer, but off on their own in the woods at the end of the lake, are the 56 one-, two-, and three-bedroom condominiums with fireplaces and complete kitchens. The old 70-room Le Chateau, once a favorite with honeymooners, now houses junior campers during the summers. It has a heated pool and its own restaurant.

Three unmemorable meals are included in the price of the clinics. Lunch is best, maybe because it's usually served outside near the lake. At dinner you have a choice of three entrees, all of them tired refugees from the era when Continental cuisine was in vogue. It's especially disappointing, partly because this is French-speaking Canada and you come expecting to dine well, and partly because you feel like you're missing the excellent restaurants in nearby St. Jovite. Booking a condominium and opting not to take meals in the lodge makes sense if food is important to you, although that does mean missing out on the socializing that goes on at dinner.

Seating in the dining room is for however many there are in your party, though there is usually at least one table for campers who want company. Coming alone thus doesn't mean having to eat alone. Jackets are recommended at dinner.

OTHER RECREATIONAL AMENITIES: Gray Rocks has virtually everything you could want in the way of summer recreation, which helps make it a superb family destination. Among the water sports available on the lake are waterskiing, rowboats, canoes, pedalboats, kayaks, sunfish, and windsurfers. There is also an 18-hole golf course, an equestrian center, jogging and fitness trails, and a children's playground. Indoors is a state-of-the-art fitness center with a lap pool, whirlpools, saunas, Nautilus equipment, and aerobics classes. You can even get a computerized personal-fitness appraisal of your cardiovascular capacity, body-fat percentage, muscle strength and endurance, and flexibility. Other options include a computerized stress profile and detailed nutrition assessment.

▶ *Gestalt*

The Gray Rocks Inn is the centerpiece of a picturesque 2,000-acre resort in Quebec's Laurentian Mountains, about an hour-and-a-half's drive north of Montreal. The main lodge overlooks Lake Ouimet in a landscape of rolling hills forested with hardwoods and evergreens. If its architecture is haphazard—the result of additions carpentered on during different decades—its setting is beautiful enough to make even the quirks of its structure charming.

There is nothing quirky about the tennis instruction. Underlying it is an approach called "The Action Method," which is the standard method adopted by Tennis Canada (the national tennis association). Simply stated, the Action Method focuses both on hitting the ball and receiving it. From the very beginning, instructors teach you how to adapt your strokes to balls coming at different speeds and heights with different spins. The emphasis throughout is not on hitting the ball in one particular way but in choosing to hit it in any of several different ways according to the situation and your objectives. In that sense it is extraordinarily pragmatic, or as Butch Staples, the former director of tennis, now president and general manager, puts it: "The Action Method is really good to teach people the realities of the game."

Philosophically, the program has evolved from instruction that was very technical to instruction that is more situational. "We teach a lot by objective," says Staples. "If their style of play is such that they feel that they want the ball to be in play—that is, they want to outlast their opponent—then we want to teach them the skills that will be consistent with how they feel. If we have another player who's very aggressive and loves going for it on the courts, we'll try to develop a

The turreted Gray Rocks Inn on Lake Ouimet is the centerpiece of a picturesque, 2,000-acre resort in Quebec's Laurentian Mountains.

style of play that's compatible with that player's interests. We try within a group setting to relate more to the individuals and their style of play."

In the same way, everything they teach has a competitive context. "We don't just teach a forehand and then a backhand," Staples adds. "We work on elements of a forehand and then relate it to a game situation and then drill it in that game situation and then actually play competitively. We teach drill-and-compete in everything we do, whether it's a drop shot or an overhead."

It bodes well when a resort's general manager has an exceptionally strong tennis background, as Staples does. Tennis is the number-one activity at Gray Rocks during the summer, and the sheer quantity of clinics and programs on the roster rivals that of any resort in the U.S. Attendance at its camps averages more than 50 players a week, reaching a zenith in early August when they fill up at 72. Even then they never exceed the optimal 4:1 student-pro ratio, which further contributes to the quality of the programs.

That many players insures a broad spectrum of levels and abundant opportunity for competition outside the regular clinics. Most come from Canada, and despite the fact that this is French-speaking Quebec, most of the instruction is conducted in English (though instructors can, when necessary, teach in French as well). Besides the morning clinics, there is more tennis scheduled every afternoon. That could be singles matches with error charting, a team doubles event, social round-robins, or a pro-am. Unfortunately, black flies also show up for many of these events, so be sure to pack an insect repellant.

The atmosphere throughout is low-key and unpretentious, except for the inexplicable preference for jackets at dinner. T-shirts are fine on the courts. One night a week, weather permitting, there is an outdoor barbecue near the lake and a live band. The bar attracts a modest crowd at night, but don't count on raucous nightlife. After a day full of activity, most campers are content to head for bed.

The accommodations and food may be unremarkable, but the setting, abundant recreation, and tennis programs rank with the best. And on a quality-for-dollar basis, Gray Rocks is hard to beat.

TRAVEL INSTRUCTIONS: The nearest airports are Mirabel, 60 miles to the southeast, and Dorval in Montreal, 78 miles to the southeast.

The Inn and Tennis Club at Manitou

Summer:

McKellar, Ontario, Canada P0G 1C0

(705) 389-2171

Winter:

251 Davenport Rd.
Toronto, Ontario, Canada M5R 1J9

(416) 967-3466

SEASON: Mid-May to mid-October.

RATES: *Very Expensive,* with the highest rates in effect during July and August. Packages include accommodations, all meals, one massage, tennis clinics, and unlimited court time.

▶ Profile

COURTS: The Inn has 13 hard courts, one of which is indoors.

COURT FEES: None.

PRO STAFF: The director of tennis is Ed Baaker, a Dutch-born teaching pro who worked at Harry Hopman's International in Florida before coming to the inn in 1983. He heads a staff of 14 to 15 pros, chosen for their personalities as much as their teaching credentials and then put through a preseason training program conducted by Baaker and the former Canadian touring pro who originated the inn's programs, Peter Burwash (see "The Designer Labels").

INSTRUCTIONAL PROGRAMS: There are two formats, each of them running three hours a day. The most basic program is a "Strokers Clinic," whose principal focus is on how to hit the ball, though it also introduces elementary strategy and tactics. The alternative, for those who already have a grasp of the fundamentals, is the Inn's "Players

Clinic," whose instruction and drills concentrate on court awareness, positioning, tactics, and competitive strategy. In both cases, the maximum student-pro ratio is 4:1 (and is often less).

SPECIAL FEATURES: Clinics typically take place in the mornings at the Inn. Those who still want more have a variety of options for the afternoon. One court is set aside for anyone interested in having his or her strokes videotaped and analyzed. One or more courts have ball machines ready for use. You can play doubles with a pro as your partner. There are always empty courts for pickup matches. And throughout the session there are men's and women's singles tournaments, in which everyone is encouraged to compete, regardless of his or her level. Winners get merchandise prizes, a trophy, and an invitation to come back in the fall—at half price—for the annual Tournament of Champions. Evenings often feature exhibition matches.

SEASONAL TENNIS EVENTS: The big event on the Inn's tennis calendar is the annual Tournament of Champions. Everyone who wins one of the weekly men's or women's singles tournaments is invited back for this ultimate contest, which takes place toward the end of the season. The players get personal tournament coaches and the chance to compete for prizes and trophies. The four-day event culminates with a 1930s All-White Tennis Ball. Contestants (and their friends or spouses) pay only half the usual rates.

Over the four-day Canadian Thanksgiving (October 12) weekend, the inn abandons its usual adults-preferred policy and encourages parents to bring their children by charging half price for children under 16. During that period, adult tennis clinics are offered free of charge and there are separate free clinics for children.

SPECIAL EVENTS: Tennis clinics take place every week of the season, but certain weeks also include special events off court, among them an epicurean weekend (when the cuisine is even more extravagant than usual), cooking schools, and jazz lovers' weekends. Dates vary, so check with the inn for up-to-date information.

LODGING AND FOOD: There are only 37 rooms at the Inn, ranging from small, simple standards (the only type without fireplaces) to junior suites with fireplace-equipped living rooms and their own whirlpools and saunas. All have terry-cloth robes and Crabtree & Evelyn soaps. Some of the rooms border the courts; others are on a hill overlooking Lake Manitouwabing.

It is no exaggeration to say that the Inn serves the finest cuisine of any tennis resort in North America, bar none. The nouvelle food alone, spectacularly presented, is reason enough to visit. The menus, which feature the freshest possible ingredients, change every two days, but a typical dinner might consist of an appetizer of pheasant pâté or ravioli stuffed with shrimp in an orange and lemon sauce, fresh tomato soup with basil, wild mushroom salad, fresh-fruit sorbet, sliced roast breast of duck in blackcurrant sauce or fresh red snapper in cucumber sauce, a selection of cheeses from France, and finally a hot or cold dessert with petits fours and chocolate truffles. In addition, each day there is one low-calorie, low-sodium, low-cholesterol selection in each category, all of them as savory and beautifully presented as the regular dishes.

Unless you request otherwise, the maitre d' typically seats parties of two together at tables for four at dinner and makes sure that no one who may have come alone has to dine alone. Jackets are required at dinner.

OTHER RECREATIONAL FACILITIES: Off to one side of the courts there is a small outdoor swimming pool, a heated whirlpool, and a sauna. On Lake Manitouwabing, the inn has a floating dock with lounge chairs and a fleet of sailboats, windsurfers, and canoes all available to guests free of charge. Fishing and boating excursions can also be arranged. The newest addition to the recreation menu is a small equestrian center, where guests can book horseback riding instruction and trail rides, and a spa, which has state-of-the-art exercise equipment, aerobics and dancercise classes, and massage therapists.

▶ Gestalt

Years passed between the first rave reviews I heard about the Inn and Tennis Club at Manitou and my own visit. It wasn't for lack of interest—after all the Inn belonged to the exclusive Relais & Châteaux association. What kept me away was that the 37-room inn was not on the road to anywhere I ever had reason to go. To fly to Toronto and then drive two and a half hours farther north seemed like an unnecessarily out-of-the-way junket for tennis, especially when there were so many other resorts closer at hand. What could Canada, a country hardly associated with magnificent tennis, offer that the U.S. could not? When I did finally get there, the most I expected was to spend a pleasant weekend. Instead I found a tiny inn whose tastefully appointed rooms, first-rate cuisine, genuinely friendly service, and superb tennis programs make it the foremost luxury tennis resort anywhere on the planet.

The Inn is located on the shores of Lake Manitouwabing in a scenic region known as the Muskoka Lakes District. Ancient glaciers

The Inn & Tennis Club at Manitou in the Muskoka Lakes District north of Toronto is the finest luxury tennis resort in the world.

gouged depressions in the Precambrian granite, filling the lakes with crystal-clear icemelt as they retreated. Later forests of evergreens and hardwoods took root. Today it has become a gentrified wilderness where wealthy Torontonians have waterfront mansions they call "summer cottages."

Arriving at the Inn after what turns out to be an easy drive, I am made to feel as welcome as a weekend guest at one of those cottages. The formalities of checking in take place at the concierge desk, a century-old table from Britain, after which I have the choice of going straight to my room or having a drink. I opt for the latter. While I'm sitting in the lounge, where the television is tuned to tennis matches, director of tennis Ed Baaker comes over to introduce himself, as he does to all arriving guests, and find out whether I'm interested in taking the clinics and, if so, in which of the two formats, Strokers or Players (see the Instructional Programs section above). At the same time, he lets me know that following the clinics there are still more on-court activities, ranging from ball-machine drills and videotape analysis to hitting with a pro, organized matches, and a singles tournament. It is the first clue to the Inn's genuine love of tennis.

But then the Inn started out as a tennis camp. Since 1958 Ben and Sheila Wise, who own and manage it, have also operated a nearby sports, art, and theater camp for teenagers. In the early 1970s, the

Wises started to offer a separate adult tennis program mainly for parents who wanted to vacation near their kids. Once it became clear that some very important people were sleeping in bunk beds just to take part in the tennis program, the Wises decided to open a little inn to give them a comfortable place to relax after a day on the courts. They furnished their inn with antiques picked up on their own travels abroad and brought in chefs from Switzerland and France to prepare the nouvelle cuisine. Sophisticated, demanding travelers themselves, they followed the simple rule of making the Inn a place they themselves would want to stay, and of striving each year to make it better. Moreover, since Ben Wise is himself an enthusiastic tennis player, they also have an undying commitment to the quality of what goes on on court.

Under Baaker and the influence of Burwash, the Inn approaches instruction with the idea of making minor changes rather than undertaking a major overhaul. "We'll pinpoint the major fault in your stroke and work on that," says Baaker. They try very hard to demystify each stroke by emphasizing what happens at the point of contact. They also introduce checkpoints, so that if strokes go awry in a match you have enough understanding to "be your own coach" (a favorite Burwash phrase) and make corrections.

The afternoon sessions begin with a theatrical—and often very humorous—introduction to some crucial aspect of singles or doubles strategy. Baaker shows up as "The Coach," a burnt-out case wearing a knee-brace, Hawaiian shirt, and sunglasses. He carries a bullhorn, the better to project a litany of tennis tips and cliches. He anchors these satiric skits, which make serious points on various aspects of strategy and tactics.

Those who want to can easily spend six hours a day on court, drilling or playing. Everyone, no matter what his or her level, is encouraged to compete in the tournament that is held each session. The finals are played on a bleachered court as spectators sip champagne. Few camps have the Inn's absolute dedication to the sheer joy of tennis—not just winning, though that is obviously important too, but playing for the love of the game.

Three-quarters of the Inn's clientele come from Canada, especially Toronto, the rest from the U.S. and overseas. Most, though not all, are couples and fall between 35 and 55 years of age. Intermediates make up the largest contingent, as they do at most camps. The Inn also gets a few beginners, though in general Wise sees a trend toward stronger players: "There are more better players than we have ever had," he says. "They come because they know that they can get some decent competition and play a lot of good tennis."

One comparison begs to be made: between the Inn and John Gar-

194

diner's Tennis Ranch in Carmel Valley, California, reviewed elsewhere in this book. They are, after all, the two most luxurious tennis camps in North America. Yet they differ in sometimes dramatic fashion.

In staying at the ranch you're made to feel like a guest in John Gardiner's home. Gardiner and his wife Monique are themselves often there. The small number of rooms—fourteen—contributes to the sense of intimacy and exclusivity: clearly not just anyone can get a reservation there. The pros, immaculately dressed ladies and gentlemen in tennis whites, show up to give the clinics but then disappear: their place is on rather than off the tennis courts. In this refined and slightly starchy atmosphere you dress for dinner, of course, sitting down at large family-style tables after serving yourself from a sideboard. The food, while more elaborate than you might prepare for yourself, has a home-cooked quality. And finally, although the ranch itself has little more than tennis and a swimming pool to offer, the galleries and shops of Carmel are nearby and so are the fabled golf courses of Pebble Beach.

It is extraordinary that the Inn could be so different. Although the Wises, like the Gardiners, are always there and have a similar dedication to providing attentive service, on and off the court, they have a completely different philosophy about what a luxury tennis camp ought to be. Ed Baaker's routine as "Coach," amusing as it is, would never be staged at Gardiner's ranch, but then the Inn doesn't take itself nearly so seriously. The pros, like all of the staff, are encouraged to be entertaining and to be a part of the social fabric of the Inn. That helps to create a real camp atmosphere, where the idea is to relax and have fun, not just with the other guests but with the staff as well.

On the other hand, the food at summer camp was never like this. The Inn depends on having a star in the kitchen—rather than, as at Gardiner's, on a collection of favorite recipes—and as a result it is culinarily light years ahead of Gardiner's traditional fare. You dress for dinner there, too; yet the Inn remains unpretentious, in large measure, I think, because the staff is encouraged to have fun with the guests.

When it comes to luxury tennis camps, the Inn and Tennis Club at Manitou sets the standard. This elegant little 37-room inn, with its fabulous cuisine and friendly manner, is the finest luxury tennis resort in the world.

TRAVEL INSTRUCTIONS: The nearest commercial airport is in Toronto, 160 miles to the south. Rental cars are readily available there and it is a pleasant two-and-a-half-hour drive up to the Inn. Alternatively, the Inn's staff can arrange for you to be met by a limousine service and driven up. The cost, for up to four people, is roughly $140 each way.

EUROPE

▶ Hotel Stanglwirt, Going/Tyrol, Austria
▶ The Palace Hotel, Gstaad, Switzerland

Hotel Stanglwirt

A-6353 Going/Tyrol, Austria
Phone: 00 43/53 58-20 00

SEASON: Year-round, although the main tennis season begins in March and lasts through October.

RATES: *Inexpensive–Moderate,* depending on the accommodations chosen and the time of year. Rates are highest from mid-July to mid-October. The basic package includes accommodations, breakfast and dinner, and three hours of daily clinics.

▶ *Profile*

COURTS: The hotel has 14 courts altogether: 8 red clay outdoors and 6 claylike Bross-Slide indoors. Only the indoor courts have lights. Adjacent to the courts is a small Austrian-style wooden hut that contains the pro shop. There is also a kiosk where players can buy drinks and snacks.

COURT FEES: *Moderate,* but complimentary on packages.

PRO STAFF: Peter Burwash International's (see "The Designer Labels") Roger Darrohn directs the program. Formerly a physical education teacher at the University of California at Davis, he joined PBI in 1978 and since then has coached over 12,000 players in fourteen countries. He has been at the hotel since 1981. He heads a staff of six teaching pros, all of whom are multi-lingual.

INSTRUCTIONAL PROGRAMS: The most comprehensive program offered runs Monday through Friday and includes three hours a day of drills and instruction and a maximum student-instructor ratio of 4:1. Although the clinics are typically taught in German, the pros can also conduct them in English (or, for that matter, French). Weekend programs are also available. So is a program for children under 13.

SPECIAL FEATURES: Some kind of tennis activity routinely takes place in the afternoons following the clinics and lunch. Mixed-up doubles round-robins, pro exhibitions, and men's and women's singles

199

tournaments are all on the calendar. On several evenings, there are videotaped tennis tips (from a Austrian television series Darrohn did—so they're in German), strategy sessions (covering everything from tennis etiquette to mental toughness), and a final awards ceremony with both serious and humorous prizes. Videotaping is a regular part of the normal clinic program.

SEASONAL TENNIS EVENTS: The weekly winners of the men's and women's singles tournaments held each week are invited back in the fall to compete in the annual Stanglwirt Cup, whose first prize is a free week-long tennis program complete with room and board.

The Austrian Open, though not staged at the hotel, is a 15-minute drive away in Kitzbühl. That Grand Prix event takes place near the beginning of August.

LODGING AND FOOD: Most people stay at the Hotel Stanglwirt, though that is not a requirement. The older section of the hotel, called the Stammhaus, dates to the nineteenth century. It contains the standard rooms (which have bath or shower) and the restaurants. The newer portion, called the Bio-Hotel, claims to be Europe's first biologically built hotel. It is constructed in Tyrolean architectural style, with wooden ceilings and 300-year-old beams, but its 80 rooms are uncharacteristically spacious and come with entirely modern appointments like walk-in closets, canopy beds, and baths with built-in whirlpools. All the rooms in both parts of the hotel have balconies with views of the valley or mountains.

Breakfast and dinner are included in the basic tennis clinic package. Breakfast is a big buffet of homemade breads, cheeses, and cold cuts. At dinner you have a choice of four menus, one of which is always natural food; Peter Burwash is a vegetarian, and so are most of his pros. There are special dinners several nights a week, among them a "Farmer's Buffet" featuring traditional Austrian dishes, and a gala six-course dinner on the last night of the clinic.

OTHER RECREATIONAL AMENITIES: Besides tennis courts, the hotel also has a riding stable featuring lessons on Lippizan horses, indoor and outdoor swimming pools, a fitness room with exercise and weight machines, three squash courts, a sauna, a solarium, Austrian bowling alleys, archery, and a masseur. There is a golf course six miles away in Kitzbühl.

▶ Gestalt

Mountain regions that have reputations as winter destinations are often at their most breathtakingly beautiful in the summer. That is
certainly true of Wilden Kaiser Mountains in the Austrian Tyrol. Just

beyond the Hotel Stanglwirt's red clay tennis courts is a three-tiered landscape that begins as pastureland, turns to deep evergreen forest higher up, and then ends as a jagged line of towering granite peaks. This court complex is, without exaggeration, one of the most beautiful places to play anywhere in the world.

As it happens, the Hotel Stanglwirt is also home to an extraordinarily successful Peter Burwash International tennis camp. From mid-March through October, this site runs nearly at capacity, attracting 40 to 48 campers each week. Most of them come from Austria and from neighboring West Germany and Switzerland. The lure is a rock-solid program based on Peter Burwash's notion that it isn't enough to correct the flaws in a player's strokes; what is crucial is to give him or her an overall understanding of the game.

There is nothing strikingly original in the Burwash organization's format. Over the course of the five-day clinics at Stanglwirt campers progress from groundstrokes through doubles strategy. As they become more proficient the pros replace straight drills with playing situations. The tenet that underlies all of this is "We Teach Individuals, Not Systems."

But though there may not be a Burwash system, there is a Burwash methodology, outlined in his book *Tennis for Life,* to which Darrohn and company subscribe. Central to the Burwash approach is the dictum that "tennis is a game of emergencies." What he means is that, against equal or better competitors, you are often going to find yourself in trouble, rushed, out of position, on the defensive. And at that point everything you've learned about the ideal way to hit a tennis ball becomes irrelevant: what matters then is simply getting the ball back. What you learn at Stanglwirt, therefore, is not only how to hit the ball in the best of all possible situations, but a sense of what to do when you're in trouble as well. It's that dual approach that makes this one of the world's top programs.

The Stanglwirt program is, however, the only one in this book whose clinics are conducted primarily in a language other than English. Most of the campers come from Austria, Germany, and German-speaking Switzerland and thus speak German (and probably English and at least one other language). I've included it not only because of its quality and large turnout, but because Darrohn is an American and his pros can teach in English when necessary.

TRAVEL INSTRUCTIONS: The nearest airport is Munich, Germany, located roughly one hour from the hotel. From there, you can either rent a car (which is likely to be less expensive if done as part of your overall travel package) or take a train from Munich to St. Johann in Austria, which is about ten minutes by cab from the hotel.   201

The Palace Hotel

3780 Gstaad, Switzerland

Phone: 030-8 31 31 or FAX: 030-4 33 44

or

Leading Hotels of the World

Phone: (212) 838-3110 or (800) 223-6800

SEASON: Selected weeks from mid-June to early September.

RATES: *Expensive.* The package includes tennis instruction, room with bath or shower, all meals, one massage, service, and taxes.

▶ *Profile*

COURTS: There are 4 red clay courts outdoors, 3 carpet courts inside in the Tennis Hall. All are set against the spectacular backdrop of the Swiss Alps.

COURT FEES: *Moderate,* but complimentary on packages.

PRO STAFF: Australian great Roy Emerson runs the sessions that take place in June and July. During the height of his career in the 1960s, "Emmo" won every major singles and doubles title at least twice, including Wimbledon, Forest Hills, Paris, and Melbourne. In addition, as a member of Australia's Davis Cup squad under Harry Hopman, he won 36 of his 40 matches. During busy weeks in the summer he has as many as eight pros helping him run his clinics. They come from all over the world; many are former tour players or notable teachers and coaches.

Niki Pilic takes over in August and September. Pilic is a former touring pro and coach of the German Davis Cup team. Finally, for one week in late August, the Palace's head pro Köbi Hermenjat, who assists both Emerson and Pilic during their sessions, directs his own program. Because Emerson is the biggest name of the three, and because he runs more sessions than either Pilic or Hermenjat, it's his programs I've reviewed below.

INSTRUCTIONAL PROGRAMS: Although the exact format of the program varies according to who is running it, the basic plan calls for four to five hours of instruction daily. The number of participants is limited to 28, except for Emerson's sessions, when class size may reach 36. Neither Emerson nor Hermenjat accept beginners. All three adhere to a 4:1 student-pro ratio.

SEASONAL TENNIS EVENTS: Gstaad is the site of the Swiss Open, usually during the early part of July.

LODGING AND FOOD: The turreted Palace Hotel has 150 rooms with wood furniture and bright, multi-colored fabrics. The Scherz family, who runs it, describes this as "rustic Swiss Baroque style." The tiled bathrooms have either a deep soaking tub or shower, heated towel racks, and hair dryers—evidence of continual upgrading. There are down comforters on the beds and maids leave Toblerone chocolate with the evening turn-down service. Most of the rooms have balconies with wrought-iron fences and orange awnings. Single rooms are available, but they are very small.

Three excellent meals are included in the package, which doesn't stop campers from occasionally heading for intimate restaurants in town for *raclette* with *rosti* or other Swiss Alps classics. Lunch at La Grande Terrasse is informal and usually takes place in tennis clothes. Gentlemen need jackets but not ties at dinner.

OTHER RECREATIONAL AMENITIES: The hotel has indoor and outdoor swimming pools, a disco, a small fitness center with aerobics classes, squash courts, and a playroom for children.

▶ *Gestalt*

Gstaad is a one-street mountain village situated at 3,600 feet above sea level in the Saane Valley of eastern Switzerland. That its winter visitors include William F. Buckley, Jr., John Kenneth Galbraith, Elizabeth Taylor, and Adnan Khashoggi and that its chalets can cost more than $5 million does not fundamentally alter its village character—or at least its village look. The castle-like Palace Hotel, which was built in 1913, is a landmark in a sea of Swiss chalets.

The largest family pension in Switzerland, the Palace has been managed since 1938 (and owned since 1947) by the Scherz family. It is revered for its loyal staff and personal service. Every waiter in the restaurants will know you by name before many days pass. The owners host a cocktail party the day you arrive, as much so they can get to know you as you, them. That same easy familiarity extends onto the tennis courts.

Roy Emerson is by nature very social, and despite his own stellar career on the circuit, he manages to make campers feel good about their own games. "We work hard, try to have a lot of fun, and try to improve players' weaknesses," says Emerson. "We do a lot of work on doubles strategy because that is what a lot of them play."

The station-to-station format means that everyone does some of the daily on-court work with Emerson himself and gets a chance to play against him. He doesn't simply introduce the drills, he actively participates in the instruction.

The structure is straightforward, beginning with groundstrokes and introducing a new set of strokes each morning. By the end of the third day, they have covered all the major strokes and move on to combination drills, ending up with a review of everything.

The instruction itself is classical, as you might expect from someone who had been coached by Harry Hopman. Players are divided into groups by level of play and worked out as vigorously as they seem to want. Emerson understandably uses many of the classic Hopman drills (see "The Designer Labels"), but he finds they have limited value for the weaker players. "We get all standards of play," notes Emerson, "and obviously if the standard is not too good we can't do a lot of [Hopman's] drills." In those cases, he works on technique instead.

"We're serious in what we do," says Emerson. "Those that can take it, we drill them pretty good. The others we take it a little easier. We try to emphasize that we're here to get a little better."

Videotaping used to be a fixture of his clinics at the Palace, but Emerson no longer uses it because he finds the campers either don't want to see themselves on video or prefer to spend the time hitting balls.

One peculiarity of the Palace setup, however, is that in rotating from court to court you must also periodically switch from the slow red clay outdoors to the fast carpet indoors and back again. It is rare for a camp to take place on two such different surfaces, because the timing required is so different. Campers at the Palace continually have to adjust.

In addition to spending five hours a day with the campers on court, Emerson and his staff have breakfast, lunch, and dinner with them. At midweek, when the groups show signs of fatigue, the whole crew picks up lunches from the Palace and rides the cable car up into the mountains for a picnic. Some walk back down, taking the afternoon off from tennis. But the afternoon session does run if anyone wants more on-court work.

The crowd typically is a mixture of Americans, Swiss, Germans, and other Europeans, a few who come as families, most old enough to have grown children. Couples predominate. Emerson usually has roughly 25 people in his clinics, though during the week before the Swiss Open he may fill up to his maximum of 36. Often there is a contingent from around Newport Beach, California, where Emerson spends part of his year. Many of the people know one another from previous visits, since they come back year after year. "One particular week [right before the Swiss Open] we have almost 85 percent of them who have been at least ten to twelve times," Emerson told me. "So we get a lot of returns. They're all pretty well established in business. They like to go on a nice vacation each year. They all like tennis."

Before and after the clinics you can hike, go hot-air ballooning, work out in the fitness center, or lie around the pool. After dinner, there is usually a group headed either for the hotel's Whiskey A Go Go disco or to one of the bars in town. Emmo is almost always part of that group, dancing with the women and telling stories from his days on the tour. The chance to hang around with Emmo adds immeasurably to the Palace's already superb program.

TRAVEL INSTRUCTIONS: The nearest airport is Geneva, roughly two hours away by car. Rather than rent a car, however, you can take the train to Montreux, where you'll be met by the Palace's vintage Rolls-Royce, provided you give them advance notice.

205